Lost Wolf

CURSE OF THE MOON - BOOK ONE

STACY CLAFLIN

www.stacyclaflin.com

Receive book updates from Stacy Claflin: sign up here.
stacyclaflin.com/newsletter

CHAPTER 1

BEADS OF SWEAT BROKE OUT along my hairline. I wiped them away, tightened my ponytail, and ran faster along the dirt trail, jumping over exposed roots and ducking under low-hanging branches. Pine trees, firs, and alders turned my path into more of an obstacle course than a trail.

A twig snapped behind me.

I glanced back, but didn't see anything. Probably just a raccoon.

My sneaker hit a root and my arms flew in front of me. I landed on my hands and knees, and slid down an incline. Rocks and branches dug into my skin until I crashed into a huckleberry bush.

I stood and dusted myself off. Blood dripped from my legs. I pulled twigs, dirt, and small rocks from the cuts.

"Nice work, Victoria," I muttered to myself.

Sasha had said I shouldn't have gone into the forest for my first jog. But having just moved to the beautiful Olympic Peninsula, I wasn't about to join a club when I had the great outdoors. Birds chirped all around and a stream bubbled nearby. It was like the woods were telling me I'd made the right choice.

Another snap.

"Who's there?" I sounded a lot braver than I felt. My heart thundered against my ribcage and I whipped my head around. My roommates had said the woods were safe, but I was also trusting people who had been strangers only a couple days earlier.

Why had I gone into the woods alone? Wasn't that how half of all horror movies started?

I thought of Sasha running on a treadmill, flirting with cute college guys. Maybe she was the smart one.

Footsteps.

"Hello?" I called.

Nothing. The birds had even stopped singing.

"Is anyone there?"

The footsteps came closer.

My pulse drummed in my ears. I fought to breathe normally.

A small gray and black wolf stepped out from behind the tree. He made eye contact with me.

I didn't move a muscle, holding its gaze.

Instead of feeling the need to run, its presence calmed me. My heart rate steadied, and I held myself back from rubbing its nuzzle.

"Are you lost, little guy?"

He stepped closer and sniffed the air.

I should've run, but was too intrigued. Would he check me out and then run off? I couldn't shake the feeling that he wanted me to pay him some attention. Or even to pet him. I wasn't sure why, but petting him felt right, natural even. How could that be? A wolf that wanted a rub down?

He took another step and then another, continuing to stare

into my eyes.

Music sounded from my pocket as my phone rang. The animal skidded back and exposed his teeth.

I reached in and rejected the call.

The wolf glanced from side to side and crept closer to me. He was close enough that I *could* have reached out and rubbed the fur. I kept my hands near my pocket.

He nudged my leg with his wet nose and sat down.

"D-do you want me to pet you?"

His nose again grazed my leg.

I hesitated, but then reached between his ears and patted the fur, surprised at how soft it was. He rested his head against my leg. I continued petting.

My phone rang again.

He jumped up and ran away.

Disappointment washed through me. That had probably been a once in a lifetime experience.

I leaned back against the tree, hoping the creature would return.

After what felt like forever—but a quick glance at my phone told me was probably only ten minutes—I decided to head back home. If the time didn't convince me to leave, the grumbling in my stomach did. Lunchtime.

I headed back the same way I came, this time paying more attention to exposed roots. Finally, I broke free of the woods.

Was it my imagination, or could I smell lunch cooking? The house was a mile away. I shook my head.

The hunger was getting to me. My nerves were frayed.

I hurried down the concrete trail until the mansion came into view. The Waldensian stood out like a sore thumb as one of the largest homes on the edge of campus. With twenty-eight bedrooms, it housed over fifty students.

Smoke came from around back. I sniffed the air. Barbecue. My mouth watered.

"Victoria!" Sasha, ran over, carrying so many grocery bags they probably outweighed her.

I grabbed several. "What's going on?"

"Landon found some patties in the freezer and he's cooking those up. We decided to throw a party."

I grimaced. "How long have those been there?"

Sasha shrugged. "No idea. I got some veggie burgers and some chicken patties. There are bound to be a lot of hot, hungry guys."

"And tons of chips." I shook the bags I'd taken. They weighed next to nothing, though full.

"Yep." As we made our way inside, she told me about all the guys she'd seen between the Waldensian and the grocery store. She'd invited every last one of them. "Put the perishables away while I get the rest."

"Sure." I dug through the bags. She'd bought enough dips and appetizers to feed an army.

Sasha came in, carrying a case of drinks in each hand. She stuck them in the fridge and then pulled her braids back into a loose ponytail. "I can't believe how hot it is. I didn't think Washington got this warm. Doesn't it rain and snow all the time?"

"Doesn't look like it, and I'm glad. I love this weather."

"Me, too. I just didn't pack for it."

I put some sandwich toppings in the fridge. "You can borrow something of mine."

Her eyes lit up. "Thank you! That cute yellow sundress?"

"Go for it."

She gave me a quick hug. "You're the best roomie ever! Can you tell Landon the food's here?"

"Yeah."

"Thank you." She squealed and ran upstairs.

The old back door groaned in protest when I opened it to poke my head outside.

Landon stood behind a smoking grill. He wore an apron that read *Kiss the Cook*, and from my angle that appeared to be the *only* thing he wore, though I was sure he had to at least have on shorts. I hoped.

"Is Sasha back with the other patties?" He turned, and I could see his shorts—very short cutoffs.

"Yeah, I just unloaded everything. I didn't think short shorts were the style for guys."

Landon grinned proudly. "When you've got legs like mine, tiny cutoffs are always in fashion."

I laughed. "Do you need any help?"

"I'm fine, but it looks like you should take care of your knees." He glanced at my legs.

"Oh, I almost forgot. Well, give a shout if you do need help."

Austin, another of our housemates, came over and smiled at me. "You can help by introducing me to all your friends. If they're half as gorgeous as you, I need to meet them all."

Heat inflamed my cheeks. "I don't have any friends, remember? I just moved here."

"You're no fun. Go away," he teased and dug through a cooler, chuckling to himself.

I went up to my room, where Sasha sat at our shared vanity wearing my dress. She spun around. "How do I look?"

"Stunning." I closed the door and pulled off my shorts.

Sasha stared at my knees. "You'd better wash that dirt out before it gets infected."

I grimaced at the thought.

She held up a blush palette next to her face. "Which one should I wear? I was thinking this one,"—she pointed to a light one, about the color of the flowers on the dress—"but I'm not sure."

"It'll be perfect." I gave her a thumbs-up and then hurried into the bathroom to fix my wounds. I sat on the counter and scrubbed, trying to ignore the sting.

After I had bandaged myself up, I went into the bedroom.

Sasha was playing with her braids. "Up or down?" She pulled them back and then let go.

"Up." I turned to my closet to figure out what I would wear. Maybe some capris to cover my burning wounds.

"You're right," she agreed.

I found a cute tank top and got dressed. My stomach rumbled.

Sasha laughed. "You'd better eat."

"Tell me about it."

Her phone rang. She glanced at it and her shoulders slumped. "My mom." She groaned. "She won't leave me alone. I swear, she checks on me every hour. You'd think I'd gone to college on the other side of the world. Ugh."

"Can't you just ignore her?" I asked, nudging her away from the vanity so I could use it.

"Obviously, you've never met her." She sighed dramatically. "You're lucky. Your parents haven't called once, have they?"

I froze, staring at my reflection.

"What?" Sasha asked.

My voice caught.

"Victoria?"

I couldn't remember my parents—or anything before I'd arrived at the Waldensian mansion, ready to start college.

CHAPTER 2

"WHAT?" SASHA ASKED. "WHAT'S WRONG?"

Other than the fact that I had no memories before a couple days earlier? "Nothing. Sorry, I guess I'm just hungry."

"You look like you've seen a ghost."

I forced a smile, meeting her gaze through the mirror. "No ghosts. I just need some food." Conversation drifted up from downstairs. "As soon as I finish my makeup."

She tilted her head.

I grabbed a tube of eyeliner. "Meet you downstairs?"

"Sure you're okay?"

I leaned toward my reflection and applied the makeup along my eyelash line. "Couldn't be better. Save a hottie for me."

She giggled. "I'm sure there'll be plenty to go around."

"See you in a few." I moved to my other eyelid.

"Okay, but if that really tall baseball player comes, he's mine. What was his name?" She paused. "It doesn't matter. I claim him."

"You've got it." I studied my eyes to make sure the liner was even.

She left the room, closing the door.

I put the lid on and dropped it, finally allowing myself to

let my realization sink in. My hands shook. How could I have no memories? Nothing. And how could I have not realized it sooner? I'd pulled into the driveway of the Waldensian and gotten out, knowing exactly what I was doing. But without a single memory from before.

My Jaguar had been packed full of my belongings—everything I would need for a successful year of college. And clearly, I knew the skills I needed. I was a pro at applying makeup, had great fashion sense, and could text like it was nobody's business.

Did I have a mom and a dad? I had to have, but trying to remember only made my head hurt. I went into my purse and dug around, finding credit and debit cards, a driver's license, and everything else that seemed to prove I was a real person with a past. Except without any clues. The only address listed was for here at the mansion.

No clues to my previous life.

I grabbed my phone and went to my contacts. Only my roommates. There were no apps for social media, either. No photos. I hadn't subscribed to any podcasts or put anything in the notes. The only thing remotely personal was the downloaded songs, but those didn't tell me anything other than the fact that I liked popular music.

Whatever past I'd had was gone, or was at least out of my reach.

How could I remember *nothing*?

What was going on? What could have possibly happened to make me forget everything?

A crash sounded outside. I went over to the window and looked into the backyard. Someone had knocked over a tin garbage can and a couple large guys were picking up the contents. The yard was filled with people.

I needed to get out there. If I couldn't remember my past, I needed to focus on the present, and that meant making lots of friends. Later, I would worry about trying to figure out why I had no memories. I finished getting ready and headed downstairs, eager to make college the best time of my life—not that I had much to compare it against.

Outside, all the food had been moved to a plastic folding table. I grabbed a paper plate and filled it, finding my appetite returning.

Landon turned to me with a smile. "What kind of patty?"

"Whatever's ready now." I held out my plate and he plopped one on my bun.

"Enjoy."

"Thanks." I found an empty plastic chair and scarfed the food down, listening to the conversation all around me. Everyone was talking about college life—sports, parties, class schedules, instructors.

Relief washed through me. Maybe having no past wouldn't be such a big deal. I couldn't hear one person discussing life back home. But of course, they were probably glad to be away. Would I ever discover my past?

"Hey, beautiful," came a deep voice on my left.

I turned and smiled at the bronzed, muscular, drop-dead gorgeous guy taking a seat next to me.

"Hi." I swallowed the last bite of my burger, trying not to stare at him. My eyes didn't want to cooperate.

He grinned, showing off perfect teeth. "What is someone as beautiful as you doing, sitting here by yourself?"

My face heated. "I-I… well, uh…" I paused and took a deep breath. "Let me start over. I figured I'd eat first and then talk to people."

He balanced his plate on his knees and held out his hand, acting as if I hadn't just made a complete fool of myself. "Then I'm in luck. I'm Carter. You are?"

"Victoria." I shook his hand. At least I had a name, even if no past. "What year are you?"

"Just a lowly sophomore," he said, with a hint of teasing in his voice.

"You went here last year?" I asked.

He nodded and bit into his hot dog. "You new?"

"Yeah. A super-lowly freshman."

Carter laughed. "You'll love it. I was kind of worried about the location—you know, small town and all that—but it's cool. Lots of parties. Seattle's not that far, but I think I only went there twice all last year." He stuffed the rest of the frank in his mouth.

"What are you studying?" I asked. Why couldn't I think of anything more interesting to talk about? I'd send him running before long.

He groaned and wiped his mouth with a napkin. "I have to declare soon. My dad's all over me about that. I have no idea what I want to do, you know?"

"What classes did you like last year? Maybe you could go in one of those directions."

"That's easy. Art history."

"I sense a but."

"That's not going to go over with my dad." His body tensed.

"So? Do what you want. It's your life."

Carter laughed bitterly. "If I major in art, they'll cut me off financially. Probably even take away my car."

"Oh."

"Do you know what you're going to study?" He twisted the cap off a beer and held it toward me.

I shook my head. "No thanks."

"Don't like beer?"

My mouth dropped. "I…"

"Oh, I get it. You're a wine cooler kind of girl." His face brightened. "I should have known you'd want something sweet." He winked.

Before I could reply, Carter jumped up and dug into a cooler. He pulled out something pink and tossed the lid into the garbage and handed it to me.

"Thanks." I sipped it. It tasted like strawberries.

Carter grinned. "See? Too classy for a regular beer."

How sad was it that a complete stranger knew what I liked better than I did?

"Of course someone as sweet as you would prefer those. You up for a dance tonight?"

"Which one is that?" I sipped the drink, hoping it would relax my nerves.

Carter leaned closer. "You can come as my guest. It's a really private, exclusive club. It's called the Jag."

I nearly choked on the drink. The Jag? Like my car was a Jaguar?

"Are you okay?" Carter's eyes widened.

"Started to go down the wrong way. I'm fine." I cleared my throat.

"Do you want to go with me?"

The club's name might have been a coincidence, but I had to find out. "I'd love to."

He smiled, leaned back, and sipped his beer. "Awesome. I thought I might have to go stag, but now I get to accompany the most beautiful girl in town."

My face flushed with heat. "What time? What should I wear?"

"I'll pick you up at seven. Wear the nicest dress you have. Like I said, it's very exclusive." He held my gaze.

"Mind my asking how you got in?"

Carter glanced to the side, a slight frown appearing. "My dad owns the place."

I stared at him, trying to put it all together. "Your dad?"

"Now you see why an art degree wouldn't fly. I pretty much have to choose business—or something closely related. As the oldest son, it's expected that I'll take it over."

"That seems…" I searched for the right word.

"Old school?"

"Yeah." I set my empty bottle on the ground.

"It is, but our family goes way back."

"But can't you just, I don't know, do what you want?" I asked.

"Then I'd have to start over with nothing. Dad won't just cut me off from finances, he'll find a way to make sure I can't get a job any higher than a janitor at a poop farm."

"Poop farm?" I laughed.

He shrugged.

"I've heard working there really sucks. Especially for the janitors."

The corners of his mouth twitched. "You get my point."

"Basically, he has the power to blackball you, no matter where you go?"

"Yep."

"That's harsh."

"It is what it is. So, you'll be ready at seven?" He rose and took my empty plate from me.

"Ten minutes early." I smiled.

"Perfect." He threw the trash away and then came back. "I'm actually looking forward to the party tonight. Thank you."

"No, thank *you*. It sounds like quite the opportunity."

"I guarantee all your friends will be jealous. Well, I have to get going. See you tonight."

"Wait."

"Yeah?"

"Don't you want to exchange numbers?"

He twisted a silver ring on his middle finger and his expression tightened. "Right. Of course." He pulled out his phone from his back pocket. The case appeared to be gold plated. He slid his finger around the screen. "What's your number?"

Feeling stupid, I pulled out mine and went into my contact list to find my number. I told him, and a few moments later, my phone rang. "Got it."

"Awesome. See you in a few hours."

"A few?" I exclaimed.

He glanced at the screen. "Okay, five."

"See you then." I leaned back and sighed. For someone with no past, things were working out pretty well. I had a date with a gorgeous guy at an exclusive club.

With nothing remotely close to nice enough to wear.

Sasha sat in the chair Carter had been in. "Who was the hottie?"

"Apparently my date tonight."

She squealed. "Where to?"

"Somewhere called the Jag. I'm going to need to get a formal dress."

Her eyes lit up. "Shopping trip!" She pulled me up to standing. We went up to our room to grab our purses and then headed for her car. She rattled on about parties and dances coming up. I wasn't sure how we'd fit any studying or sleeping into our schedules with so many social activities.

It was nice to have something else to focus on other than my past—or lack thereof.

I had a blast trying on dresses. Sasha and I snapped pictures of each other in all the ones we liked. I ended up choosing a floor-length teal one with straps that criss-crossed in the back and a shimmery bodice.

"You're sickeningly beautiful," Sasha said.

"Uh, thanks?"

She nudged me and snickered. "That's a compliment."

"Then you're sickeningly stunning."

Sasha beamed. "You're the best. What did you think of that white dress on me?"

"The one with the lace?" I asked and went back into my dressing room.

"Yeah. Did it look too much like a wedding dress?"

"Not at all."

"I'm going to get it. I heard the sororities host formal

dances all the time. We can pretend to be potential recruits."

"Sounds like fun," I agreed. "As long as there aren't any initiations involved."

"During a dance?" The door closed in the next dressing room. "If that happens, we'll hightail out of there."

"Okay. I may as well get as much use out of this dress as possible for what it costs."

When we got back home, the backyard was even more crowded. Landon came in and washed his hands as we passed the kitchen.

He glanced at me. "I saw you talking to Carter Jag."

I stumbled into Sasha, unable to believe what I'd just heard. "What did you say?"

Landon's brows squished together. "I saw you talking with Carter Jag earlier."

I gasped for air. His *last name* was Jag?

Heart thundering, I stared between the two of them. The room spun. I took a deep breath to keep from running out of the room.

CHAPTER 3

"YEAH," LANDON SAID. "HIS FAMILY owns—"

"The Jag." I leaned against the wall for support.

What was the deal with jaguars showing up everywhere?

"Right. He and all the super-rich kids always hang out together. I've never seen him at any of my parties. In fact, I can't say I've even seen him talking to any of my friends."

I swallowed. "Interesting. He probably doesn't invite people to parties at the Jag, either, does he?"

Landon's eyes nearly bulged out of his head. "Did he…?"

"He's picking me up at seven." I bit my lower lip.

"Really?" Landon stepped closer to me. "Get pictures. Lots of 'em."

"Okay."

"No, I'm serious. There are so many rumors about that place, but I've never seen so much as a picture of the inside. No one else has that I know of, either."

Sasha stared at me. "How'd you manage to get into the most exclusive place on the peninsula?"

"You've got me. Carter just invited me."

"Find out if he has any brothers."

I closed my eyes and took a deep breath. "He said he's the oldest brother."

She grabbed my arm. "Come on. We've got to get you ready."

"Right." I opened my eyes and followed her upstairs, lost in thought. How could a girl with no past find herself with an invite to the Jag? Unless it was some cosmic joke. Either it was, or going there would shed some light on what was going on.

There were too many jaguar references for it to be a coincidence.

Once in our room, Sasha pulled out her phone and scrolled around the screen. "There's a makeup tutorial we've got to follow. You're going to be so hot, you'll set the place on fire."

I shook my head.

"Here it is. What do you think of the look?" She showed me the screen. The girl in the video looked like she belonged on the red carpet.

"Gorgeous," I whispered.

"Wash your face while I get this video set up on my laptop."

"Okay." I trudged into the bathroom, still trying to pull my thoughts together. Nothing made sense.

When I came out, Sasha was swearing at her computer.

"What's the matter?"

"Stupid thing won't start." She chucked it on her bed. "I'm going to have to get a new one. Can we use yours?"

"Sure." I found the backpack where I'd seen it while unpacking and set it on Sasha's dresser, closest to the vanity. When it powered on, I nearly passed out.

The desktop image was a jaguar lounging in a tree.

"Don't just stand there," Sasha said. "Open your browser."

"Of course." I shook my head to clear my thoughts. It didn't work.

I opened the browser and Sasha found the video. "Sit. I've got work to do."

"Should I get the dress on first?"

"And risk spilling something on it? No way." She guided me to the vanity and got to work.

I let my mind wander as she followed the video and chatted excitedly about my date. It was impossible to piece everything together when the majority of the puzzle was missing. I really hoped Carter and the club would offer something—even a small clue would help.

Jaguars obviously meant something, but what?

"Done," Sasha said, interrupting my thoughts.

"That was fast."

"Because you were in your own world," she teased. "Day-dreaming about Carter?"

"You caught me." I sighed.

"Hang onto that one."

"I'll try."

"You gotta get me in. I'm dying to see the club now. What do you think?"

I studied my reflection, barely recognizing myself. "Wow. You should become a makeup artist."

She scrunched her face. "My mom would love that. She and my aunt own a beauty parlor in the Bronx."

"You don't want to carry on the business?"

"Not back home. Maybe in the city or something—*if* I even choose that route. Maybe my creative writing class this quarter will send me in a whole new direction."

I turned back to the mirror. "You definitely have a talent with this."

"Meh. I can use it on my daughters."

"You have children?" I teased.

"I'm going to have five. All girls."

"Really?" I tugged at my hair, trying to figure out what to do with it. "Does your future husband know?"

"It's going to be his idea." She winked. "Do you want your hair up or down?"

"What do you think?"

She closed out the video and brought up a ton of hair images. "It's up to you, darling."

I scrolled through the pictures while she looked at herself in the mirror. "I'm going to have to get my braids done again." She sighed dramatically.

"Why not go natural?"

Sasha laughed and fell on her bed. "That's funny."

"Why?"

"I'll have an afro that'll reach to the ceiling."

"Can't you just straighten it?" I asked.

"Promise me you'll never go into the hair industry."

I turned away, embarrassed. "Why not?"

"Do you know how long straightening locks like mine would take? I don't have time for that. Braids. Then I don't have to worry about my hair every single morning."

"If you say so. Back to my hair. What should we do with it tonight?"

She studied my hair, holding it out and rubbing it between her fingers. "It's nice and thick with a great texture. We can do a lot." She leaned over, glanced at the screen, and pointed to a wavy style with half the hair in a loose bun at the base of the head. "That would look so beautiful on you."

"You don't think it would cover the straps in the back?"

Sasha pursed her lips. "Hmm. Good point, but you could pull half of it over the front. Best of both worlds, don't you think?"

"Yeah, that might work."

"We'll try it, and if it doesn't work, I'll do an updo."

She got to work, and before long, my phone buzzed.

"It's Carter." Blood drained from my head.

"We'd better get that dress on you!"

I accepted the call. "Hi, Carter, I'll be right down."

"I'll be waiting." His voice was so smooth it made it easy to picture him in a tux.

The call ended. I put my phone down and squealed.

Smiling, Sasha pulled my dress out of the bag and unzipped it. "Step inside."

I did and she zipped it back up.

She stepped back and looked me over. "You could be on the cover of *Glamour* magazine."

Curious, I went into the bathroom and looked in the full-length mirror. My mouth gaped. Though I wasn't sure what to expect at the exclusive party, I was sure I wouldn't have any trouble fitting in.

"Come on," Sasha called. "Can't leave that hot guy waiting."

I hurried out, slid on my new, sparkly silver pumps, and grabbed my purse.

"You can't take that," Sasha exclaimed.

"Why not?"

She rolled her eyes. "You've got to be kidding me. It's a good thing you have me." She went into her closet and pulled out a tiny sparkly clutch.

"Will my phone even fit in there?"

"Of course. That and your wallet and a few makeup items. All you need for a date."

"You're the expert." I dumped the contents of my purse onto my bed and stuffed what I could into the miniature bag.

Sasha gave me a once-over. "Girl, you're going to be the best looking one in the place."

"Stop." But I couldn't help beaming. "Do you really think so?"

"Of course. If I was your mom, I'd be taking a million pictures right now. Wait, gimme your camera. I'll take some so you can send them to her."

My chest constricted. Maybe one day I could.

"Hand it over."

Fumbling, I pulled it out of the clutch.

She grabbed my phone and held it up. "Say cheese."

I forced a smile, feeling the start of a lump in my throat.

The flash shone a couple times and Sasha studied the screen. "Perfect."

"Come on, we've made Carter wait long enough."

My knees felt weak. I reached for my phone.

She shook her head. "I'll need pictures of the two of you."

I couldn't argue with that.

We headed downstairs. I could hear Carter before I saw him. He was discussing baseball with Landon. We came into the kitchen.

Carter had his back to us, but Landon looked at me and

whistled. "Lookin' good, roomie."

Sasha pushed me closer to the guys. "I know, right? Makes me want to go out somewhere fancy."

Carter turned around and our gazes met. His hair was slicked back and he was even more gorgeous in a tux. I almost dropped the handbag.

"You look beautiful." He picked up a plastic box from the table, pulled out a corsage with white roses, and slid it onto my wrist.

"Stand over by the wall," Sasha directed. "Picture time."

Carter flashed me a handsome smile and put his arm around my shoulders. We stood where Sasha pointed, in front of an empty wall.

She snapped a few pictures and handed me my phone. "I'm so jealous."

I glanced down at the image on the screen. We did look great—he was gorgeous and I barely recognized myself. I slid the phone into the clutch. "I'm sorry it took me a little longer to get ready than I thought."

"Not a problem. You were well worth the wait."

Sasha raised her brows. "See?" she mouthed. Then she turned to Carter. "Have fun, you two. Bring her back by midnight."

"What?"

"I'm kidding!" She laughed and grabbed my arm. "I want to hear everything when you get back."

Maybe I didn't need a mom with Sasha as my roommate. "Sure."

Sounds of shattering glass came from the backyard.

Landon groaned. "I better get out there. Things are starting to get rowdy. See you guys!"

I gave a little wave and Carter, who still had his arm around me, led me toward the front door.

Sasha caught my gaze and gave me a thumbs-up. I smiled, my heart thundering in my chest.

"Is your friend always like that?" Carter asked and chuckled.

"I'm not really sure. We just met a couple days ago."

"Right. Well, it's nice to have someone who cares."

I couldn't deny that.

He stopped in front of a cherry-red Ferrari and unlocked it with a remote.

My mouth nearly dropped to the ground. Next to his car, my black Jaguar seemed like a run-of-the-mill sedan.

Carter removed his arm from my shoulders and opened the passenger door. "M'lady."

I hurried over and climbed in. It smelled of leather, and I sank into the super-comfortable seat. It was so soft and supple and conformed to me as I sank in. It relaxed me, and almost made me forget my troubles—much in the same way Carter did.

He got into the driver's seat and started the engine. It purred like a kitten. He turned to me, a devious smile on his face. "Wanna see how fast she can go?"

My eyes lit up. "Yeah, of course."

"Once we get off the main road, we'll have a nearly straight shot to the Jag. I'll show you there."

"I can't wait."

He turned on the music, and the same song played as on my phone when I received a call.

"You okay?" He pulled out of the parking spot.

"It, uh… I was just listening to that song earlier."

Carter tapped his temple. "Great minds." He pulled out onto the main road.

Every other car slowed for him. Quite a few pulled out phones and snapped pictures.

"Is it always like this?"

"Yeah, especially at the beginning of the year. Give 'em a few weeks, and everyone will be used to seeing her around." He pulled off the main road. "You ready to see what she can do?"

I hoped so. "Let's see."

Carter punched the gas, sending the back of my head into the headrest. Everything outside seemed to pass in a shapeless blur.

"This is unbelievable," I gushed.

"You haven't seen anything yet. Wait until you see how she handles the corner coming up."

I couldn't see a corner.

He turned the steering wheel to the right and we took a sharp turn so smoothly I didn't even feel a thing.

"Wow," I whispered.

"Now prepare to really be impressed." He slowed down and pulled into a parking lot. Most every car parked was a luxury vehicle, many as impressive as the Ferrari.

The building in front of us stood tall and sleek, black with no windows in sight. The three letters—Jag—stood out, the same color as Carter's car.

He turned to me. "Are you ready to see the inside?"

My breath caught. Ready or not, that's where we were headed.

CHAPTER 4

CARTER AND I WALKED AROUND the building to where a long line led to a single door. Two enormous men wearing all black stood at either side, checking IDs against their tablets.

My feet hurt just thinking about standing in the line.

Carter laced his fingers through mine and marched to the two burly guys.

Everyone in line stared at us. Their chatter quieted.

"Ringo," Carter said.

The nearest bouncer turned to us and he broke into a grin. "Carter, my man. Come on in."

Both of the huge men moved out of our way and opened the door. The couple in the front of the line tried to go through, but Ringo blocked them with one arm and shook his head.

Carter tugged on my hand, and I followed him inside. The door slammed behind us.

It took my eyes a moment to adjust to the darkened hallway. Tiny lights lined the floor at the wall. The hall went off in two directions. Loud music with a strong beat sounded from the far end.

He squeezed my hand. "Do you want to start with dinner or dancing?"

"Can we eat first?"

"Whatever you'd like." He led me down the quieter hall and we stepped into a formal restaurant.

Waiters in suits hurried about, taking food and orders. I couldn't see a single empty table.

A man with salt and pepper hair wearing a tux came over to us, smiling warmly. "Greetings, Carter." He nodded to me.

"Hello, Mac. Is a table available?" Carter asked.

"For you? Always. Would you like to dine with your father or at your own table?"

Carter arched a brow.

Mac nodded. "Your own table. I understand. Hold on just a moment." He scurried away.

I glanced around the dim restaurant. Fancy artwork decorated the walls. Everything seemed to be gold-plated. Overhead lamps lit each table illuminating the guests, all dressed in formal wear. Compared to all the other women, I was nothing special. I would fit in, but barely.

Why had Carter brought me? If he never spoke to most people at school, why stop by our barbecue and invite me? Could it have something to do with my elusive past?

Mac returned. "Your favorite table is ready for you."

We followed him, zigging and zagging around booths full of happy customers. People laughed and toasted each other. Finally, we stopped at a corner booth. Two tall candles sat on the middle of the table on either side of a champagne bottle.

Carter let go of my hand and gestured for me to sit. He sat across from me and turned to Mac. "Thank you."

Mac nodded and then rushed away.

"So, this is your favorite table?" I couldn't help wondering how often he brought guests here. Was I merely one of many?

He adjusted himself in the seat. "It's my favorite place to study."

"Study?" I exclaimed.

"It's much quieter during the day."

A server came over and placed a plate of dark bread in the middle of the table and then set three sauce cups around the basket. He poured champagne into the glasses. "Are you ready to order, Master Jag?"

Carter cleared his throat and turned to me. "Do you know what you'd like?"

I glanced around for the menus.

"Order what you'd like. No limitations here—unless you're looking for a rare delicacy from another country. You'll have to order that ahead of time."

I stared at him, unable to speak.

"Master?" asked the server, staring at Carter.

"We'll need a few minutes."

The server bowed and walked away.

"Master?" I asked.

Carter shook his head. "My dad likes things old school."

"Right, you said that."

He nodded. "If you like lobster, I recommend that. Our fishermen go to a spot that no one else knows about, and the seafood is second to none."

"You have your own—? Never mind. Lobster sounds wonderful."

"Dig in." He took a piece of bread and dipped it in garlic butter.

I took one and dipped it in a creamy sauce. It tasted like

crab and melted in my mouth.

The server returned. "Have you decided, Master Jag?"

"We'll both have a lobster from today's catch."

"Would you like to kill it yourself?"

My eyes nearly popped out of my head.

Carter glanced at me. "No thank you. We'll let the chef take care of that."

"Very well." The server bowed and left again.

Three violinists and a harpist came our way and stood in the middle of the adjoining booths.

I arched a brow at Carter, who nodded toward the musicians. He appeared amused.

They set up their instruments and played a soft, romantic melody that lulled me into a trance.

After the song ended, I shook my head to clear it. I couldn't tell how much time had passed. Everyone else clapped. I blinked a few times and joined them. The musicians picked up their things and moved to a different part of the restaurant.

I turned to Carter. "This place is amazing."

He rested his chin in his palm. "It's fun to watch it through the eyes of an outsider. Especially one as lovely as you."

My face flushed, and I sipped my champagne. I wondered how far out of my element I was. Without any memories, it was hard to judge, but with or without them, it was impossible to not be impressed. It didn't feel like my normal stomping grounds.

Carter took another piece of bread. "Have you registered for your classes already?"

I nodded. "Nothing exciting this quarter other than psychology."

"Really? I have psych, too. Wonder if we have the same one."

The way things were going, it would have surprised me if we didn't. "Could be."

He pulled out his phone and slid his finger around the screen. "One o'clock with Massaro."

"Sounds familiar." I pulled out my phone and checked. "That's the one."

Carter grinned. "I'm glad you'll be there. I heard he can be a real jerk when he wants to be. What else do you have?"

I glanced over my schedule. "Intro to Statistics and World Geography."

He sipped his drink. "I aced both, so let me know if you need any help. You know where I study." He glanced around the table.

"Thanks."

"Johnson for geography? You'll like her."

I nodded. "And Foley for stats."

His face clouded over.

"Something wrong with him, too?" I asked.

Carter sat taller and his brows came together. "He's new. I wouldn't know."

I tilted my head. "Sure you haven't heard of him?"

The server arrived and placed the two lobsters in front of us. He held up a pepper grater as long as his arm. "Pepper?"

"Please," Carter said.

Once we both had our dishes seasoned, the server again left.

The grin had returned to Carter's face. "Dig in and tell me

this isn't the best you've tasted."

I forced a smile. It wouldn't be hard to say that.

"Go on." He stuck a forkful into his mouth and closed his eyes. "It doesn't get any better than this."

Curious, I stabbed the largest piece and took a bite. The taste exploded in my mouth. "Oh, my."

Carter flicked a nod. "Told you. Oh, and be sure to save room for dessert."

We ate in silence as my taste buds screamed in delight. Even the side vegetables were mind-meltingly delicious. It was hard not to scarf everything down, but I kept control, making eye contact with him every so often and smiling.

As soon as the plates had been emptied, the server returned. "Would you like more, or some dessert, perhaps?"

I leaned back. "As much as I'd love some more, I hear the dessert is just as good."

"Very well. What would you like?"

"Good question." I turned to Carter. "What do you recommend?"

He chuckled. "Just about anything, but then again, I've never found a sweet that disagreed with me. Pick your favorite, and we'll have two."

My mind went blank. "I, uh, don't really have a favorite."

"Really? No favorite?"

I shrugged. "Not really."

He turned to the server. "Bring us tonight's special."

The server balanced the plates and bowed. "Coming right up." He spun around and left.

"What's the special?" I asked.

"No idea, but it'll be good. Did you like the dinner?"

"It was hard to save room for dessert."

"Yeah, once you eat at the Jag, everything else pales in comparison. I hope you won't be too full to dance." His eyes shone.

I studied his handsome face and let my gaze linger down to his muscular arms before looking back into his eyes. "I don't think that'll be a problem."

A slow smile crept across his face. "I'm so glad I ran into you at the party. You're such a breath of fresh air compared to everyone around here."

Did he mean at the club or in town? I didn't have the chance to ask, because a loud sizzling noise distracted me.

Our server was headed our way, carrying two flaming dishes.

I turned to Carter. "Is that our dessert?"

"It most certainly is."

A moment later, the two fiery plates were in front of us. Underneath the flames was an enormous slice of cake that looked like layers of sponge cake, ice cream and meringue.

"Enjoy." The server bowed and hurried away.

My eyes widened as I stared.

"Blow it out," Carter said. "If you just watch the show, your dessert will be charred."

I watched him blow his out, and I imitated him. The sweet smell arose and made my mouth water. "What is this?"

"Pure heaven." He took a bite and closed his eyes. He opened them and winked. "If you mean the name, it's called Baked Alaska. Dig in."

I grabbed my fork and scooped as much as I could. All the flavors worked together to create something I was sure I'd never tasted before.

"A rare rum gives it that kick," Carter said. "Father has it imported from a dangerous little town in Russia."

"Not Alaska?" I took another bite, letting it melt on my tongue.

"Where's the challenge in that?" He ate the last of his and pushed the empty plate to the edge of the table. "Are you going to be able to finish that?"

Half of my enormous slice remained. "I'm going to try."

Carter chuckled. "It's hard to leave any on the plate, I know. Once when I—" He sat taller and stared at something behind me.

"What is it?" I asked.

He groaned and scooted away from the booth's edge. "It's my father with some out of town guests."

"You don't want to talk to him?"

"Not if I can avoid it."

I pushed my plate toward him. "Help me finish this—I hate to see it go to waste—and then we can sneak to the dance floor."

His expression relaxed. "I like the way you think." He picked up his fork, and soon we had the plate emptied.

"Are you ready to dance?" I asked, just as eager to have his arms wrapped around me again as I was to burn off some serious calories.

Carter sat taller and glanced behind me. "He's distracted. Let's go."

"We don't have to pay?"

"Not when my last name is Jag. Come on."

I reached for Sasha's clutch and followed Carter out of the

restaurant. We went down the dimmed hallway again, following the loud music. Laughter and happy screams sounded as we neared.

"Sounds like a real party in there."

"It really is." He put his arm around me and ushered me inside. The enormous room was as dark as the hall, but with multi-colored lights all around. Most of the dancers wore glowing or flashing lights and multicolored lasers danced around the ceiling. On the second floor, the DJ had a massive setup, and he wore a mask—jaguar, of course—with lit whiskers and eyes. He danced around, encouraging everyone else to move with the music.

A large bouncer stepped in front of us we walked in. He took one look at Carter and went back to his place. "Master Jag, do you need anything? Martini?"

"Just here to dance." He turned to me. "Unless you want a drink?"

I shook my head. "I'm stuffed."

"Have fun," the bouncer said. "If you need anything, just say the word."

"Can you keep my purse somewhere safe?" I asked.

"You can rest assured no one will touch it while it's with us."

I handed it to him. "Thank you."

He handed us small mesh bags with what looked like pot-pourri inside. I sniffed it. It smelled like catnip.

Carter held his up to his face and took a deep breath and held it in before placing the bag in his coat pocket. "Let's dance." His face lit up and he held his hand out for me.

"Okay. What am I supposed to do with this?"

He took it from me, sniffed it, and handed it back to the bouncer. Then Carter laced his fingers through mine and led me to the middle of the dance floor. He danced like a professional, moving precisely with every beat of the music.

Panic struck me. I had no idea if I could dance. What if I had no rhythm?

He motioned for me to join him.

What was the worst that could happen? I gave him my best smile and moved to the music. It felt natural and our moves matched each other perfectly.

Several around us whistled and cat-called, cheering us on. The crowd backed up, giving us room. I spun around shook my hips, laughing and having the time of my life—all three days of it that I could remember. I had years to make up for, and I suddenly resolved to do it all in that one night on the dance floor.

The cheers around us only pushed me forward. I moved in step with the beat and with Carter. We couldn't have done better if we'd spent years working on the routine.

We continued for the next several songs until a slower tune began. Carter pulled me close and I put my hands around his waist.

He stared into my eyes. "I'm having such a great time. Where did you learn to dance like that?"

I wished I knew. "Just comes naturally."

"No, seriously. I spent years in lessons."

"Maybe I did, too." I smiled, trying to be mysterious.

Over the next few songs, we glided around the floor like two professionals. I loved the feel of being in his arms. Judging by the look in his eyes, he felt the same way.

After the third slow song ended, overhead lights came on and everyone stopped dancing.

"Is it closing time?" I asked.

Carter shook his head, his eyes shining with excitement. "The DJ is taking a quick break. Then the party really starts."

CHAPTER 5

BRIGHT LIGHT SHONE ON MY face.

"Rise and shine, sunshine," came Sasha's annoyingly perky voice.

I rolled over and pulled my covers over my head. "Go away."

"We have lunch and then orientation, remember?"

Every muscle ached. "I don't care."

"Are you going in your pajamas?" She yanked on my comforter.

I grasped it with more force. "Take notes for me."

"I can't. We don't have any of the same classes."

"As long as I can find my way around when they actually start, I'll be fine."

"Come on." She pulled the cover off me.

I glared at her, but then had to cover my eyes from the awful brightness.

"Get in the shower. I'm not going alone."

"Take Landon."

"He's not a freshman." Sasha pulled on my arm. "You're my roommate."

"Technically, everyone who lives in the Waldensian is a roommate."

"You're the only one who shares a *room* with me, girl-friend. Get in the shower before I throw you in."

I moaned. "What time is it?"

"Eleven."

"How can you be so perky at this early hour?" I mumbled.

"Because I didn't come home at six."

Everything from the night before flooded back.

"What did you guys *do* all night?" Sasha teased.

"Danced."

"Seriously?"

"Until it closed. Then we watched the stars fade, parked in his Ferrari. Then he brought me back here."

"Hold up. Did you say Ferrari?" she exclaimed.

"Cherry red."

She sat on the bed. "Girl, seriously?"

"Yes. Do you see why I'm so tired?"

"Hang on to that guy. Does he really own the club?"

I sat up and groaned, trying to force my eyes open. "His dad does."

"Did you get pictures?"

Pain shot through my head. "I forgot."

"You didn't get any?"

"I just woke up. Would you please leave me alone?"

"It went well, right? You'll probably be back. Get pictures next time. Lots of them, okay? Us peasant-folk want to see inside."

"I'm getting in the shower."

"You can tell me what it's like, though. What is the—?"

"Can you start some coffee? I'm going to need a gallon."

Sasha laughed. "I think Landon already started some. Hurry up, I don't want to be late."

I got up and tripped over my pumps.

"You really shouldn't leave those lying around," Sasha teased.

"So helpful." I kicked them under my nightstand and made my way into the bathroom. The light in there was almost as harsh as the sun. I looked in the mirror and immediately regretted it. My hair stuck out in every direction, my un-washed makeup was smeared all over my face, and I had dark circles under my eyes.

I was so sore that even my bones ached.

Sasha pounded on the door. "You didn't fall back to sleep did you?"

"You're the most annoying roomie ever!"

"I'll take that as a compliment."

"You would." I turned on the shower as hot as it would go, climbed in, and let the stream run over me. It soothed my muscles, but my bones wouldn't be comforted. I turned up the temperature, but it didn't help.

"Hurry up," Sasha called.

"I am!" I lathered up my hair and rushed through the shower.

By the time I was done, I felt like a new person—except for my bones. They continued hurting. I found some painkillers in the cabinet and took a couple. Then I got ready as quickly as I could, making sure to conceal the shadows under my eyes.

I adjusted the towel and went into the bedroom.

Sasha shoved a coffee at me. "Hurry up, or we're going to miss lunch. All the freshman from the Waldensian are eating together, so we at least don't have to worry about reservations."

"Got it." I sniffed the coffee steam and held it in before gulping it down. It was bitter, but I didn't care. The jolt of energy was just what I needed. Then I made my way to my closet and pulled out a gray and white yoga tank.

My roommate stared at me like I was crazy.

"What's wrong?"

"Are you seriously thinking about wearing that to orientation?"

I held it up. "It's cute."

"For the gym." She put her hands to her face. "Thank the stars that you got me as a roomie, girlfriend. Move aside."

Sasha flipped through my closet. "Remind me to take you shopping again this afternoon. Especially if you want to impress that sexy, rich, Ferrari-driving boyfriend of yours."

"Boyfriend? That's a little premature. We just met."

She snapped her attention to me. "You spent the whole night with him last night."

"He didn't even kiss me goodnight."

"Twenty bucks says you'll hear from him before dinner."

I shrugged. He'd told me that I would hear from him soon.

Sasha went to my dresser, rummaged through the drawers, and tossed some jeggings and a lacy purple top at me. "Put those on. I can't believe you were going to wear exercise clothes."

"These?" I exclaimed, holding up the pants. "Did you notice it's summer? I'm going to melt."

She shook her head, muttering to herself. "Your legs are cut up, remember?"

"Oh yeah. Still, I'm going to fry."

"At least you know you'll be smokin' hot."

When we got to the restaurant, everyone was already ordering burgers. After dining at the Jag, it was a bit of a disappointment, but it was fun to hang out with the other freshmen. We were all excited to get the lowdown on our upcoming year.

Once we got onto campus, we had to go to the stadium for the orientation. The sun beat down on us.

Sasha leaned over and whispered, "I thought it was supposed to rain all year around here."

"And the vampires sparkle, too."

She glared at me and then laughed. "We're on the other side of the forest from Forks."

"Maybe that's where it rains."

A microphone squeaked over the loudspeakers. Groans sounded all around us.

Down on the field, several people stood on a platform. A heavy, balding guy was adjusting the microphone. "I'd like to extend a warm welcome to our newest Freshman Class. We have an exciting year planned. You all should have received a link to our handbook. If you haven't read it already, be sure to get it done before tomorrow morning."

"I'll get right on that," Sasha muttered.

I snickered. "I thought you couldn't wait for the orientation."

"To check out the guys." She glanced around. "And it looks like we're in for a good year."

Though after the night I'd just had, I only had interest in one particular guy.

The various staff took their turns filling us in on tedious

details about our upcoming education while we roasted in the sun. Finally, the first guy returned to the podium and told us to break into groups with our staff advisers.

Sasha turned to me. "Who's your adviser?"

"Foley, I think. He's my stats teacher."

"I got some intern. Maybe he's young and hot."

I shook my head. "Do you think about anything else?"

"No, not really. See you back at the house."

"Bye." I adjusted my purse over my shoulder and made my way to a courtyard with a pretty fountain. At least it was shaded. A group already sat next to a little garden under some maple trees.

I sat near the edge of the group, as close to the fountain as possible, hoping for a little spray to cool me.

The instructor stood with his back to us, shuffling through some papers.

I yawned, the coffee already losing its hold on me.

A pretty redhead who didn't look old enough to drive turned to me. "Bored already?" She giggled.

"Late night."

"Gotcha. Yeah, I know how that goes. I hear this guy is new. Hopefully he knows more than we do, right?"

I nodded. "Let's hope."

"My name's Grace. What's yours?" She held her hand out.

"Victoria." We shook hands.

She fiddled with a book bag. "I'm so nervous. Aren't you?"

"Should I be?" I had enough to worry about without getting anxious about school.

Grace leaned closer to me and whispered. "I'm only fifteen. Maybe that's why my nerves are on fire. You think anyone will care about my age?"

My brows came together. "Fifteen? Are you a genius or something?"

She giggled. "Hardly. I'm homeschooled and blew through my studies. If I keep doing well, I could graduate college at nineteen. Cool, huh?"

"I can't imagine hitting the real world now."

"Oh, I'm not going to work after that. Grad school. I'm going to study—"

"Attention, please," Professor Foley said and turned around.

Grace snapped her attention toward the front. I followed suit.

"Welcome," he continued.

I studied his profile. There was something familiar about him.

My heart raced at the thought.

He continued speaking, focused on the other side of the group. I couldn't understand a word he said. The longer I stared at him, the more convinced I became that somehow I knew him. Or at least had seen him somewhere.

His hair was dark and thick, his skin tanned to perfection. He had stunning features and a gorgeous profile. It was hard to believe he was old enough to be a professor. He was younger by far than all the others I'd seen. A magazine cover would have been a more fitting place for him.

Professor Foley turned toward my side of the group. "And be sure to ask questions. That's what we're here..." His voice trailed off as our gazes met. His face paled and his eyes widened. His expression held something. Horror? Shock?

Whatever it was, he continued staring at me.

I was frozen in place. My heart thundered in my chest, threatening to break through my ribcage. I knew him. Without a doubt, we had spent time together. I just couldn't remember any of it. My palms had grazed that stubble and my eyes had stared into those deep blue eyes. Even with the distance, I recalled that he often smelled of woodsy aftershave and soap.

Those around me whispered, bringing me back to the present.

Professor Foley cleared his throat and glanced around at the other students. "Excuse me. As I was saying, the faculty is here to help you. Just don't wait until the final hour."

"What was that?" Grace whispered.

My mouth gaped and I shook my head.

"You know him or something?"

"Shh," I snapped.

"Sorry." She scooted away.

My hands shook. I sat on them to get them to stop.

Foley stopped talking, and everyone paired off. Grace glanced at me, her expression pensive.

I nodded and tried to push the instructor out of my mind. But how could I? He was my only clue to my past. Part of me longed to run around the other students and throw my arms around him.

Grace came over. "I wasn't trying to bother you before."

"I know. Sorry. What are we supposed to do?"

"We're supposed to discuss…"

My gaze wandered back over to Professor Foley. He was speaking to a couple students and smiling. My chest constricted. Oh, that smile. It had taken my breath away countless times, though I couldn't remember a single one of them.

"Did you hear what I said?" Grace asked.

I shook my head.

"How are you going to pass this class if you're going gaga over the teacher?"

My face heated and I pulled my attention back to her. "What are we supposed to do?"

She shrugged. "Basically just go over the map and find all the important places. The cafeteria, clinic, our classes. That sort of stuff."

I pulled out my phone and found the campus map. "There's our stats building. Let's see… there's my geography building—all the way across campus. Great." I looked at her. "How are you getting around?"

"My mom's dropping me off in the mornings, then I'm going to walk." She shrugged.

"Where are your classes?"

"My other two are kinda by your geography building."

"I can give you a ride."

"Really? You'd do that?"

"Yeah, my car fits two, but no more. It's a Jaguar."

Her eyes widened. "I'll have to ask my mom, but that would be so cool." She leaned closer and whispered, "Cute professor, three o'clock."

I spun around, and sure enough, he was headed our way. My stomach squeezed tight, and I fought to breathe normally.

My voice caught. What would I say to him without looking like a fool?

CHAPTER 6

Toby

I WALKED TOWARD VICTORIA WITH a million thoughts swarming my mind. I'd spent so much time and energy searching for her, and then the moment my mind was elsewhere, she just appeared.

It had been so many painful years we'd been apart, especially given how we'd been ripped from each other's arms. The hope of ever seeing her again had all but vanished for a long time.

Yet there she sat, like any college freshman in orientation. She was anything but ordinary. And she certainly hadn't been born anywhere near the time her classmates had been, though she didn't appear any older.

My pulse drummed in my ears as I headed her way. When she'd looked at me, I saw a flicker of recognition—surprise, really—but nothing more.

What had they done to her?

How would I keep myself from picking her up, swinging her around, and giving her such a passionate kiss that her toes would curl?

She was alive. Alive. And right in front of me.

As I neared her and the redhead, the other girl whispered to Victoria. She whipped around and again, our gazes met.

I wanted to shout from the rooftops. My sweet Victoria was alive and right here. Enrolled in one of my courses. I would see her every day for the next three months.

She was just as beautiful as I remembered.

Her eyes widened as I neared. They seemed more filled with curiosity than joy or any other emotion I would have expected.

The crushing reality hit me.

Victoria didn't know me.

I swallowed, stood taller, and plastered on a fake smile. "Hello, ladies. Do you two need any help?"

She held my eye contact, but didn't say anything.

"I think we found everything," said the other girl.

I kneeled down to their level and focused on the redhead because I didn't trust myself to look at Victoria yet. "Well, if you have any questions, just let me know. That's what I'm here for."

"Thanks, Professor Foley," Victoria said.

The formality in her tone nearly killed me. Almost as much as not being able to wrap my arms around her and breathe in her almond-scented shampoo that I loved so much.

I turned to her and opened my mouth, but as soon as I gazed into her eyes, I couldn't remember what I was going to say.

She stared back, an intense expression on her face. That was the look she had when trying to figure something out.

Oh, how I wanted to cup her chin and tell her everything would be all right. She was alive and only about a foot away.

How could things not be okay?

Aside from the fact that she obviously couldn't remember any of our time together. That was like an arrow to the heart. Worse, actually. I could pull an arrow out, but this felt more like my heart was being torn in two.

I would have to handle it with delicate care.

If I was barely more than a stranger, I would have to regain her trust. Without all our memories, she would have nothing to draw from.

But I had promised her I would never give up on her—on us. I'd sworn my undying love to her just before she'd died in my arms.

My phone buzzed in my pocket, reminding me that I needed to conclude the powwow.

"You both have my office number and email address. Don't hesitate to ask anything."

The younger girl's face lit up. "Thanks!"

Victoria nodded, her alluring eyes still wide. She seemed to want to say more.

I tried to give her a reassuring smile. "I've got to wrap things up. It was nice to talk with you two." I rose and returned to the front of the group. It was hard not to stare at Victoria as I spoke to the students and then sent them on their way.

I gathered my things and looked around. Victoria had already taken off.

My heart sank to the ground and fell through to the other side of the world.

It was little consolation that I would see her the next day in class. How would I be able to teach math with her sitting there, having no idea who I was? That woman was the love of my life, and even with her death, I'd been unable to truly love another.

"Hey, Foley!"

I shook my head and turned toward the entrance of the courtyard.

Roger, who had the office next to mine, stood there, rolling up his sleeves. He worked out every day and loved to show it off. "A bunch of us are going to lunch. Want to come?"

"Going to pass this time." I slung my bag over my shoulder and hurried over to him. "I need to make sure I'm ready for tomorrow."

"First day jitters?" he asked. We headed for our office building.

I shrugged. "Something like that."

"You taught high school before this, right?"

"Yeah."

"This is no different, really."

"I sense an *except* coming." I arched a brow.

Roger laughed. "Except the ladies are legal."

"Seriously?" I exclaimed. "You're going to go there?"

"Easy there," he said. "I was just joking. Did I step on a nerve?"

He had, but I wasn't going to let him know. I shook my head. "Like you said, jitters."

I thought back to a fleeting relationship I'd had years earlier while trying to get over Victoria, but it hadn't worked. And now Victoria was back. I rubbed my temples, trying to make sense of it all.

"Well, I'd never put my job on the line like that," Roger said, bringing me back from my thoughts.

My stomach twisted, and I suddenly realized that not only did Victoria have no idea who I was, but she was now my student. Not that I couldn't find another job if push came to shove. Since I aged so slowly, I moved around fairly often to avoid questions, but I didn't care to be fired. Even though Victoria would be worth any hardship.

I'd already chosen her over my natural family so long ago.

"What's with you?" Roger slapped my back. "You're not usually so quiet."

"Must be the impending full moon."

Roger groaned. "Seriously? Right at the first day? The students always go cray-cray then."

"Tell me about it." Although most of the kids I'd worked with over the years went nuts on the full moon for entirely different reasons than my colleague was referring to.

He stopped in front of our building. "Sure you don't want to join us? That hot new art history professor is going."

I shook my head. "Thanks, but I have some things to take care of at home."

"Your loss. See you tomorrow."

"Have fun." I went inside and up the stairs to my office. The entire floor was empty. I sighed in relief and slunk into my chair.

Did Victoria even know she was a werewolf? What would she do tonight? Would she go into the forest?

I sat up in my chair.

That was it. Maybe if we ran into each other in our wolf form, I could help her remember everything. Communication was so much easier as animals. Primal. Whoever had messed with her memories wouldn't be able to control her during the full moon.

The office felt like it was closing in on me. I grabbed my bag, headed for the parking lot, and jumped into my camouflage Hummer. The heat nearly suffocated me, so I cranked the AC and bolted off campus.

When I reached my private dirt road, I hit the gas, barreling down the long path to my home. Once the wrought iron gate came into view, I remote unlocked it, waited for it to open, drove through, and locked it behind me.

I parked and stared at my newly painted, light blue Victorian-era mansion and fought to rein in my thoughts. My pack needed me to focus. How could I though, now that I knew Victoria was so close?

Why hadn't any of the locator spells worked to find her? Especially since we were living in the same town?

I pulled out my phone and texted the witch who had been helping me find her.

Toby: I found her!

Gessilyn: What?! Where?

Toby: Campus.

Gessilyn: Can't believe it! So happy 4u!

How would I reply to that? I should have been thrilled, but I felt like punching something.

Gessilyn: U OK?

Toby: V can't remember me.

Gessilyn: O no. Was afraid of that.

Toby: I should've known.

Gessilyn: Need anything?

Toby: Got a memory spell?

Gessilyn: Not sure. Will look.

Toby: OK. Call u l8r.

Gessilyn: Day or nite.

Toby: Thx.

I took a deep breath and put my phone back. For once, I wished the full moon was out. More than anything, I wanted to shift and run the length of the forest. I hated being restricted by the moon's phases.

Maybe a human run would help. It had to be better than sitting in my driveway. I got out of the Hummer and locked it.

A breeze blew by. I could smell several of my wolves. They were probably sleeping, preparing for the long night ahead of us. I would, too, if I thought sleep was a possibility.

I rubbed my temples. The familiar ache set into my bones, warning me of the impending shift.

Inside, the house was quiet. I stared at the newly-remodeled entryway and sniffed again. All the young wolves were home. They needed their rest most of all because turning into their wolf form was still so painful. I didn't miss those days.

Footsteps sounded on the staircase. Jet, one of my pack assistants, came downstairs. He arched a brow. "You're home early."

I hesitated, unsure if I wanted to talk about Victoria.

He stopped at the foot of the stairs. "Everything okay?"

"No, but I can't focus on it."

Brick, one of the pack guards, came in from the kitchen and turned to Jet. "Hey, Yamamoto. You left your phone down here." He handed it to him.

"Oh, yeah. Thanks." He turned back to me. "Sure you don't need something?" Protectiveness and loyalty were written all over his face. "Someone giving us trouble in town again?"

I shook my head. "Not since we ran those mutts off. No, this is something else."

Jet and Brick exchanged a concerned look.

"It doesn't affect you guys. If it did, I'd tell you."

"If it's going to distract you on the full moon, I think it does concern us." Jet's mouth curved down.

Anger flared, but I bit my tongue, not wanting to take it out on one of my best wolves. Tempers always grew during the full moon.

His eyes narrowed. "No disrespect meant, but we deserve to know what's going on. At least I do as the highest-ranked pack member."

I clenched my fists. "I need to go for a run. We'll talk after I get back."

Jet's eyes nearly popped out of his head. "A run *now*? We need to rest."

The wolf inside me was starting to force his way out early. A growl escaped my mouth. I forced him away and stared Jet down. "Stand down. I said this doesn't concern you."

"Yes, sir." Jet's nostrils flared and he stormed up the stairs, muttering to himself.

It had been a risk bringing him into my pack. He had been born alpha of his own pack, but instead chose to stay with me. We had more power struggles than any other wolf I'd encountered. He was also more loyal than any other.

"Sir?" Brick stared at me.

I counted to ten. "I need to clear my head before the others wake. I'll be back long before dusk."

"Okay. Do you want me to prepare dinner?"

"Crap." Usually, I prepared the big full moon meal. Cooking tended to calm me. We all ate ravenously before shifting, barely stopping to use our hands, much less utensils.

Brick tilted his head. "It's not a problem."

I glanced at a clock on the wall. "If I'm not back in ninety minutes, you can start. The fridge is stocked."

He flicked a nod in my direction.

"Can you put this in my room for me?" I held out my bag.

"You're going to run in slacks?"

"Right now, I don't care."

Brick took my bag and headed upstairs.

I went outside and stared at the woods. Hopefully a run would help, though the only thing that would truly help would be to have Victoria back in my arms—and I would stop at nothing until that happened.

CHAPTER 7

Victoria

I PACED MY ROOM, HOLDING back tears. Why was I so sure I knew Professor Foley? And not just generally? I could recall the feel of his embrace. I was certain of the scent of his aftershave. Even his kisses—when I closed my eyes, I could feel those gorgeous lips on mine. I could taste the familiar minty sweetness.

And why wouldn't my bones stop hurting? Irritation set in and I rubbed my neck.

Why on earth couldn't I remember anything before I'd arrived in my shiny black Jaguar?

I picked up a fluffy beige teddy bear from my bed and stared at it. "Are you special? Or just some stupid random toy?" I chucked it at the bed.

"Whoa," Sasha said. "What'd the bear do to piss you off?"

"How long have you been standing there?" I snapped.

"Long enough to see you throw the poor teddy."

I scowled.

"What's the matter?" She gave me a sympathetic glance and closed the door.

How could I explain anything without sounding like a nut

job? No memories before arriving, and now I was certain I'd had a romantic relationship with my *professor*. He looked about thirty, and I was eighteen. Or at least I thought I was—that was what my driver's license showed.

Sasha put an arm around me. "Take a deep breath. I'm sure whatever it is will be okay."

I grumbled. A sharp pain ran down my spine. I gasped and gritted my teeth.

"Do you need to go to the clinic?"

"No. I'm fine. Really."

She shook her head. "Do you need something to eat?"

My stomach growled at the mention of food. I was ravenous.

"Come on." She grabbed my arm and pulled me toward the door.

I rolled my eyes. "Fine."

Down in the kitchen, Landon sat at the table, texting. He glanced up. "How are—what's wrong?"

"Girl needs some food," Sasha said.

He arched a brow. "You look pale."

I shrugged.

Landon jumped up. "We've got plenty for sub sandwiches."

The two of them pulled out the fixings. I opened a jar of pickles and scarfed them all down.

Sasha arched a brow. "Sure you're not knocked up?"

I shook my head, but really, how would I know if I was? Maybe I was, and the shock of it had created a serious case of amnesia. But I didn't care. I just needed to eat more food.

Sharp pains shot through my shoulders. I grimaced, determined not to cry out. It seemed to work. Neither of them noticed my agony.

Landon and Sasha piled lunch meat and cheese on white bread.

I grabbed a tomato and took a bite, sending juice and seeds flying in several directions.

"Can't you wait a couple minutes?" Sasha wrinkled her brow.

"No." I bit into the tomato more carefully, and managed to eat the rest without making a further mess. Then I reached for some cheese, but Sasha shooed me away.

"Fine," I grumbled and went into the cabinet. I pulled out a jar of peanut butter and scooped some out with my fingers.

"Gross," Landon said. "Ever heard of a spoon?"

I glared at him and ate it.

He shook his head and turned to Sasha. "I thought all you girls went out for lunch."

"We did."

"What'd she eat? A piece of lettuce?"

"Funny." I scooped more peanut butter into my hand.

"You know what?" he asked. "Just keep that jar. I'll buy a new one."

"Here." Sasha handed me a six-inch sub. The scents of meat, onions, and condiments made my mouth water.

I grabbed it without a word and had to force myself to stop and chew. Though it seemed easier. I ran my tongue along my teeth. Had they always been this sharp?

She stared at me. "How did you eat that so fast?"

"Hungry." I turned around and grabbed the one Landon made. It smelled even better than Sasha's.

"Hey," he exclaimed.

I bit into it without apology. This one had peppers—that was why it smelled so good. It tasted even better.

"I'll just make another." Landon's brows came together. He turned to Sasha. "Maybe you're onto something with being knocked up."

She turned to me. "Are you?"

My mouth was too full to answer.

"Maybe we should take you to the all-you-can-eat place," Landon said. "I can't afford to give you any more of my food."

My stomach growled.

Sasha slapped her forehead. "You're hungry after all that?"

I turned to Landon. "Where's that restaurant you mentioned?"

He gave me the directions. "Just don't put them out of business."

"Funny."

"Maybe we should get you to that clinic," Sasha said. "This isn't normal."

"I'm just hungry—ow!" I doubled over as every bone in my body radiated pain.

"That definitely isn't normal," Landon said. He grabbed my arms and pulled me to the table. "What hurts?"

"Everything," I moaned and slumped into the hard chair. The pain finally started to ease. "I think I need to lie down."

Sasha and Landon exchanged a worried glance.

"Sorry about all this, guys. Next time the kitchen's a mess, I've got it." I forced myself to stand and went upstairs, clinging to the railing for support.

They were talking about me, but I couldn't focus on a

word because my bones were starting to hurt again. I finally made it to my room and climbed into bed. I knew they were right—whatever was going on with me wasn't normal.

Nothing added up. No memories, jaguars everywhere, some kind of connection with my professor, and now the ravenous hunger and bone pain. It felt like my skeleton wanted to explode.

I grasped some blankets and squeezed, trying not to cry out as a new wave hit. Would I survive this… whatever it was?

My stomach growled again. There was no way I could eat while dealing with this. What was my body thinking? I writhed and kicked, all the while biting my tongue to keep from screaming out.

If I couldn't convince Sasha and Landon that I was getting better, they'd take me to a doctor. With symptoms like these, I'd likely wind up locked away. I just needed to find a way to dig around enough to figure out what was going on.

It was *my* memories and my body. There was no reason I couldn't find out what was going on—once the pain and hunger left. I didn't know which one was worse.

But it was starting to piss me off. College was supposed to be one of the best times of life—the first shot at freedom. Time to hang out with cool people and have fun without parents controlling everything. Blessed independence.

All I had was one big, crazy mystery that would make me look twice as nuts if I told anyone. The only thing I wanted was to know what was going on. Was that so much to ask?

My phone played a tune from somewhere in the room.

I groaned. It was probably Carter. I vaguely recalled making plans with him again. Dinner?

My mouth watered and my stomach roared thinking about food at the Jag. Maybe I could even meet others and ask some questions to hopefully get more pieces to this puzzle.

The song on my phone continued. I pulled myself out of bed and crawled on all fours to the bathroom. I'd seen some painkillers in there, hadn't I?

My legs ached, the pain dulling. Heat radiated up and down my spine. Hunger continued tearing through me—I was tempted to peel the paint off the wall and eat that. Instead, I lay on the little fuzzy pink rug and stared at the ceiling.

Inside the bedroom, my phone played its song again.

Carter would think I was ignoring him. I had to at least talk to him. If only I could pull myself up and find some medicine. Then I'd be fine.

Right. That would make everything better. I rolled my eyes.

With any luck, hanging out with Carter would at least distract me from everything else. Maybe if I was really fortunate, I might find some answers, but I wasn't going to hold my breath.

I had to accept the fact that I might not ever remember anything about my life before arriving here. Not that I would stop looking, but I had to focus on school and building my future. I didn't need a past to build a future.

Groaning, I grabbed onto the handle of a drawer and pulled myself up without flinging the drawer open. When I got to my knees, I clung to the counter and heaved myself up. I went through the cabinet, knocking things down until I found some ibuprofen. Once I got past the childproof cap, I poured four onto my palm—twice the recommended amount, but I was in at least twice as much pain as was normal.

I swallowed them with some water and then stumbled back to the bed. At least I could walk. Improvement was good. Right?

"Are you okay?"

I jumped and turned to Sasha by the door. She arched a brow. "What's going on—seriously?"

"Probably just nerves." I climbed into bed and closed my eyes. "I'm feeling better already."

"Is that what all the noise was in the bathroom?"

"You saying you never knocked anything over?" I asked.

"I've never eaten like I just saw you eat. You scarfed more than two quarterbacks do after a game. No joke."

"As long as I didn't eat more than a fullback."

She snorted. "At least you've got a sense of humor. But really, what's going on? Is this normal?"

"Maybe."

"You haven't talked to your family since you got here, have you?"

Tears stung my eyes. "Nope."

"Call them. Maybe this is genetic—something your Great-Aunt Gertrude had and passed to you."

"Later."

She came over and handed me my phone. "Looks like you missed some calls from that hottie, Carter. And some texts. Want me to check them for you?"

I pulled a pillow over my face. Couldn't the world just disappear for a while?

The phone sounded again.

"Want me to answer?" Sasha asked.

"No."

"Hi, Carter," she practically sang.

I sat up and stared at her.

She had my phone up to her face and was nodding. "She's here, but how do I put this delicately? She's having... lady problems."

"What?" I threw a pillow at her.

"Mmm hmm." She tossed it back. "Tonight? I'll ask her."

"Do I want to know?" I mumbled.

"He wants to take you back to the Jag. He promises to have you home in time for a full night of beauty sleep for your first day of classes."

I rubbed my aching neck.

What did I have to lose?

CHAPTER 8

Toby

I STARED AT THE MOON as the rest of my pack ran off in other directions, howling and chasing each other. My inner wolf clawed to get out, but I was fighting it—not that I could hold out much longer.

The curse of the moon.

I narrowed my eyes and cursed it for cursing me and my kind.

Pain ran through my spine as my bones shifted and prepared to change shape. I clenched my teeth and removed my clothes, adding them to the pile.

My body threw me to the ground and I landed on all fours as my wolf escaped. Fur popped out, slicing through my skin. I gritted my teeth. Fighting the process only made it worse.

I closed my eyes and waited until I could feel paws on the ground. When I opened my eyes, everything seemed brighter. I did love the night vision and heightened senses.

My wolf urged me to join the pack.

Not tonight.

Our nose sniffed out Jet, Brick, and the others.

I shook our head.

A low growl rumbled from our throat.

Typically, we werewolves were one with our inner wolves, but the exception was when we had differing motives. The wolf longed to run with the pack—our family. I needed to find Victoria—our other half.

I parked our hindquarters on the ground.

Our pack queen is nearby. We have to find her. She needs us.

My wolf stared at the moon and howled, calling out to the others.

You'd leave her to fend for herself?

Another growl escaped our mouth.

He wasn't going to win tonight. Not when Victoria was probably frightened somewhere not far away. What if she had shifted around others?

My wolf lowered our nose, submitting to my leadership. Finally. He missed Victoria's wolf form as much as I missed her in her human form.

I raised our nose and sniffed the air, weeding out the unimportant smells.

A slight breeze brought a familiar aroma.

Victoria.

She had to be several miles away, given how faint the scent was. I put our nose to work to make sure it was coming from the direction I thought.

It was.

A howl sounded in the distance. The pack was looking for us.

I returned the call, letting them know we would join them later.

A call of protest sounded.

I howled a final time to let them know my mind was made up. Jet would be happy to be the temporary alpha, anyway.

My wolf rose and took a step toward Victoria's scent. We melded together and then burst into a run, going past the house and eventually down a dirt road which led us through more trees.

We came to a large, dark structure with a bright sign. I couldn't make out what it read from my angle. I did, however, recognize that all of the cars in the parking lot were extremely expensive, many imported.

A heavy feline scent hung in the air, and it wasn't from house cats.

Shifters.

I slowed down to a near-crawl and walked around the immense building. A wide variety of odors assaulted our nose, everything from food to perfumes. I could even smell strange plant life—they had to have been imported like the cars.

Around the back of the building, I finally saw windows. People danced inside, appearing to have the time of their lives. Music sounded from inside, loud enough that I could feel the beat on the ground.

I paced, keeping my focus on the party. Victoria's scent lingered, and it was stronger here. It seemed to be coming from inside, but that didn't make any sense. Why would a wolf be in there? Especially among feline shifters?

Rumors abounded of jaguars and cougars, but this was the first real proof I had of any of it. Though I couldn't tell if what I smelled was jaguar or cougar, I had a feeling I'd soon know the difference.

My wolf and I sat, focusing all the more on the dancers. I could sense that he wanted to leave, not that I could blame him. We were in dangerous territory, and if any of the other shifters caught wind of us it might get ugly. No way we could take on an entire pack—or herd, or whatever cats traveled in.

Then I saw her. Not only was Victoria in human form—during the full moon—but she was dancing with a tall, muscular man.

A low growl escaped our throat. I wasn't sure if that was from me or my wolf. I didn't care.

What was she doing with that guy?

I growled, exposing our teeth. I would tear him apart.

My wolf urged me to back down.

Have you lost your mind?

An annoying feeling of calmness washed over me.

Stop it!

He didn't. Another few minutes of this, and I would curl up and go to sleep.

A thought crossed my mind—I knew nothing of what had happened to her during our time apart. Running inside to fight wouldn't solve anything.

Back before her death, we had been in rival packs. Both of our fathers were alphas, and had expressly forbidden us from seeing each other. We had both been chosen to marry others from our respective packs.

Not that any of that had kept me from falling head over paws for her.

My wolf finally relented with his force to calm me. I brought my focus back to Victoria.

I let out a yelp.

She was wearing a white lacy dress. I jumped up and paced. This couldn't be a wedding, could it? She hadn't somehow been turned into a cat shifter?

No. It wasn't possible.

Victoria was a *wolf*.

Yet she was human during the full moon.

What had they done to her?

I growled and inched toward the building.

A twig snapped nearby.

It was only someone taking a bag of trash to the dumpster. He didn't even look my way.

I snapped my neck back toward Victoria. That pompous jerk held her close and spoke into her ear. She threw her head back and laughed.

My wolf urged me to return to the pack.

Never.

A wave of calm pulsated through me.

Sometimes I hated him. It was my turn to give in to his leadership. Later, I would probably agree that he was right. But right then, staring at Victoria in the arms of another man—a feline shifter—nothing other than an attack made sense.

Why was she wearing what looked like a wedding dress? Could that just be the style of formal wear this year?

My wolf stepped away from the building. He'd calmed the fight out of me. When he burst into a run, I merely went along for the ride. I would need to find out as much as I could the next day when she showed up to class.

That was it. Tomorrow was the first day of classes. She wouldn't be getting married right now.

My own relief washed through me.

I'd overreacted, and my wolf had been right.

We traveled through the woods, again passing my home. The air pressed our fur back like a heavy wind blows down blades of grass. Our pack's scents grew stronger.

My wolf called out to them.

Joyful howls sounded in return. All except Jet's.

He would get over it.

Our pace slowed as we neared the others. We were near the Faeble, a lively bar open to all supernatural creatures. Often, after shifting back to human form, we would stop in for something to drink to relax after the grueling changes of shifting. The owner let us keep spare clothing around back.

I, for one, was ready for both shifting back *and* a strong drink.

One quick glance at the moon told me it would be a while. My wolf urged me to go on a hunt.

Wouldn't you rather curl up and sleep? Busy day tomorrow.

He growled. I would have, too, if I could only be in my preferred form one day a month.

I lowered our nose to our chest.

My wolf burst into a run, sniffing for something to chase. Our mouth watered and our stomach growled at the thought. He wanted to go after a deer, always preferring the thrill of getting a larger animal.

I couldn't stop thinking about Victoria in the arms of that feline. None of it made any sense. Obviously, she didn't remember me, but what else had changed? One didn't just stop being a werewolf. Sure, we could fall in love with other species, but not become one.

As my wolf ran through the woods, I blocked him out and

tried to make sense of everything. The more I thought about it, the more it made my brain hurt. Or wait…

No, that was the familiar ache of the impending shift.

My wolf's disappointment ran through us. It was so strong, it nearly felt like my own, except that I was all too aware of how badly I wanted back into my human form.

I had to find out what was going on with Victoria.

Pain shot through our spine. I gave into it, eager to be human for the next month. My wolf fought it.

Next time, we need to get on the same page.

His resistance ran through me.

In this form, our uniting was on me. When I gave into the monthly change and went with the flow, it was as though we were one and the same. Times like this reminded me that we were two forming one.

Our front legs ached. It was about to happen. I looked around. We weren't as near the Faeble as I would have liked. Sure, I was comfortable in my own skin, and my pack was plenty used to seeing each other in the nude given the nature of our changes, but I avoided running through the woods without any clothes if I could.

I'd run into people more often than I preferred—and *they* weren't nearly so forgiving about guys running around naked.

Clumps of fur dropped to the ground. I fought the bone pain and ran toward the bar.

I could smell the others nearby. Some were already in human form while others were still changing. The younger ones tended to have less control over the changes and often turned first.

Being over a century myself, it was unusual for my wolf

and me to be at such odds. We were old friends and had been through a lot together, including loving and losing Victoria.

My wolf stopped us and put our nose to the dirt. Pain ran from the tip of our tail upwards through our spine, spread out to all four extremities and finally crashed into our neck and skull. The crunching was so loud, I couldn't tell where the shift began. It was easy to know when it had ended, though. Rocks and twigs dug into my sensitive human flesh.

I stood and pulled some leaves from my side. Stinging nettle. Great. I pulled some more off and thanked my wolf for his choice of where to stop.

The sounds of conversation reached me from nearby. The Faeble was only a hundred yards away. I ran for the back, where the spare clothes were stashed in some old lockers.

Jet was already getting dressed. He stared at my side. "Run into trouble?"

"Stinging nettle. I'll be fine."

He punched me in the arm. "What doesn't kill you, right?"

"Yeah, I'm sure this'll make me plenty stronger." I opened the locker where I'd stored some of my clothes and got dressed. "I could sure use a drink."

"You and your wolf were at odds tonight. What was up?"

I pulled on my jeans. "That obvious?"

"Dude." He arched a brow. "Totally not like you."

"It happens to everyone." I shrugged like it was no big deal.

"Yeah, but not *you*."

"I'm made of flesh, blood, and fur just like the rest of you." I pulled my shirt on and found some socks and shoes. Only a couple more outfits remained. I'd have to restock soon.

"If you say so."

A few more guys came over and threw their clothes on. We all headed inside. Music greeted us from the nightly live band as soon as the door opened. Lively conversation buzzed around from all directions and I could smell a wide variety of creatures, as usual.

Some of our pack were already seated, so we joined them. Jet grabbed a seat from another table. A siren in a fedora glared at him, but didn't say anything.

The waitress came over and took our orders. Each of us ordered strong drinks—they tended to help us ease back into being human.

I laughed and joked with everyone, but my mind was back at the large building Victoria had been dancing in with the cat. I needed to find out everything I could about both the shifters and their club.

There had never been a jaguar here at the Faeble as far as I knew, so if I couldn't find anything out from Victoria, I was going to have to get creative.

Either way, I would get to the bottom of all this no matter the cost. Nothing else mattered.

CHAPTER 9

Victoria

MY FAVORITE SONG INTERRUPTED A deep sleep. I groaned, hoping it would stop.

It didn't.

"Would you turn that off?" Sasha asked. "I've got another hour to sleep."

I reached for my nightstand, with my eyes still closed, and found my phone. The music grew louder as I brought it closer. I found the snooze button and jammed the phone under my pillow.

A moment later—or at least that was how it felt—the song played again.

"Guess I better get up," I mumbled. The last thing I needed was to be late for class on my first day of college. I was setting the stage for my entire college career. No pressure.

I opened my eyes and turned off my alarm.

"What were you doing out so late?" Sasha mumbled. "I heard you come in at, like, two or something."

"I lost track of time." I yawned and stared at my pillow, wishing I could flop back onto it for another five or six hours.

"Dancing with Carter again?"

"Yeah. It's so much fun at the Jag."

"Did you get pictures this time?" she asked.

"Sorry, I forgot again."

"Some friend you are."

"Didn't you want more sleep?"

"Yep." She flipped over and pulled the blankets over her head. "You're the one who wanted a ten o'clock class."

"It sounded good at the time."

"Live and learn."

She was right. I'd just have to make sure I got to bed at a decent hour in the future. Maybe dancing with Carter would have to be a weekends-only thing. We could still do dinner other nights.

I forced myself out of bed and stared at my clothes. They all seemed so boring after wearing formal dresses the previous two nights. "Thanks again for letting me borrow your dress last night."

Sasha mumbled something.

I picked a gray tank top with splotches of pink and some cute denim cutoffs and headed for the shower. The hot water soothed my bones. The ache lingered, but the harsh pains seemed to have disappeared.

When I got out of the bathroom, Sasha was in her bed, texting. She glanced up and nodded with approval. "Cute. I see you did your eyeliner like I showed you."

"Yeah, I like how it makes my eyes catlike."

"Definitely suits you, girl. Good luck today."

"You, too." I grabbed my already packed backpack and my purse. It was kind of awkward with both. I'd need to figure something else out.

Sasha's forehead wrinkled. "A backpack? Really? What is this—the third grade?"

I frowned. "I saw plenty of people with those at orientation."

"And how many of them are dating Carter Jag?"

"Who said we're exclusive?"

"Two nights in a row and plans for studying this afternoon? I'd call that serious."

"We'll see. I gotta go."

"Better eat breakfast. I'd hate to see you empty out the cafeteria."

I grabbed one of my pillows and chucked it at her. "Funny."

"You're never going to live that down. I hope you realize that."

"Just wait until you do something crazy."

She snickered. "I don't do crazy. Well, not like that. I'm more likely to get drunk and dance in someone's yard, singing old 90s songs. In my bikini."

"Nice. See you later."

"We'll go shopping tonight."

"For what?" I asked.

Sasha rolled her eyes. "For a better bag. Just try not to ruin your reputation today with that ugly thing."

"Won't dating Carter make up for that?"

"Let's hope. I have a reputation to manage, also. Can't be roomie of a geek."

I threw my other pillow at her and went downstairs. The TV blared from the living room, but I had the kitchen to myself. I dug my frozen waffles out of the freezer and ate them quickly. I was surprised I had any appetite left over after all I'd eaten the night before. After pigging out on sandwiches, I'd eaten two main dishes at the Jag.

Carter had been amused by my appetite—not knowing about how much I'd eaten earlier—and luckily hadn't been put off by it. The sparkle in his eyes actually made me think he enjoyed seeing me scarf down so much. Most girls probably tried to impress him by barely eating, but I'd been so ravenous I'd had no other choice except to give in to my appetite.

I'd had such a great time dancing with him, but the entire time I felt pulled outside. In fact, I'd glanced out the window so many times, he insisted we just dance in front of it. For some reason, the moon was so gorgeous I couldn't stop staring.

But now it was the first day, and if I didn't hurry, I'd find myself late for my first class. I hopped in my Jaguar and drove as fast as I dared until I reached the parking lot nearest my class.

Once I found the room, it was nearly full. I recognized most of the faces from the orientation.

Grace waved me over to where she sat on the far side of the room, halfway back. She patted the desk next to her. "I saved it for you."

I sat down. "Thanks."

"I can't believe you were almost late on the first day."

"Life happens." I pulled my laptop out of my backpack.

Professor Foley entered the room, chatting and laughing with a couple guys wearing school football uniforms. He set his things on the front desk and arranged them.

Grace rattled on about a band, but I couldn't stop watching

the teacher. He was so gorgeous, as evidenced by the three pretty students who had jumped up and now surrounded him, chatting and obviously flirting.

Something deep within me awoke with fury. I had to literally force myself to stay in my seat, gripping the sides so tightly that my knuckles turned white. I wanted to tear those girls to pieces.

"You okay?" Grace asked.

I gritted my teeth. "Fine."

"That vein in your forehead is going to explode if you're not careful."

Not that I cared. Those twits were practically all over him. If it would have been socially acceptable for them to actually crawl on top of him, I was sure they would have.

I sniffed the air. I could actually smell their lust and desire.

Okay, I was losing it. I shook my head. How could I smell their emotions? I had to get control of myself. Who cared if they were flirting with Professor Foley? Why should I, when I had Carter to focus on?

I turned back to Grace. Now she was talking about a virtual game her mom didn't like. I tried to focus on what she was saying, but Toby's aftershave wafted over to me.

Wait.

Toby?

I didn't know Professor Foley's first name. I hadn't even seen it anywhere.

Or had I? I found the online course syllabus.

Introduction to Statistics
Professor T. Foley

My breath caught. His name actually did start with a T.

Maybe I remembered reading that and just gave him the name in my mind.

That had to be it. There was no other explanation. Not that smelling his aftershave or the desire of those girls all the way from my seat made any sense, either.

He stepped back and told everyone to take their seats. His gaze ran across the classroom and stopped when it landed on me.

My heart jumped into my throat and my pulse raced. We stared at each other for a moment before he continued looking around the room. I shook.

What was it about him that sent me into such a frenzy? I didn't feel this out of sorts even when Carter laced his fingers through mine or when he held me close as we danced to slow, romantic music.

Toby—Professor Foley—introduced himself again and then told us to open the syllabus. He went over the expectations of the class and told us that he was available for anyone who needed help.

"Call my number or email me, day or night." His gaze held mine for a moment. "If I'm available, I'll help you then. If not, I'll get back to you as soon as I can. I want all of you to succeed." He scanned the rest of the room, explaining the schedule. "And there will be a pop quiz every Wednesday."

Half the class laughed.

"I'm telling you so you know to be prepared for it—and to be here. I know the ten o'clock classes tend to be considered early, but don't miss any because you're tired. You can't make the quizzes up. I hope you're taking notes."

The sounds of laptop keypads being struck sounded all around the room.

Professor Foley smiled.

It was such a beautiful sight. I nearly melted into the chair. It was hard to breathe as he grinned. I wanted to reach out and stroke his stubble. To lean in close and smell his musky personal scent.

He gazed into my eyes again from the front of the room. It was like he wanted the exact same thing.

I swallowed. How would I ever learn math in such conditions?

He turned from me and spoke, but I couldn't understand a word that came from those gorgeous lips.

Maybe what I needed was a new teacher. Except that I'd been one of the last to register for classes and nothing else was available.

Somehow I made it through the rest of the class. He had us take an assessment quiz to find out where we all stood.

After he collected the papers, he said, "This will help me figure out how fast or slow to move through the material. I don't want anyone overwhelmed or bored." He smiled again.

I looked away. No way would I allow myself to get sucked into that vortex again.

When the class was done, I bolted into the hall without a word. I couldn't look at him for another moment. More than anything, I wanted to. Oh, how I wanted to get lost in those eyes and feel those luscious lips on mine.

Stop.

I sat on a bench, closed my eyes, and tried not to think of him. His beautiful, smiling face was the first image in my mind.

What had Carter said the other day?

Poop farm. I pictured piles of dung. Many piles. Everywhere. Covering all kinds of things.

"You okay?" Grace's voice broke through my disgusting thoughts.

I looked up. "Just tired."

"Something going on between you and the teacher?"

"No."

"You still willing to drive me to the other side of campus?"

I blinked my eyes a few times. Right. I had about ten minutes to get to my geography class. Then I would have time for lunch before psychology. Maybe that class would help me figure out what was wrong with me.

"Sure." I rose. "We'd better hurry."

CHAPTER 10

Victoria

BY THE TIME I STUMBLED out of my geography class, I had a roaring headache. Carter had been right about Johnson being nice, but she had loaded us with work. It was almost like she thought we had nothing else in our lives other than her course.

One look at the world map told me that I had never put any serious time into learning most of the countries. I knew the major ones, but could barely find anything else by memory.

My stomach rumbled. I didn't feel like running back to the Waldensian, so I checked the campus map and saw the main cafeteria was only a couple buildings away.

I stuffed the map into my backpack and followed the mob outside. The sun beat down on me, so I hurried over to the cafeteria. A line of people extended out the door.

Wonderful. I hurried over to the back, hoping it wouldn't take too long. If it did, then I would have to plan on eating lunch at home in the future. I made small talk with the girl in front of me while we wound our way inside and up the stairs to the register. At least the line went pretty fast.

"Twelve dollars," the cashier said without looking at me.

He readjusted his backwards baseball cap.

"Seriously?" I exclaimed.

He shrugged. "It's cheaper if you get a meal plan."

"I'll have to look into that." I dug into my purse and found a ten and no change. "Do you at least take credit cards?"

"Sure."

I handed him one. He compared the picture on the card to me and swiped it through the machine. I waited for him to hand me the receipt, but instead he swiped it again.

"What's going on?" I asked.

"You sure the card is current?"

"Yeah, what's the problem?"

He swiped it one more time and studied the screen before handing it back to me. "You'd better call your bank."

I groaned. "I checked the balance two days ago."

"Got another one?"

I dug into my purse for my debit card and handed that to him.

"Hurry up," someone shouted from the line.

"Yeah," said another. "We're hungry."

My shoulders slunk. "Sorry."

The cashier handed the card back. "This one doesn't work, either. Got cash?"

"Ten dollars." My face and the back of my neck heated.

He shrugged. "Sorry. Can't help you."

Professor Foley walked by, carrying a tray with a double cheeseburger and fries.

My head heated all the more.

He turned and smiled. "Hi Victoria." Concern washed over his face. "Is everything okay?"

I straightened my back. "Yeah, I'm just going to have to skip lunch today."

"You don't have enough to cover it?"

"Apparently not." I looked away.

"That's no way to start your first day. I'll cover it."

I stared at him. "I can't ask you to do that."

"You're not. I'm offering." He dug into his back pocket and handed the cashier a card. "I've got her meal."

He shrugged, ran the card, and handed the receipt to Toby—Professor Foley. Why did I keep wanting to call him by his first name? If that was even really his name.

The cashier turned to me. "Head on in. Trays are straight ahead."

"Thanks," I mumbled and turned to Professor Foley. "I swear I'll pay you back tomorrow. I don't know what's going on with my cards. Maybe someone hacked into my account."

"Computers make mistakes all the time. Well, have a nice lunch."

"Uh, thanks. You, too."

He held my gaze like he wanted to say more.

I couldn't pull away from his enchanting eyes. Again, I found myself wanting to throw myself at him.

He cleared his throat. "Well, I usually sit near the back if… uh, you don't find anywhere else to sit."

My voice caught. I nodded and hurried over to the trays, nearly running into a guy wearing black skinny jeans and thick eyeliner.

"Sorry," I muttered.

"Whatever." He glared at me before taking his silverware.

My college career was off to a *fabulous* start. I sighed and grabbed a tray. What would I do if I couldn't sort out my money situation? I didn't even know who was supplying the funds.

What kind of daughter doesn't even keep her parents' contact info in her phone?

Suddenly, I felt so small and helpless. Not knowing my past was more than just annoying and embarrassing. It was beginning to look like it might be dangerous.

I got in line for food and piled on things without paying attention. What if someone stopped paying for my car? How would I get around? Or what if my college payments came to an end?

The noise around me grew louder. Everyone around me felt closer, like they were pressing into me. I jumped out of line and ran toward the tables. I couldn't breathe.

All sound merged into a cacophony. The room grew hot. I sat at the nearest empty table and stared at my plate. My stomach rumbled, but I couldn't feel the hunger anymore.

I ran my hands through the length of my hair and tried to breathe. Still, only shallow breaths came.

What was I going to do? Who was I leaning on to pay my bills? What if I'd done something wrong, and this was a warning? If only they would have let me know what I'd done to offend them. Or was I supposed to somehow know, but since I couldn't remember anything at all, I didn't know where I'd gone wrong?

What was I doing? How had I thought I could get through the school year without knowing anything about my past?

My stomach twisted in tight knots. I probably should have just walked away after the card was declined. My time would have been better spent calling the banks to find out what was going on. Now I would feel guilty if I didn't eat what Toby— Professor Foley—had paid for.

Wait. Had he asked me to eat at his table?

I looked around and spotted him at a table near the back of the room. A group of pretty girls sat around him, giggling and talking with him.

Well, at least he wouldn't miss me. He'd probably already forgotten all about me. I glanced at my plate, but still felt guilty about not eating it. I'd just pay him back, but I didn't even have the means to do that. Plus, I knew I'd be hungry once my emotions calmed down. Since I'd been given the opportunity to eat, I needed to take advantage of that.

Who knew what would happen once my stash of groceries dwindled? I needed to figure that out along with everything else—my tuition, rent, car payments, and whatever else I could think of when I could think straight.

Surely, I wouldn't end up on the streets. Or would I?

I had to stop thinking so catastrophically. There could be some simple reason for the cards not working. It didn't mean my Jaguar would be repossessed and that Landon would throw me out. I'd gotten those things somehow, and I could find a way to keep them.

People started getting up from their tables in droves. I glanced at a clock. There was only about fifteen minutes until my next class started. I scarfed down the food on my plate, despite not being hungry. Then I followed the crowd and returned my tray.

My mouth was parched since I'd forgotten to grab something to drink. I found the soda machine and filled a plastic cup with too-sweet iced tea and drank it.

I was tempted to skip my next class to figure out my finances, but that could wait an hour. I couldn't miss my first day. At least the building was close. And my heart had stopped racing. Maybe eating had been a good idea after all. It didn't feel like the world was going to crumble around me anymore.

Once inside, I found the classroom easily enough. It was on the first floor. I walked in and froze.

Carter sat in the middle of the room. My mind spun back to our first date, and I remembered he was in the same psychology course.

He glanced up and smiled wide, lighting up his entire face.

I slid my bag off and walked over to him and sat to his right. "It's nice to see a friendly face."

His expression darkened. "You're not having a good first day?"

Part of me wanted to talk about something else, but I found myself spilling my money problems to the one guy who had probably never once had to worry about anything like that. "I nearly didn't get lunch today because I had no money. It was awful—right in front of so many people."

Carter's brow wrinkled.

"My cards were declined." I frowned.

"It happens. System glitches or a new employee pushes a wrong button. One time—"

"But two different cards?" I asked. "Not even from the same bank."

He wrinkled his brow. "That is odd. Want me to look into it for you?"

"Thanks, but it's my problem."

"Well, I happen to want to help. Did you eat anything?"

I nodded. "Someone took pity on me and paid for my meal."

"Tell you what. Make your calls and then send me a text. We'll go study at the Jag, okay? Either to celebrate or commiserate. Sound good?"

"Do I need a formal dress?"

"Not for a weekday afternoon. You're fine."

I breathed a sigh of relief. Even though I hadn't unloaded all my problems, at least I had someone to talk with about some of them.

The professor walked in. He was a large man with thinning hair and a thick beard. He wore a scowl on his face. "Take your seats, everyone," he ordered and then set his things on the table as everyone scrambled to sit.

Carter and I exchanged a curious expression.

"Remember what I said about Massaro?" he whispered. "Grumpy old man."

Professor Massaro hit his desk, causing several people to jump. "Let me get this out of the way," he said. "If you don't plan on taking this course seriously, I suggest you leave now. Some people think of psychology as an easy elective, but I assure you it's not. It's one of the most important fields out there, and if you're looking for something to breeze through while you focus on Calculus or Thermonuclear Physics—get out!"

One kid ran from the room.

A few chuckles sounded around the class.

"Do you find this funny?" the professor bellowed.

The room went silent.

I could hear her typing in the background. "It's been frozen."

"What does that mean? Why?"

"It was issued by the main card holder. You'll have to ask him."

How was I going to do that? "Who is that?"

"I can't give out that information."

"But it's my card! My name's on the account."

"Yes, but it's been frozen."

"I know that! That's why I called you."

"You'll need to speak with the main account holder. Is there anything else I can help you with?"

"You can't tell me anything about my money?"

"Not beyond what I've already said."

"Why can't you at least give me his name?" I exclaimed.

"Because I have a note on the account not to."

I threw my head back and dug the tree bark into my scalp. "Thanks for your help." I ended the call.

After a few deep breaths, I called the next company, but didn't have any better luck.

Whoever controlled my finances didn't want to be found.

CHAPTER 11

Toby

I TOOK ANOTHER SWIG OF my drink and slammed the glass on the bar.

"Easy there." Tap mixed a drink, sprinkled in some faerie dust, and then dumped in ice. "What's eating you up?"

"Nothing I feel like talking about."

"I suppose that's why you're here in the afternoon without any of your pack mates." He added the drink to a round tray with some others and stepped out from behind the bar. Tap went from eye level to four feet as he stepped from his platform behind the bar.

"Want some help?" I asked.

The troll shook his head. "I'm fine. It's just not usually so busy around here in the afternoons. Maybe I'll hire one of your college pups."

"Just don't call them pups to their faces."

"Noted." He went to the next room and handed the drinks to a group of witches.

I took another sip and became aware of the loud buzz of conversation around the Faeble. It wasn't often I came in the afternoon, but when I had, it'd never been this busy.

Perhaps I wasn't the only supernatural creature having a bad first day. It was a college town, and the number of inhabitants had tripled, if not quadrupled, in the last several days.

Someone sat next to me, but I didn't turn to them. I had no interest in talking about Victoria or my overwhelming disappointment concerning her memory loss or complete lack of interest in me. Even providing her lunch hadn't phased her.

"What has you tied in knots, sugar-cup?"

I held in a groan and turned. My eyes nearly popped from my head and the glass shook in my hands. I set my glass down and scooted away.

The tall, slender blonde smiled. "Don't worry, handsome. I'm not here for you."

"I-I… you're a valkyrie." My heart thundered against my ribcage.

Her grin turned crooked. "Like I said, I'm not here for you."

My mouth dropped.

"You… you…"

"I take souls. Yes, I know." She leaned against the bar and yawned.

"What are you doing here?" I wasn't sure I could take any more bad news—and a valkyrie couldn't mean anything good.

Tap sauntered back over to the bar. He grinned when he saw the angel of death. "Soleil."

She leaned her chin against her palm. "Tap, my old friend. How are you?"

"Much happier now that I'm running the Faeble. I got tired of fighting the ogres for my lake. You want your usual?"

"Yeah, but go easy on the unicorn horn flakes. I don't like my drinks too sweet."

Tap muttered something about picky valkyries.

Soleil turned to me. "Isn't he adorable?"

I stared at the tough-as-nails tattooed troll mixing the drink at hyper speed. "Uh, if you say so."

The valkyrie shoved me, and I struggled to stay on the barstool. "Well, I find him cute as can be."

Tap turned around and handed her a tall rainbow-colored drink. "Light on the flakes."

She sipped it and closed her eyes. "Perfect."

I eyed Tap. "How do you two know each other?"

He gave a slight nod, seeming to understand my unasked question—why was an angel of death sitting next to me?

Tap leaned against the bar. "Soleil and I met centuries ago during a particularly bloody revolution against my people. We quickly became friends."

"I helped him defeat the ogres he mentioned earlier."

"Until they came back with their cousins." Tap grimaced.

"That was practically fifty years later." Soleil shook her head.

"I suppose, but like I said, I'm much happier running this place." He turned and mixed more drinks.

Soleil and I sipped our drinks in silence. I hoped to sneak out unnoticed once mine was gone, or better yet, that she'd leave.

"So, what has a gorgeous wolf such as yourself so upset?" she asked.

"Girl trouble," Tap answered for me as he poured yellow alcohol into a cup.

"Ah." The valkyrie nodded as though that explained everything. "Maybe I can help."

"I'd like to keep her alive, actually."

"You know, I don't take the souls of everyone I come in contact with. Tap will tell you."

"She doesn't," he assured me. "I'm living proof."

"Great."

"What's the problem?" Soleil asked.

"She can't remember him," Tap said.

I glared at him. "Thanks."

"Give her a chance, she could get to the bottom of this quicker than anyone else in here."

"Really?" I turned to her, suddenly curious.

Soleil nodded, her expression an odd mixture of knowing and boredom. "Care to hear more?"

"You should," Tap said.

Why had I told him anything at all?

The valkyrie shrugged and sipped the rainbow concoction. "Whatevs."

I took a deep breath. "What does it involve?"

Her face lit up. "You want my help?"

"I'll hear you out."

Tap gave me an encouraging nod before taking another tray to patrons.

Soleil put her glass down. "All I have to do is drink a little of someone's essence. I can learn a lot that way."

I stared at her. "Drink her essence?" I exclaimed. "What does that even mean?"

"Let me show you."

Tap walked by, his tray empty.

Soleil stared at him.

"What?" he asked, stepping back up to his platform.

"I need to show wolfy, here, that drinking someone's essence isn't the kiss of death. I save that for the ones I have to kill."

"Of course," I said.

"It's close, though." Tap mixed another concoction.

"Wait, what?" I exclaimed.

"I can show you." Soleil leaned close.

I shook my head. "No way."

"Tap?" she asked. "It was your idea."

"Mine?"

"Come on." She batted her eyelashes.

"Fine. Just a little, okay?"

She clapped her hands.

My stomach twisted. What had I just gotten my friend into?

He leaned over the bar, across from the valkyrie. She stretched toward him, and as she did, wings pressed through her shirt. They spread out, one nearly knocking me over. I jumped out of the way just in time.

Soleil put her hands on Tap's cheeks and closed her eyes. He closed his, also. She opened her mouth, but didn't kiss him. His mouth opened, seemingly in response to hers. A couple inches remained between them.

After a few moments, I wondered if they were playing me. But then a light purple mist appeared from Tap's mouth.

I stumbled back, knocking over my stool.

Soleil widened her mouth and the mist swirled in a circular pattern until it entered her mouth.

I stared back and forth between them, never having seen anything like that.

Tap seemed okay. He wasn't resisting in any way.

She let go of his face and closed her mouth, breaking the flow of the swirls. The remaining purple mist returned to Tap's mouth. Her wings disappeared into her back, leaving her shirt torn and bloody.

His eyes flew open. Peace and relaxation flooded his expression.

Soleil's eyes remained closed for a minute. She opened them and leaned back, staring toward the ceiling.

I arched a brow at Tap. He took a deep breath, but didn't respond.

"What was that?" I asked.

Her mouth curved upward. "Like I said, drinking his essence."

"Did it hurt?"

Tap smiled. "Heavens, no."

Soleil giggled. "It's pleasant on both sides—unless of course it turns into a kiss of death. Then it's only fun for me."

"What exactly does that do?"

She leaned on her palm again and studied Tap. "So, a trickster has been giving you issues?"

He blinked a few times and moved to mix a drink. "You tell us, essence-drinker."

"You think he came from the south somewhere. He's been playing pranks on your customers."

Tap nodded. "Shaved a young wraith bald as she ate appetizers over there a few days ago." He nodded toward a table in the middle of the room. "All her hair was gone before anyone noticed—even her."

"This is all interesting," I said, "but what does it have to do with Victoria and me?"

Soleil sat up straight. "Oh, pretty name. Not one you hear much anymore."

"It was pretty common when we were young." I sighed. "How do you think sucking her soul is going to help us?"

The valkyrie scowled. "Drinking her essence. It's an entirely different thing. I can see into her thoughts and experiences. If she can't remember you, I might be the only way to find out what's behind that. You two were in love?"

My heart constricted. "Madly."

She frowned and tilted her head. "Tell Soleil everything."

"Can't you just suck—drink—my essence to find out?"

"I could, but I like to hear people tell their stories."

"She does." Tap disappeared with another tray of drinks.

"So, what happened, wolfy?"

"My name's Tobias, but everyone calls me Toby."

"Ah, Tobias. Another one that's been left by the wayside. Tell Auntie Soleil your troubles." She twirled a blonde strand around her finger and stared intently at me with her dark green eyes. Her gaze seemed to bore into my soul—it probably did, given her nature.

I squirmed, finished off my drink, and then returned the stiff stare. "We grew up in rival packs, but we were always drawn to each other. As we grew older, we'd sneak off together whenever we could. We'd planned to run away and start our own pack... but that didn't work so well."

"Meaning?"

"She died in my arms." I looked away and cleared my

throat before the quirky blonde angel of death could see my eyes misting.

"Aw, that's horribly tragic." Soleil sighed dramatically. "And now she's back to life, and can't remember anything? Or just you?"

I shrugged and swirled the ice in my otherwise empty glass.

"Leave it to me to figure out the missing pieces to your puzzle."

"Why do you care?"

"Why wouldn't I?" she countered.

"Don't you have better things to do than to play match-maker for werewolves?" I asked.

"Not really. I'm taking a break from my mission."

I turned to her. "What do you mean?"

She blew air up, making her bangs bounce around. "I'm searching for a vindictive dictator who doesn't wish to be found. My superiors won't be surprised if I'm here on earth for a few decades. Gives me some time to play and have fun."

"Oh."

"Anything else I should know about the beautiful young werewolf?" She took a sip of her drink.

"Victoria didn't shift on the full moon."

Soleil choked and put her glass down. "How's that possible? I thought the moon forced you guys to change."

I frowned. "It does. There's no way around it—or at least there isn't supposed to be."

She cleared her throat. "I'm certainly no expert on other species, but I thought it was totally impossible to avoid the full moon."

"Me, too—and I once was alpha over a great many packs. If someone had figured out a way to avoid the curse of the moon, I'd have heard about it."

Soleil took a deep breath. "Now I really want to drink her essence."

"How are you going to do that? Just walk up and offer a kiss?"

She laughed. "Good one. No, I've been around a great many millennia, and I've picked up a trick or two in that time. You got a picture? Location?"

I pulled out my wallet and showed her my favorite picture of Victoria.

"What a beauty. Where's she staying?"

"Not sure, exactly. She's a student at the university, though. Somehow, she ended up in my statistics class."

"You're a student, too? Are you following her?"

"I'm a professor."

"Sexy."

"So, do you want something in exchange for your essence-sucking?"

"Drinking," she corrected. "And no, that's plenty payment." She licked her lips. "There isn't anything tastier or more fulfilling than the essence of a supernatural."

"Aside from taking the entire soul." Tap returned to his place behind the bar.

"Clearly." Soleil finished off her drink. "Well, I'm going to make like a baby and head out. I'm dying to know what's keeping a werewolf from shifting at the full moon."

"Wait," I said.

She turned to me, brows arched.

My teeth gritted. I didn't want to say what I needed to.

"Yes?" Soleil asked.

"You might find her with the jaguar shifters. They have a—"

"Club. I'm quite familiar with it. Let me tell you what I know."

CHAPTER 12

Victoria

CARTER LOOKED AT ME FROM behind his laptop. "How's it going?"

I groaned. "Massaro's a jerk."

The server came by. "Would you like more appetizers, or are you ready for dinner?"

"Could I just get some more sparkling cider?" I asked.

He nodded and turned to Carter. "Master Jag?"

"I wouldn't mind some crab cakes."

"Coming right up." He disappeared.

"How's the essay coming along?" Carter asked.

"Great, but no matter what I do, I can't get it to exactly three thousand words. First I had two-thousand-ninety-six, then three-thousand-fifteen. Now I'm eight words under. Why does the word count matter so much?"

"Because he likes to make people miserable."

"Mission accomplished," I muttered.

"Want me to have a look?"

I shrugged. "You have yours to worry about."

"It's done. Scoot over." Carter came around to my side of the booth and sat next to me, pressing his side against mine.

He angled my laptop toward him and read under his breath. "That's really good. You said you're eight words short?"

"Yep."

He scanned the screen. "Oh, we can beef up this one with some extra words." He typed. "Perfect. What do you think?"

I read it over and looked down at the word count. Exactly three thousand words. "You're a lifesaver."

Carter put his arm around my shoulders. "Nah. You did all the hard work, and I was serious about it being great. Did you have really good grades in high school?"

Tears blurred my vision. If only I knew.

"What's the matter?" he exclaimed. "Are you okay?"

My nose grew warm and my lips trembled. "It's been the crappiest day, that's all."

He squeezed my shoulders. "I hope I helped somewhat."

I blinked and a tear fell to my face. "You did."

"Do you want to talk about it?" He ran his fingers through my hair.

Did I dare? It would be so nice to tell him everything. Maybe he could even help—he certainly had the resources. Another tear escaped and ran down my face.

Carter brushed his finger under my eyes and held my gaze. "You can tell me anything. I could never judge you."

Another tear escaped. He leaned closer and kissed it. Then he trailed kisses down to the edge of my mouth.

My heart beat out of control. There was no way he couldn't feel that—knowing how nervous I was. He brushed his lips against mine and cupped my chin.

All my worries seemed to melt away into the background. He continued to kiss me gently, sweetly. I relaxed and kissed him back, wanting to forget about everything else in my life. I just wanted to melt into him.

Someone cleared his throat on the other side of Carter. "Your crab cakes and cider."

Carter let go of my chin and waved at the server without pulling himself away from my lips.

"Master Jag, your father has arrived with Shu Hwang."

Carter groaned and then pulled away from me. "Thank you. If he asks about me, tell him I'll find him in a while."

The server bowed and walked away.

"Is everything okay?" I asked, still recovering from the kiss.

He nodded. "Just one of Father's overseas business associates. He likes me to sit in on the meetings so I'll know what to do when my time comes. He can't wait for me to become his partner so he can shove stuff like that in my lap, but I don't want to burden you with that. You were about to tell me what's weighing you down." He gazed into my eyes.

I took a deep breath. "It's going to sound crazy."

Carter kissed my nose. "Never."

"You don't know what I'm dealing with, though."

"Try me."

I opened my mouth, but nothing came. It was too insane to say out loud.

He ran the back of his fingers along my cheeks. "I promise, you can't tell me anything crazier than I've already heard."

"What do you mean?"

"You'd never believe some of the things I hear around here. The Jag is home to a great many wild secrets."

My mouth went dry, so I grabbed my sparkling cider and emptied the glass. "I can't remember anything," I spit out.

His brows came together. "What do you mean?"

"I have no memories before arriving here on the Peninsula." I blinked away more tears. "Somehow I drove here in my packed Jaguar, all set for college life."

He rubbed his stubble. "So, you're saying you don't know who your family is?"

I shook my head.

"You don't remember going to school? Sports?"

"No," I whispered, fighting back a sob.

"And nobody's tried contacting you? You can't find them online?"

I leaned my head against his shoulder. "My phone and laptop were practically on factory settings." Minus the jaguar images. "And I don't know who's controlling my money, but they've cut off access. The banks won't tell me who he—or she—is."

"Wait." He leaned back and looked at me. "You have no money?"

My cheeks warmed. "Ten dollars in my purse."

He swore. "None of your cards work?"

"Nope."

"Are you kidding me?"

I studied him. "What's wrong?"

"You've been left high and dry. What about your bills—tuition, car? Rent?"

"I don't know."

"I can't believe this!"

"There's not much I can do. I don't know who to talk to."

His face contorted. "I can't believe this."

"You already said that. I think I'm going to have to find a

job. It's obvious I can't rely on my family, or whoever has been funding all my stuff."

"No, you're not finding anything. You can work here."

"Here?" I exclaimed. "Doing what?"

"Whatever you want. Serving food. Overseeing the servers. Setting up the dance hall. Anything that sounds good."

My mouth gaped.

"We pay top dollar and provide the best benefits you'll find. If you work afternoons, you'll even have time to get some of your studying in."

"But—"

"Nothing. You need work. I'm here all the time. It'll give me an excuse to see you." His expression softened and he brushed his lips across mine. "Give me a minute. I need to speak with my father. Stay here."

I nodded, too shocked to respond. Not only did he not question my sanity, but he wanted to help—by getting me a job at the Jag? My head spun.

A tall blonde with intense green eyes stopped at the table. "Are you Victoria?"

I studied her. "Do I know you?"

"No, but I've seen you around here a lot lately. Carter seems to have taken to you." She sat across from me.

"You know Carter?" I asked, feeling a twinge of jealousy. She was gorgeous.

She held out a hand across the table. "I'm Soleil."

I shook her hand. "Nice to meet you."

"Where are you from?"

My emotions were too raw. "Around."

"Yeah, me, too. Don't you just love the Jag?" She glanced

up at the fancy overhead light, just above our heads. "They put so much detail into everything. I'll bet even the custodian's closet is pretty."

"Maybe."

"What did you do before moving here?"

"I went to high school."

Her forehead wrinkled. "Really?"

"What else? I'm here for college."

Soleil's mouth formed a straight line as she studied me. "You seem more mature than the average freshman."

I shrugged. "Maybe I've been through more than them."

"Oh, that sounds interesting. I bet you have some great stories to share."

"Not really." I leaned over and glanced down the restaurant, hoping to see Carter. He was nowhere in sight.

"Carter's talking with his dad and some old but handsome Asian guy."

"So, you come here often?" I made myself comfortable.

"More lately. How do you like your classes? Got anything interesting?"

I stared at her. Why was she taking such an interest in me? Because I was spending time with Carter? Everyone at the club treated the Jags like they were royalty.

"Have you seen that new math instructor?" Soleil fanned herself. "Think he has a girlfriend?"

"How would I know?"

She glanced around and then leaned over the table. "Mind if I ask you something personal?"

"Go ahead." It wasn't likely I'd be able to answer. Then maybe she'd get bored with me and find someone more interesting.

Soleil curled her finger, indicating for me to lean toward her.

I did.

She opened her mouth, but didn't speak. Something from deep within me pulled up through my throat. It was smooth, like silk, and glided up through my mouth and out. My eyes shut on their own, and a warm tingle ran through my body, massaging my every fiber. A slight breeze fanned my skin. The pulling sensation continued and the tingle grew warmer. My body went limp, and suddenly, my problems didn't seem to matter anymore.

Everything stopped. My back straightened and my eyes opened. I blinked several times and fought to find my voice. "What... what was that?"

Soleil looked deep in thought and confused. "Interesting."

"What?"

"I've never seen anything like that."

"Like what? What did you do?"

She glanced to the side. "Looks like Carter's about to head back. It was so nice to meet you, Victoria. We'll speak again soon, okay?"

"Um, sure."

Soleil smiled, her eyes seeming even greener than before. Almost unnaturally green.

Without a word, she slid from the booth and hurried away.

I leaned back against the seat, trying to figure out what had just happened. A slight tingle remained from our interaction— whatever that had been. I wanted more.

Carter appeared and slid next to me again. "Sorry that took

so long. I hope you don't mind, I ordered us some dinner. No sense in you worrying about that. If you need to get home, I can have them box it up for you."

I scooted closer to him and leaned my head against his chest. "I'm happy here."

He put his arm around me. "I'm glad to hear it." He kissed the top of my head. "By the way, Father said you can either work as a manager in the dance hall or help in the spa. Apparently, they're short-staffed."

"Spa?" I exclaimed.

Carter laughed. "I always forget we have one. The last thing on my mind is getting a pedicure."

"Really?" I teased. "I pictured you with a mud mask, cucumbers on your eyes, and someone shaping your nails."

"I wouldn't mind seeing you get pampered like that. In fact, how does that sound after dinner?"

My mouth dropped open. "I couldn't…"

"Couldn't say no? Perfect. Besides, it'll give you a chance to see what it's like in there. You can decide if you'd rather work there or in the dance hall."

One corner of my mouth twitched. "Well, I don't see how I can say no when you put it that way."

The server arrived with two steaming plates of food. I pushed my laptop to the other side of the table, and he set the plates in front of us. The one in front of me was lobster and the one Carter had was a fancy steak.

"Anything else?" asked the server.

"A bottle of our best white wine," Carter said. "Oh, and red, too."

"Coming right up." He bowed and left.

Carter removed his arm from me and scooted over. "If you'd prefer the steak, you can have it. I'm fine either way."

I studied the two plates. "Lobster sounds wonderful."

We dug in, and I was glad to have a distraction from all my problems. Plus, relaxation lingered from my interaction with Soleil and also Carter's kiss earlier.

"Father wants me to return to his meeting with Mr. Hwang, so feel free to take all the time you want in the spa. Get a full body massage if you want."

"So, if I work there, I can get pampered anytime I want?"

Carter chuckled. "You can, anyway."

We ate our dinner and then packed up our laptops.

"I'll show you to the spa," he said and took my backpack from me, "but then I have to return to business. Feel free to interrupt me when you're done—please do, actually. Those meetings tend to bore me to tears."

He led me down a dimmed hallway I'd never seen. We arrived at two enormous glass doors. He opened one and gestured for me to go through. I entered a wide-open entry with a sprawling gold desk. Mirrors lined one wall that led down a brightly lit hallway.

On the other side was a waiting room with luxurious-looking leather sofas. Paintings of hot springs, mountains, and cherry blossoms lined the walls. A long fish tank with coral and bright fish sat in the corner. Soft instrumental music played in the background.

I took Carter's hand and walked over to the tank. I could identify most of the fish. That made me sad because I had no idea why I knew their names.

"Hello," came a soothing feminine voice from behind. A slender, beautiful girl about my age with hair flowing to her waist smiled at us. She gave a slight bow. "I'm Yurika. May I help you?"

Carter nodded. "This is my special guest, Victoria. Anything she wants is hers—and on the house."

Yurika clasped her hands. "My pleasure, Victoria. What can we get you started with?"

"One other thing," Carter said.

"Yes?" Yurika turned to him.

"If she likes it here, she may decide to assist you."

The girl's eyes lit up. "Oh, delightful. Things have been harried since—"

"Yes," Carter interrupted. "For now, she's the most important guest here. After her treatment, feel free to ask her about assisting—only if she's interested."

Yurika bowed. "Yes, Master Jag." She turned to me. "Are you ready, my lady?"

I glanced at Carter. He pressed his palms on either side of my face and his mouth came down on mine. Before I could react, he pulled away. "Enjoy yourself, beautiful. You deserve it."

My breath caught.

He held my gaze for a moment and then spun around and left. I couldn't look away from the closed door.

"What would you like to start with, my lady?" Yurika asked.

I turned to her, unable to answer.

"My suggestion is a facial when you're stressed. Clear your skin and your mind." She smiled sweetly.

"Okay."

She looped her arm through mine. "Follow me."

CHAPTER 13

Toby

I PACED THE LENGTH OF the bar.

Tap shot me an annoyed glance. "You're scaring away my patrons."

"Seriously?" I fanned my arm around the busy room. Not a single customer was paying me an ounce of attention.

"Friend, you're driving me nuts." The troll scowled at me.

"Where is she?" I exclaimed.

"Soleil will be here when she's done. Do you think she can just walk into the Jag and tell your girlfriend to pucker up?"

"That would be nice."

"You and I both know it wouldn't go over well. Go home. I'll send her your way when she gets back. It could be hours." His bushy brows furrowed.

"I doubt my pack will be very excited about a valkyrie showing up."

"You're the alpha. Tell them to get over it."

My skin bristled at the thought. "I'm not a traditional alpha, Tap. I'd think you'd know that by now."

"You mean you're not your father."

A low growl escaped my throat.

"See? That's exactly what you meant."

"Right. I'm not a *traditional* alpha. I don't treat my guys like dirt or the women like objects." The wolf inside me clawed to get out and attack something. Being that it was so close to the full moon, turning was possible but it would wreak havoc physically. I pushed him down.

"You can still tell your pack to chill when Soleil arrives. They're doing pretty well with that vampire in your home." Tap arched a brow.

I nodded, but didn't want to mention that I *had* used the alpha card to convince some of them to relax. Anyone following me knew I was against the ancient werewolf-vampire animosity. Hatred, really. Too many wars had been fought, too many lives lost. It was pointless.

Any werewolf who followed me had to agree to act in peace toward all other supernaturals.

"They are doing okay with her, right?" Tap asked, breaking my thoughts.

"Yeah, no one would dare cross either Jet or me." Ziamara was the lone vampire living in my home because she was Jet's wife. They'd met under my watch, years earlier when I'd been training Jet.

"So, they'll be fine with Soleil."

"An angel of death is of a slightly different caliber than a vampire."

"How so?" I asked.

"I'm pretty sure our blood isn't toxic to valkyries."

"Fine. Sit down and have a drink. Just stop your bloody pacing."

"Oh, all right. You win."

Tap wandered over to the liquor. "What do you want?"

"Surprise me." I pressed my face against my palms and shook my head. What would Soleil learn about Victoria? If she couldn't remember me, what else had she forgotten? And along the same lines, how much would the valkyrie be able to read if Victoria herself didn't know the answers?

A glass hit the counter next to my elbow.

"Try that," Tap grunted.

I glanced up to see the same rainbow drink Soleil had ordered earlier. "What *is* that?"

"I said try it." He folded his arms.

It bubbled and seemed to shine with glitter.

"Seems a little girly for me."

"Wuss," Tap muttered.

I grabbed the glass and swallowed the drink in one gulp. It tasted of citrus and other fruits, and practically fizzled and popped in my mouth. The sensations continued down my throat and into my stomach.

"That wasn't so bad, was it?"

It left me with a strange mixture of relaxation and energy. I wasn't as worried as I'd been, nor did I feel like pacing—I was ready to run a marathon.

"You wanna head home, and I'll send the valkyrie after you?"

I wiped my mouth. "Yeah, sure."

Half of Tap's mouth curved up. "Glad to hear it. See you later."

"Have you been to my house?"

"The old Moonhaven mansion."

I nodded. We just called it Moonhaven, though that wasn't

an important detail. As long as he could point Soleil there. "Thanks, Tap."

"Hope she remembers you."

"Me, too." I ran my fingers through my hair, hoping Soleil found something we could work with, and rose from the stool.

Someone bumped into me. "Hey, watch it."

I turned to see a vampire baring his fangs at me.

"Put those away," I told him. "My blood could kill you."

He jumped toward me, hissing. "I have a silver blade in my pocket, pal. That could kill *you*." He shoved my shoulder.

"I don't allow fighting in here," Tap said. "You wanna hang out at the Faeble, you get along with everyone."

The vampire's eyes turned red as he glared at Tap. "I could take you, shorty."

"You think so, huh?" Tap came around the bar and held up a fist toward the vampire. "Ever fought a troll?"

"Always wanted to." He lunged for Tap.

I grabbed his shoulders and threw him across the room. "Play by the rules or go home."

He rubbed his head and looked at his palm. "I'm bleeding. You two are going to pay." He ran toward us.

Several others from around the room jumped up from their tables and surrounded the vampire. He was outnumbered by about a dozen angry supernaturals.

"You mess with Tap, you mess with all of us," said a siren.

"Use your song on him," said a water faerie.

"Or I could send him to Valhalla." Soleil stepped around the group and glared at the vampire. Her wings spread open and her eyes turned black.

The vampire stumbled back, his pale skin now white as a

sheet. "You're… you're…"

A smile spread across her face. "A valkyrie, yes. They don't like vampires in Valhalla."

He scrambled away, but Soleil blocked him with a wing, sending him to the ground. The vampire pulled himself up with a barstool. "I'm leaving, okay?"

Soleil shook her head, her eyes still deathly black.

"What?" the vampire squeaked.

"You owe Tap an apology for coming into his place of business and insulting him."

"I-I…"

She stepped closer to him. "He opens up the Faeble to all supernaturals—even the occasional pet human. All he asks is that everyone put aside their differences and get along. Is that really so much to ask of those he serves?"

The vampire gulped and shook his head. He turned to Tap. "I'm sorry, I didn't know. My friends, they told me to come in here and stand my ground against a werewolf. We-we could smell him from the woods. I was just turned a couple weeks ago, so I don't know all the rules."

Soleil put her hands on her hips. "Then I suggest you learn them. Around here, we stick together."

Tap stepped near the trembling vampire. "Wars have been started from less. If that's what you want—"

"No. I'm sorry. I'll j-just leave."

"Maybe you should."

The vampire ran past the group, stumbling over his own feet. Several others laughed and shook their heads.

"Stupid newbie," muttered the siren and went back to his seat.

Soleil's eyes turned back to green. They seemed a much more vibrant shade than when I'd spoken with her earlier. "Sometimes it pays to be an angel of death." She winked at Tap.

"I could've taken him," Tap huffed and headed back his place behind the counter.

"Oh, I know," Soleil practically sang. She grinned at me.

"Did you find Victoria?" I asked, ready to get down to business.

Her expression sobered. "Yeah. You want to go somewhere more private to talk?"

My heart plummeted. "Bad news?"

"Well..."

I turned to Tap. "Any of your private rooms available?"

He gestured down the hallway. "Take your pick."

"Lead the way, sailor," Soleil said.

"Sailor?" I asked.

She shrugged.

I went down the hall and into the first available room.

"What did you find out?" I closed the door behind us.

Soleil and I sat across the table from each other. She stared at me with her deep green eyes. I couldn't pull my attention away from them. The color was mesmerizing. That was probably one way she lured her prey.

"Her memory has been wiped—"

"Permanently?" I exclaimed.

"I wouldn't know, but I couldn't access what she didn't know. So there's that. Make of it what you will. But I was still able to pick up plenty for us to work with."

The room seemed to spin around me. "What *did* you find

out?"

"She can't access any memories before she came here, and she suspects it has something to do with the jaguars, but has no idea they're shifters. In fact, it appears she has no idea about the supernatural world at all."

My mouth dropped. "But that wouldn't keep her from turning on the full moon."

"No, but being spelled would."

"Spelled? You mean by a witch?"

"I don't know of anyone else who casts spells."

"The curse can be broken with a spell?" I slunk into the chair.

"Seems to be." Soleil smacked her lips. "Spells always leave a foul taste in my mouth. Bleh."

"Tell me everything. Don't leave anything out." I sat up straight and stared at her.

"She feels a connection with you—"

"I knew it. I could see it in her eyes."

Soleil frowned. "It's not much, though. She doubts her own feelings."

My shoulders slumped. "Oh."

"But if I were you, I'd go after her. Make it so she can't doubt. Whatever you two had together, it was strong enough to leave remnants despite that spell. She can't remember her family or anything else about her past, but she does remember you."

"What, exactly?"

Light pink colored her cheeks. "This is where drinking people's essence gets uncomfortable. I experience their memories and feelings as though they were my own."

"Meaning?"

"Though she hasn't gotten close to you, she knows you smell good, feel nice, and are a great kisser. Every time she looks at you, those memories bubble to the surface."

My pulse raced. "That's something I can work with. If I brush my hand against hers, she might remember more. I can find the cologne I used to wear—"

"Aftershave. She liked the way it smelled with your soap."

"That's right," I whispered.

"But there's something you need to know." Her tone shot fear through to my very core.

"What?"

"She seems to be building a relationship with one of the young jaguars."

"Why?"

"He keeps taking her to the Jag. I've never seen anywhere nicer, outside of a castle. I can't blame the girl. I'd start to fall for someone who took me there, too."

"No wonder she wasn't impressed with me buying her lunch today at the cafeteria."

Soleil put her hand on mine. "She's confused. Feels alone. Don't take it personally."

"Is there a way to get her memories back?"

"If I were you, I'd find a witch and try to get to the bottom of the spell. I'd also try to spend as much time with her as possible. Tutor her or something, but don't sit around while that young leader woos her."

"He's a leader?"

She nodded. "Next in line to be their version of an alpha."

"Why are the jaguars interested in her? They view werewolves as bottom feeders. Trailer trash. Algae in the pool of life."

"They like her." Soleil shrugged. "She's a daughter of an alpha. Maybe they don't have one in the jaguar world. Jags have to marry by a certain age, or they can't be alpha, right?"

"I wouldn't know. How close is the guy who's pursuing her?"

"No idea, sorry."

I rubbed my aching neck. "None of this makes sense."

"She's back from the dead and remembers your sexy kisses. Use that to your advantage."

"I'm her professor!"

"What's more important? The love of your life or a job? If you really need money—"

"I don't. It's just to blend in with the humans. They already whisper about us because we live on private property in the middle of the woods. You wouldn't believe some of the rumors going around."

"Then don't worry about getting fired. Once Victoria remembers you, you guys can go anywhere. You can even just stay in the woods."

"And we need to act fast. Her body's going to start to deteriorate if she doesn't shift soon."

"Maybe the spell protects her from that. But I'd be more worried about the jaguar. He's probably close to the age of marrying."

"So?"

"He could be banished from his place in his family if he doesn't marry in time—and he definitely has his sights on Victoria."

My nostrils flared. "If he marries her, he won't live to see his next day."

CHAPTER 14

Toby

BRICK CAME INTO MY STUDY. "Dinner's ready."

"I'm not going to eat with you guys tonight."

He tilted his head. "Everything okay?"

"No."

"Food will help. Time with your pack, too."

"I appreciate your concern, but not tonight." I felt bad saying no because meal times were so important to the pack—dinner in particular. We had large appetites and we tended to bond over a good feast.

"You're our alpha. It won't be the same without you."

"I said no," I snapped.

Brick stood taller and his expression turned stoic. "Yes, sir."

"Wait, Brick."

He spun around and left the room.

I stared at my—blank—notes for the next day's lessons and threw them across the room. "Damn it!"

Not much stung worse than being at odds with anyone in my pack. The only thing worse was being apart from Victoria—and knowing that a pompous jaguar was trying to win her over that very moment. The thought of the arrogant jerk staring into her eyes and running his hands through her hair was enough to distract me from everything else.

I was going to have to wing it in class the next day. Luckily I knew math like the back of my hand.

Grumbling and shuffling sounded from the kitchen. I needed to get my mind off Victoria long enough to get through dinner.

Sighing, I picked up the strewn papers and shoved them on my desk. I took a deep breath and stormed into the kitchen.

A dozen sets of eyes glanced up at me. Eleven of my pack mates and one rainbow-haired vampire.

"Toby?" Jet asked, eying me warily.

"I'm just on edge." I turned to Brick. "I apologize for the way I spoke to you in there."

He looked down. "You don't have to, sir."

"Yes I do, and in front of everyone. I have no right to snap at you—any of you." I took a deep breath. "I haven't told you what's going on, and you deserve to know."

They all exchanged curious and worried glances.

I sat at my spot at the head of the long table and took another deep breath. "Victoria is here on the Peninsula."

Gasps and whispers filled the table.

"Why isn't she *here*?" asked Ziamara. She was not only the lone vampire in Moonhaven, but the only female, too. She was probably eager for Victoria to join us.

My mouth formed a straight line as I considered my wording. "She's having some memory issues."

"What do you mean?" Jet asked.

I hated to say it out loud, but I had to tell my family. "She doesn't remember me."

"Sir!" Brick exclaimed.

"She also doesn't realize she's a werewolf. Someone found a way to get around the curse, and she hasn't shifted."

Mouths dropped and eyes widened.

"I'm trying to figure out how to resolve all of this."

"Have you talked to Gessilyn?" Ziamara asked.

"Not yet. I'm working with someone named Soleil. If she stops in here, I want everyone to welcome her."

"What is she?" asked Dillon, one of my newer pack members.

"Don't freak out," I said.

"I think you just assured we would," Jet said.

"She's on our side." I narrowed my eyes.

"What is she?" Dillon asked again.

"A valkyrie."

Gasps and worried exclamations went around the table. A few jumped out of their chairs.

"I said to remain calm," I reminded them. "Soleil isn't here for any werewolves. She's friends with Tap and is taking a break from hunting a dictator."

Everyone grumbled.

"Come on," Ziamara said. "If Toby and Tap trust her, she's safe."

"Easy for you to say," Dillon snapped. "You have no soul for her to take."

"Hey!" Jet jumped from his seat, knocking it over. "Take that back, fool."

"Face it, she's a vampire." Dillon narrowed his eyes. "No soul."

Jet ran over and pulled Dillon from his chair by the collar. "If you've spent five minutes with her, you'd know better."

"She's dead, stupid."

Jet balled his fist and hit Dillon across the face. "Want to say that again?"

Dillon wiped some blood from his nose. "It's the truth."

"Learn to respect your leaders." Jet threw him across the kitchen.

I jumped up. "Enough!" I narrowed my eyes at Dillon. "You will respect Jet as the assistant alpha. And when I'm not here, you treat him as alpha. Got it?"

Dillon rubbed his back and nodded. "Yeah."

I glared at everyone around the table. "That goes for everyone. We're a peaceful pack, remember? We don't fight unless provoked."

"Thank you," Jet said.

"I meant by outsiders. Sit," I ordered.

Everyone took their seats.

"You all need to relax. I know I do, as well. You're probably on edge because I am. Do I have your word that no matter who comes to our home, you'll treat them with respect? Witch, valkyrie, anything."

"Vampire," Dillon muttered.

Jet raised a fist at him.

"Do I need to send you two to your rooms?" I asked.

They both looked at me like I was crazy.

"I'd send you outside to burn off your energy, but I'm afraid only one of you would return."

Jet shot Dillon a smug look. Dillon rolled his eyes.

"Why do I feel like I'm running a daycare rather than a

pack?"

"He started it," Dillon said.

"Shut it," Brick barked. "Both of you."

Dillon and Jet glared at each other.

My patience was wearing thin, and if they kept it up, I would risk losing my cool. I'd led packs long enough to know how little time it took for a couple of young wolves to wreak havoc. "You two need to stop right now."

The two of them both looked down.

"We are a pack, and sometimes not being a natural-born family, that makes things harder."

Dillon glanced at Ziamara.

"We all treat each other with respect. You disrespect each other, you disrespect me."

A few heads snapped their attention toward me.

"That's right," I said. "Look at Brick, he doesn't get into petty scuffles. He's mature and—"

"A guard." Dillon scoffed. "I'd rather be a leader."

"Is that what this is about?" I leaned forward.

He shrugged.

I was too tired to deal with this and everything else. "Maybe sending you two out into the woods to work this out like pups is the best solution."

Jet's expression tightened. "I'm up for it."

"Me, too." Dillon cracked his knuckles.

Ziamara peered at him from around Jet. She put her hand on her husband's shoulder. "Hey Dillon, how do you feel about a vampire bite?"

"It'll hurt you a lot worse than it'll hurt me, babe."

"Watch it," Jet warned.

"I'll risk it," Ziamara said. "You think Toby would let me stay here without plenty of werewolf venom cure on hand?"

"Do you ever get tired of rainbow-colored hair?" Dillon asked her. "I sure get tired of it."

The doorbell rang.

"Thank God." I rose from my seat. "You two work this out however you need to—just leave Zia out of it. I'm going to talk with the valkyrie about Victoria."

Several eyes widened.

"I told you, she's not going to hurt anyone—as tempted as I am to have her deal with you two." I stared at Jet and Dillon.

Both of their faces paled.

The doorbell rang again. I hurried to the front door.

"I was beginning to think I had the wrong house." Soleil gave me a playful smirk.

"You know of any other Victorian home in the middle of huge acreage?"

She shrugged. "I didn't know of this place before today. Could be others."

"So, what's going on?" I asked. "I wasn't expecting you here so soon."

"I'm trying to scope out your girlfriend's life, but she's apparently working at the Jag—and they've wised up to me. I couldn't get in this time. They—"

"She's *working* there?" I exclaimed. "Doing what?"

"That's what I'm trying to find out. You might have to ask her, though."

I sighed, feeling more defeated by the moment.

"Probably waitressing or something. Speaking of food, I'm starving. You got some dinner?"

A slow smile crept across my face thinking of the pack meeting her. It might help them to chill. "We're having dinner now. Why don't you join us? You should meet the other wolves, anyway."

"Thanks." She stepped inside.

I led her to the kitchen, but before she entered, I glanced at my pack. "I have someone I'd like you to meet. Everyone, this is Soleil."

They all sat up in their seats, their eyes wide and faces paling.

She stepped inside and waved her fingers. "Hi, boys. I hope you're not giving Toby any trouble."

Dillon dropped his fork.

Soleil turned to him. "Ever seen a valkyrie in action?"

"N-no. I swear, I meant no harm."

Her eyes turned black. "Behave, or you'll see what I can really do."

"I-I... Yes, ma'am."

Jet chuckled.

I pulled out a vacant seat. "Soleil is going to join us for our meal. I know you'll all show her the same respect you'd show any other guest."

Mutterings of *yes* went around the table as she sat.

"What are you boys talking about?" Soleil piled some fried chicken and mashed potatoes onto her plate.

"Want to tell her, Dillon?" Ziamara asked, a hint of teasing in her voice.

Dillon shook his head and shoveled food into his mouth. He looked at Brick. "Tastes great. Thanks."

Zia grinned.

"You guys helping Toby with Victoria?"

"Not much we've been able to do," Jet said. "But now, I guess that's changed. Do you have any ideas?"

"Did any of you know her before she died?" Soleil asked. "We need as many people and things as possible to jog her memory. Who knows what will crack the spell?"

"It would have to be Toby," Brick said. "You should have seen how in love those two were. Never seen anything like it."

"You knew her?" Soleil asked and poured gravy over everything on her plate.

Brick nodded. "Me and Sal." He gestured to my other guard.

"You two been with Toby all this time?" Soleil bit into her chicken and closed her eyes. "Oh Valhalla, this is so good." She looked back at Brick. "You made this? You from the south?"

He nodded. "I did, and Mama grew up there."

"Props to your mama for teaching you to get this right. Anyway, you and Sal have to get in with Victoria if you can. And all three of you have to think about things that will spark memories. Like, if you used to cook this before, make it for her—and be sure to invite me."

Brick chuckled, clearly enjoying the praise. "You can take the leftovers home."

Soleil turned to me. "I like this guy."

"Me, too. That's why I keep him around."

"Where are you staying?" Brick asked.

"Here and there." She dug into the potatoes.

"What does that mean?" Brick tilted his head.

"Depends on the day. Not sure where I'm going tonight."

"You should stay here," Brick said and then he turned to

me, wide-eyed. "I mean, if you think that's a good idea, sir."

"I'm more than happy to provide a place for her to stay." I looked at Soleil. "We have several spare rooms if you'd like to claim one for a while."

She leaned close and whispered, "Does he always cook?"

"Mostly, yeah. I like to cook before the full moon, though."

Soleil stared at Brick's muscles before meeting his gaze. "You're something else."

He shrugged, but also smiled.

Ziamara caught my attention and grinned.

I turned to Soleil and Brick, who were still staring at each other. "We'll have to work together in finding Victoria."

"Definitely." Soleil sighed. "Brick and I will have to spend a lot of time together figuring out a way to break through her memory."

He grinned. If his wolf were out, he'd be wagging his tail and nuzzling up to her.

CHAPTER 15

Victoria

I STUMBLED INTO THE STATISTICS classroom, barely able to keep my eyes open. Even though I'd gone to bed exhausted the night before, I couldn't get my mind to settle down. There was just so much to think about, and now I couldn't focus on any of it.

"You okay?" Grace asked as I sat next to her.

"Yeah, sure." I sipped my latte, hoping the extra shot I'd ordered would help.

Grace gave me a once-over. "Did you get drunk last night or something?"

I nearly spit out my coffee. "No. Aren't you too young to know about that?"

She snorted. "I'm fifteen, not stupid."

"Sorry. I was just up late, that's all. Got a new job."

"Really?" she exclaimed.

"Why is that surprising?" I nursed my latte.

Grace shrugged. "I guess I figured since you drive a Jaguar, you must be sp—I mean, uh, well off. You know, like you wouldn't need to work."

"You think I'm spoiled?"

Her face turned red. "I didn't mean that. I swear."

"Trust me, I have as many problems as anyone else. And it looks like I'm meant to learn the value of hard work."

She breathed a sigh of apparent relief. "Where're you working?"

"A place called the Jag."

Her mouth dropped. She stared at me. "Serious?"

I nodded.

"Doing what?"

"Learning the ropes in the spa. I'm greeting people when they arrive and in the slow times, they're teaching me how to do manicures and pedicures."

Her eyes lit up. "Is it fun?"

"So far, but I'm not looking forward to touching people's smelly feet."

Grace snorted.

"What?"

"People who go there aren't gonna stink."

"Guess I'll find out."

Professor Foley came in and started setting his things up. Some of the girls crowded around his table, but he sent them back to their seats.

Relief flooded through me. I watched as he opened his laptop and organized some papers. His hair looked so soft, I could actually feel it between my fingers. I could smell the woodsy, masculine scent of his aftershave.

Grace said something in the background, but I couldn't make it out. I didn't care. I just wanted to know if Toby smelled the way I seemed to remember. If his stubble would tickle as I trailed kisses down to his lips—

"Victoria."

Annoyed, I turned to Grace. "What?" I snapped.

She frowned and turned to her laptop. "Never mind."

"Sorry."

"Whatever. Didn't mean to bother you."

Toby—Professor Foley—cleared his throat and told everyone to open their text books. Some people pulled out physical books, while others turned on their tablets. I'd forgotten both. Great.

He scanned the class as he spoke, skipping over me. He held Grace's gaze for a few moments before moving onto the next student.

I felt the sting of… what? Rejection? Disappointment?

Why did I care? I was probably just imagining that we had a past together. It was ridiculous. He was older than me—a professor, for heaven's sake! I was just a freshman who couldn't remember anything.

I was grasping for straws—embarrassingly too eager to find things that weren't there. He was hot, and I just *wanted* to smell and feel his hair. Which was ridiculous, especially considering what I was building with Carter. He was gorgeous, too—and I *knew* what he smelled and tasted like. Purely wonderful. Plus, he'd gone out of his way to bring me to the club and even get me a job.

He was who I needed to focus on. Not an out-of-reach professor who already had gobs of girls clamoring for his attention. What was I, besides some girl who couldn't even keep her credit cards up to date? That was probably why he wouldn't look at me. He might even regret having helped me with lunch. As soon as I received my first paycheck, the first thing I was going to do was to repay him. Then hopefully we could just be a normal student and instructor.

Grace poked me.

I looked up. Professor Foley and the entire class was looking at me.

My face burned.

"Answer him," Grace muttered.

"Can you repeat the question?" I cleared my throat.

He smiled, instantly relaxing me. "I asked if you have any questions about the syllabus."

Oh, good. An easy question. I shook my head. "It was perfectly clear. My favorite, actually."

A few people snickered around me.

My face warmed again.

Toby's smiled widened and the kindness in his eyes nearly melted me into a puddle. "I'm glad to hear it." He turned and asked another kid something about the syllabus.

I slumped down in the seat, my heart thundering against my chest.

"Maybe you need more coffee," Grace whispered.

Or a cold shower.

Toby moved to the white board and started writing numbers with a red pen. He turned around. "Statistics is my favorite math course, and I hope to help you all enjoy it as much as I do."

Some people groaned and others giggled.

I didn't know how I'd learn a single thing with him teaching. Looking at that gorgeous face was too much of a distraction, especially when our gazes met. Somehow I needed to find a way to break my attraction to him. It would be the only way I could survive with a decent grade.

He started speaking about the real-world uses for statistics, and it piqued my interest. I followed along, typing notes, finally able to concentrate as I stared at the screen.

It seemed like time sped by, and before I knew it, the class was over.

"Can I ride with you to the other side of campus?" Grace asked. "I promise not to annoy you. Well, I'll try not to."

"Yeah, sure." I slid my laptop into my bag.

"Sorry about earlier."

"Don't worry about it. I'm sure it was me. I gotta get more sleep."

"Yeah, don't you know coffee's bad for you?"

I held my latte close. "No, it's liquid heaven."

She laughed and then we headed for the door.

"Victoria," Toby said.

I froze and then turned to him, unable to find my voice.

He smiled sweetly. "It seems like you might be having trouble, is there anything I can help with?"

My mouth gaped and the room heated by at least ten degrees. Or was that me?

"Since we eat lunch at the same time, why don't we talk then?"

A group of girls stared at me, jealousy covering all of their faces. If looks could kill, I'd be dead on the floor.

I glanced back at Toby. "Okay. Thanks."

He grinned, seeming genuinely happy. "Perfect, I'll see you then."

A curvy brunette with too much makeup stepped forward. "Can we make it a study group, Professor Foley?" She batted her eyelashes.

"Shoot me an email, and we'll set up a meeting in my office."

Her face fell, and she left the room, muttering. The other girls followed, consoling her.

Toby didn't seem to notice. He turned back to me. "Maybe we can find somewhere to eat outside. The weather's so nice this time of year, it would be a shame not to take advantage of it."

I nodded, unable to stop looking into his beautiful eyes. I could get lost in them if I let myself.

"Perfect. See you in an hour."

Grace tugged on my arm. "We gotta go, or we'll be late."

"See you then," I whispered to Toby and then pulled my gaze from him.

Geography proved to be a good distraction, and by the time I made it to the cafeteria—paying with cash that Carter had given me—I felt more grounded when Toby found me at the soda fountains.

"Are you ready to discuss statistics?" His eyes crinkled in the corners when he smiled at me.

"As ready as I'm ever going to be." I cringed, hoping that everything coming from my mouth over lunch wouldn't sound so stupid. "Thanks for helping me out."

"My pleasure. I saw a shaded bench outside. Hopefully it's still free."

I followed him outside, balancing my tray. He led me to a picnic bench that had a couple squirrels fighting over a nut. Toby shooed them away and brushed off the table.

We sat and ate quietly for a few minutes. After I'd finished my chicken salad, I glanced up and found him looking at me. As we stared into each other's eyes, I couldn't help noticing how at ease I felt. Like I was home.

Or crazy. He was my professor.

I pulled my gaze away and picked at some fruit.

Something inside of me urged me to ask him if we'd met before. I told it to be quiet. It said no, that I needed to talk with him.

My theory about going crazy was looking more like a possibility than ever before. Except that crazy people didn't know they were crazy, did they?

I sighed.

"Is everything all right?" he asked.

"I'm just tired. You know, trying to get used to college life."

"It's pretty different from high school, isn't it?" He tapped the table. The look on his face made me think he knew something about what I couldn't remember.

That only proved I was losing it.

"What was high school like for you?" he asked.

I shrugged. "You know."

Toby shook his head. "Tell me."

"I thought we were here to discuss statistics."

He straightened his back. "I'm just trying to get a feel for your background. Were you good at math?"

I bit my lower lip. "Maybe."

"You don't know?" His eyes were kind. Concerned.

The world seemed to spin around, out of control.

"Is something the matter?"

I studied his face. The urge to pull him close and make

everything better was strong. My arms wanted to reach out for him. But it was ridiculous. I was crazy.

He cleared his throat and leaned a little closer. "If it's stressing you out too much, we can change the subject. What do you want to talk about?"

My pulse picked up speed. "I don't know." I looked down at my food, but I'd lost whatever appetite had remained.

What was wrong with me?

Something inside me nudged me to tell him.

Now I was hearing voices, to top everything off. Tears misted my eyes. I tried blinking them away.

"Victoria?"

I glanced up at him. A single teardrop clung to an eyelash.

His mouth dropped. "Are you all right?"

"Yeah, fine." I wiped my eye, brushing away the tear. "Everything's great."

Toby frowned and put his hand on top of mine. His skin was so soft... his touch, so familiar.

The voice inside of me screamed to tell him everything.

I swallowed, ready to burst into tears. I couldn't lose it in the middle of the bustling campus. In a matter of minutes, people would pour out from the cafeteria and the surrounding buildings. But somehow, crying in front of the man in front of me seemed infinitely worse.

He removed his hand from mine and cleared his throat. "Just know that if you need to talk about anything, I'm here. Not just as a math instructor or faculty adviser." He pulled out a business card. "This is my personal cell phone number. Call anytime you need something, okay?"

I nodded and stuck the card in my bag. The voice inside

urged me to talk about what was going on. I rose and picked up my tray. "Thanks, Toby. The—" I froze, realizing I'd just called him by his first name.

Our gazes locked. His eyes widened and his pupils dilated. Something else registered on his face. Surprise? Hope? It was hard to tell, though it had to be shock. He'd never told our class his first name.

"I-I'm sorry," I stammered. "I don't know where that came from, Professor Foley. I meant no disrespect. I'm sorry."

I grabbed my tray and ran into the cafeteria.

CHAPTER 16

Victoria

I SLUMPED INTO THE SEAT and closed my eyes. Around me, everyone discussed how mean Massaro was for making us write the papers at exactly three thousand words. At least I wasn't the only one annoyed, but at this point, it was the least of my concerns.

Someone sat next to me.

"Are you okay?" Carter asked.

"Yeah." I didn't open my eyes.

"You emailed in your paper, right?" he asked.

"This morning, before my first class."

"What's the matter, then?"

"I'm just tired."

He patted my hand—the same one Toby had touched.

My eyes flew open, and I gasped for air.

Carter studied me. "Maybe I should tell Yurika you need to work a little earlier."

I shrugged. "I don't want to be a pain. I'll work around her schedule."

"What would help you get more sleep? Studying earlier?"

"Not having to write a paper with an exact word count," I

mumbled.

He chuckled. "Let me rephrase that. Is there anything I have any control over that I can help with?"

"I wish. No, I probably just need to get used to college life."

Carter leaned close and whispered in my ear, his breath tickling my skin. "I'm sure it would be a lot easier if you could remember your life, right?"

I nodded and rested against him. "That would definitely help."

He kissed my cheek. "We'll see what we can do about that."

"How?"

"Maybe we'll find the answers in this class. It is psychology."

"I'm not going to hold my breath."

"Why not?"

"I've never heard of an intro psych course solving anyone's problems."

His lips curved into a smile. "There's always a first time for everything. And besides, it's not like your memory is the best."

That comment hit me like a slap to the face. I scooted away from him.

"Wait, I didn't mean—"

"Someone didn't send me their assignment," Massaro bellowed as he entered the classroom. "Which one of you bold souls dared to defy me? You'd best admit it now since I already know who you are."

Silence hung in the air. Despite all my problems, I pitied the person who hadn't turned in the assignment.

"Nobody wants to take responsibility?" He dropped his bag

onto the table. The sound echoed all around.

He narrowed his eyes and glanced around the room. "It would be better for the person to stand up now and admit her shortcoming."

Massaro paced the room, taking the time to make eye contact with each student individually.

Finally, he stopped. "I'm almost impressed with this student's brazenness. But I urge her to speak up now."

The only sounds in the room were of people breathing.

"Who is Victoria Bernhardt?"

My throat closed up.

"I thought you said you sent it," Carter whispered.

"Where is Miss Bernhardt?" Massaro demanded.

I raised my hand.

He came over to me, glowering. "Why didn't you do your assignment?"

"I did." It barely came out as more than a whisper.

"I don't have it." His eyes narrowed and walked over to my desk, towering over me.

"But I sent it."

"When?"

My entire body shook. "This morning, around nine."

"Sure you sent it to the right email?" He leaned down, closer to me.

"Y-yes. I double checked."

He shook his head, making a tsk noise. "Yet *four* hours later, I still don't have it."

I sat up straight. "I can prove it. It's in my sent folder."

"You'd better hope so. Show me now."

Carter met my gaze as I pulled out my laptop. My hands

shook so bad, I nearly dropped it. Once my email was open, I was so nervous, I had to type my password four times before I got it right.

I scrolled over to my sent messages and showed him. "See? It's right here. There's your email address, and it shows I sent it at five after nine, exactly."

He narrowed his eyes. "Open it."

I did and then scrolled through my exactly three thousand word essay.

"Leta Hollingworth. Good choice, though I was looking for someone a little lesser known. Resend it, and if I don't reply, print it out and hand it to me tomorrow. Got it?"

"Yes. Thank you."

He turned around and opened his own laptop. "Turn to page twenty-two of your text books."

I slunk down in the chair, still shaking. Somehow I made it through the class, but once Carter and I were outside the building, I couldn't recall anything Massaro had said after humiliating me.

Carter turned to me. "I'm so sorry you had to deal with that."

"At least I could prove I'd sent it."

"Still, that sucked a big one. I had to keep myself from punching that jerk in the throat."

"It wasn't his fault the email never showed."

"Yeah, but he didn't have to treat you like that." Carter's face pinched. "I still have half a mind to go back in there and—"

"Don't. He has something to prove, and I don't want him taking it out on you. If I have to print out my assignment, I will."

He frowned. "If you're sure, I'll drop it."

"Thank you."

"I gotta get to my next class. Study at the Jag again?"

"Yeah, that would be great."

He pulled me close, embraced me, and kissed the top of my head. "It'll all be fine. Maybe take a nap. I'll call you when I'm ready to head over."

I stared into his eyes. "Thank you. You make me feel sane."

Carter ran the back of his fingers along my jawline. "My pleasure, and you're as sane as they come. I'm serious about that nap." He brushed his lips across mine and walked away.

I watched him until he was out of sight. He really did make me feel normal, which given the circumstances of my life, was a miracle.

A group of four girls came over to me.

"Are you dating Carter Jag?" asked a girl with wavy auburn hair.

"You're so lucky," gushed a blonde. "He barely gives anyone the time of day."

"Have you been to the Jag?" asked the first girl.

My head spun. "Yeah and yeah."

They all squealed.

"What's it like?" asked a redhead, her eyes wide.

"It's really nice," I said. "Look, I have to get going."

"Are you the one who had lunch with Professor Foley?" asked the fourth girl.

"Um, yeah. He was helping me with stats."

The blonde stepped closer to me. "Can you rub some of your hot-guy magnet on me? Oh-em-gee. You're, like, the luckiest girl on campus."

"Right?" The redhead scowled at me. "Save some hotties for other people. So selfish."

"Seriously, I have to go." I adjusted the strap on my backpack and ran for the Waldensian.

Once I got to my room, I found Sasha sitting on her bed, blasting music and typing on her laptop. "Hey! How's it going?"

"Worst day ever." I kicked my shoes off and threw myself on my bed.

She turned the music down. "That bad?"

"Worse. The only good thing is that things can only get better from here."

"Ouch. Can I help?"

"I just need a nap."

"No problem. I can scram. I have a study group soon, anyway."

"Thanks." I pulled my covers back.

"Oh, your dad called not long ago."

The blood drained from my head. "What?"

"Yeah, he called the landline. Nice guy."

My mouth gaped.

"Have a nice nap." Sasha smiled. "Don't forget to call your dad later. Sounded like he really wanted to talk to you."

"I… Did you get his number?"

Her brows came together. "I didn't think I needed to. You don't have it?"

"Uh, never mind. Sorry, like I said—bad day."

She gave me a sympathetic glance. "Take that nap. Seems like you need it."

"I will."

Sasha gathered some things and left the room.

I flopped onto my pillow and pulled the covers up. My dad had called? And talked with Sasha? Why hadn't he called the cell phone? Or was he expecting the service to be cut off?

I dug into my bag and checked my phone. Full service. Everything seemed fine—except for the lack of contacts.

Was there another phone somewhere with all my memories? Pictures of friends and family? Toby?

It was too much to think about, and I didn't want to think of my professor. Not after the way lunch had gone. If he didn't think I was nuts before, he was sure to after the way I'd ran off.

I glanced back and forth between my phone and pillow. As tired as I was, I doubted I could sleep now. I got up and checked the caller ID on the phone. A blocked number. Of course. Maybe there was a way to find out the number my dad had called from.

A half hour later, my online search had yielded nothing useful. The number was blocked, so there was no way I could find it.

Maybe I just needed to take Carter's advice and get some sleep. I still had to study and then work.

At least I had a parent. Maybe whatever Sasha had said convinced him to give me access to the money again. Not that I'd stop working. If this had taught me anything, it was that I needed to make sure I could take care of myself.

I yawned. Maybe a power nap would help. If nothing else, I'd at least feel a little better. I climbed back into bed and closed my eyes. It was too bright to sleep. I pulled one of the pillows over my eyes. Much better.

My body gave into the exhaustion and stress. I fell into

what felt like a deep sleep...

Dark woods surrounded me. I could see a few stars between tree branches. The metallic odor of blood hung in the air. Shouts and cries sounded not far away. A wolf howled somewhere in the distance.

A tree fell behind me, landing with a harsh thud. I jumped and turned around.

"Victoria!"

I spun around again.

Toby ran toward me, covered in blood. "They're going to kill us. We have to leave now."

Fear tore through me. "But my sister—"

"They won't hurt her. She's done nothing wrong. Come on."

"She covered for us. They'll kill her."

A shot rang through the air. Something hit the tree next to Toby's head.

I screamed.

Toby covered my mouth and put an arm around my shoulders. He guided me around the fallen tree, and then we ran, darting around bushes and low-hanging branches.

Footsteps thundered near us. A group of men blocked our path, bearing hatchets. I recognized Toby's father. His eyes narrowed and he aimed his blade at me.

I sat up in bed, drenched in sweat and gasping for air.

The dream had felt so real.

I threw aside the covers and jumped onto the floor. The smell of blood and gunpowder mixed with Toby's rugged scent lingered in my nostrils. I had to get out of there. Away from everything.

My pulse drummed in my ears as I ran down the stairs.

"Are you okay?" Landon called from the kitchen.

"I'm going for a run."

"Without any shoes?"

I glanced down at my bare feet. "Yeah." It didn't matter. I'd had enough of it all—and it was only the second day of classes. I ran out the front door and headed straight for the patch of woods near the Waldensian.

Rocks and twigs dug into the soles of my feet. It felt good in a way—physical pain was better than emotional.

My feet pushed harder, and I finally made it to a small path. Several fire pits were nearby, all littered with bottles and wrappers. I ran faster, feeling the burn in my lungs and legs. Sharper rocks pricked my feet, but I didn't let that slow me down.

It wasn't until I could barely breathe that I stopped. I leaned against a tree and gasped for air. Everything around me seemed blurry. I couldn't remember what'd had me so stressed.

Good.

I huffed and puffed, breathing in the clean, fresh air. Somehow I knew I'd always loved the woods because of all the wonderful smells. Today, it was a pleasant mixture of soil, pine needles, berries, and something musky. I sniffed the air, zoning in on the musky scent. Though I couldn't place it, it struck me as familiar.

A gray and black wolf walked up to me. I gave it a double-take. It was the same one I'd seen when jogging a few days earlier.

It sniffed my leg and then plunked its backside on the

ground.

"You again?" I exclaimed. "What's the deal, big guy?"

The animal nuzzled its nose against my leg and pushed its head underneath my hands.

"And now you want to be petted?"

I had some interesting luck—at least it wasn't attacking me. I rubbed its ears and the top of its head, half-expecting it to bite me despite how things had gone before. Instead, its tail wagged and whipped against the ground.

It seemed to remind me of something. Maybe I'd had a dog growing up that had acted similarly.

"If we're going to keep running into each other, I should give you a name. What do you think?"

He continued wagging his tail.

I studied the cute face. "You seem like an Alex. Sound good?" Not only that, but it was a name that could belong to a male or a female.

The wolf continued to rub against me, apparently agreeing, or maybe just enjoying the attention. Maybe it wasn't a wolf, but just a lost dog. How would I know the difference? I felt confident that it was a wolf, but really, why was I so sure?

I slid down to sitting and the animal sniffed my face, rubbing its wet nose on my skin. Though I should've been concerned, I wasn't. I closed my eyes and he rested his head in my lap.

After a while, I woke with a start. The wolf glanced up at me, seeming to question what was going on. I rubbed my eyes.

"I think I'm supposed to meet Carter." I jumped up and ran toward the mansion, groggy and with slow reflexes. A low-hanging branch hit me in the face and as I rubbed my face, I tripped over a root and tumbled to the ground. I rolled a few feet, picking up dirt and leaves in my hair.

I tried dusting myself off, but it was pointless—I'd need a shower. As I ran, more twigs and pebbles dug into my feet.

Once I finally reached the Waldensian, the cherry-red Ferrari sat in front.

My stomach dropped. I didn't want him seeing me like this.

CHAPTER 17

Toby

I CLOSED THE OFFICE DOOR. My afternoon class had felt like it went on for an eternity. I still couldn't get over the fact that Victoria had called me by my first name. I hadn't told any of the students what it was.

Somehow she'd remembered. It had freaked her out, but she'd remembered.

A mixture of hope and frustration filled me as I watched her run into the cafeteria after our lunch together. It continued to run through me, making it hard to focus on anything else.

Despite her inability to remember our life together, it was still there. It was just a matter of breaking the barrier, and it was already cracking.

The sound of her voice saying my name continued rolling around in my mind. I couldn't stop thinking of the look in her eyes when I'd put my hand on hers.

Things were clicking—her memories awakening. I just needed to find a way to help the process along without sending her running every time.

Knock, knock.

I sat in my chair and grabbed a stack of papers so I'd look

busy. "Come in."

The door opened and Roger came in. "Some of us have a weekly poker game, and a spot just opened up. Interested?"

His question caught me off guard. "I'm not really a gambling man."

"Oh, it's just for fun. I've never lost more than forty bucks. Drinks, snacks, and guy time."

I thought of my unruly pack the previous night and wasn't sure I needed more testosterone-filled time.

Roger closed the door and walked to my desk. "Let me level with you."

I arched a brow.

"It wasn't easy convincing the others to let you in."

"Why's that?"

"No one trusts you, but if you join us—"

"What? Why doesn't anyone trust me?"

He took a deep breath and sat in the student seat across from me. "Look at all the facts, man. You're new and young, yet you have a reference list longer than anyone else."

I shrugged like it was no big deal. "I've moved around and taken my career seriously."

Roger scooted closer and rested his arms on the desk. "You live in the middle of the woods on a huge property."

"Something wrong with that?" I tilted my head.

"Only the fact that everyone in town is curious about that place. It was abandoned so long, it became common knowledge that it was haunted. And now a mysterious new professor comes to town and renovates it with a bunch of college kids." He held my gaze. "People are talking—a lot."

I took a deep breath. In trying to lay low, I'd only managed to raise everyone's suspicions. "I assure you it's not haunted, and nothing weird is going on with anyone living there. They're my family."

"Family? You've got every race in there from white to Asian to Samoan."

"There's been a lot of adoption. And besides, you forgot Hispanic and African. I have an equal opportunity family."

Roger chuckled and leaned back. "You don't have to explain anything to me. I like you, and I'm sure you have your reasons. You strike me as a guy who just likes his privacy. Nothing wrong with that. Join the game, and it'll show everyone that you're a normal guy."

I ran my hands through my hair. "It's weekly?"

"Every Friday night. Vinny from the history department brings his famous moonshine—I'm telling you that alone makes it worth it. But it's a ton of fun."

I took a deep breath. Did I really have time for a weekly game? On the other hand, I knew how fast things could go south when the locals didn't trust us. I held back a shudder.

"Can I get back to you?" I asked.

His eyes lit up. "Let me know by tomorrow."

"Okay."

"Think seriously about it."

I tipped my head. "I will."

He got up. "See you tomorrow."

"Bye, and thanks for the invite."

Once the door closed behind him, I rubbed my temples. I almost had no choice except to join the weekly card games. I'd thought that becoming a professor would help stave off questions and doubts, but apparently not. I'd have to talk with the pack and see what everyone thought. A weekly game on top of my job just felt like too much of a commitment.

I opened my wallet and pulled out my picture of Victoria. Oh, how I longed for the days when we were both in love with each other. I really had to get to the bottom of that mystery. Figuring that out was far more important than a game—unless not going would put my pack in harm's way.

I'd had one home burned down. I didn't want that to happen again.

"I wish I could talk with you about this," I whispered to the picture.

Another thing I wished was that I still had all my old photos of her. But they'd been destroyed in the fire, and that had been before the days of digital photography. Nothing was stored on some remote cloud. Back then, clouds had only existed in the sky.

My phone vibrated. I pulled it out of my pocket and saw I had a new text from Gessilyn. She'd probably expected to hear back from me by now.

> **Gessilyn:** *U OK?*
> **Toby:** *No*
> **Gessilyn:** *Want 2 get 2gether?*
> **Toby:** *Yeah*
> **Gessilyn:** *Free now?*

I checked my schedule. I didn't have any student appointments, but it would only be a matter of time until they filled my afternoons.

> **Toby:** *Yes*

Gessilyn: *Ur place?*

Toby: *Gimme 20 min*

Gessilyn: *OK*

At least I had a witch on my side. She had ways of finding things out that no one else I knew did. And she wasn't just any witch, either. She was the high witch and could do things others only dreamed about.

I gathered my things and locked my office. Down the hall, I could hear Roger talking about the poker game.

When I got home, Dillon was staring out a window, muttering to himself.

"Everything all right?" I asked.

He glanced at me. "Fine."

"Talk to me."

"Honestly?"

I set my bag down. "Of course."

"Sometimes I wish I lived in a normal pack."

"You mean one with a harsh alpha who demands unyielding obedience?"

Dillon frowned. "I mean one that didn't allow other species in."

"Did Ziamara use your hairspray again?"

He glared at me. "No. I was taking a leak when your witch friend jumped through the mirror."

I held in a laugh, but a smile escaped.

"It's not funny," he snapped.

"No, I'm sure it wasn't." I cleared my throat. "I'll talk to her about traveling through a different mirror."

"Yeah, well, tell her I hope she enjoyed the show, because

that's all she's getting." He stormed past me and went outside, slamming the door behind him.

At least I never had to worry about life being boring. I sniffed the air and smelled the scent of a witch in the kitchen. It smelled like someone else was with her.

I went into the kitchen. Brick was laughing with Gessilyn and Soleil. Gessilyn, as usual, looked more like a fitness instructor than a witch with her yoga pants, pink racerback tank top, and a blonde ponytail.

They all stopped laughing when I came in.

"Don't stop on my account." I went into the fridge and grabbed some juice. I sat next to Gessilyn. "Dillon says hi."

Her face flushed red. "I should probably place a rune on a different mirror for traveling here. You don't mind, do you?"

I chuckled. "The guys who use the downstairs bathroom would probably appreciate it."

"You won't tell Killian about that, will you?"

"Your secrets are safe with me, but he'll probably find it funny, too."

"I know. That's the problem."

"Did we miss something?" Soleil asked.

"Nothing important." I took a swig of my juice. "But something big did happen today."

"What?" Gessilyn asked.

They all leaned closer.

"Victoria accidentally called me Toby." I could still hardly believe it. "I never told her my first name."

"Really?" Soleil asked. "You sure she didn't find out some other way?"

"I wouldn't know, but she was so shaken up, she ran off."

"Do you think she remembers anything else?" Gessilyn's eyes widened. "We might be getting close. Soleil filled me in on what she found out."

I turned to Soleil. "Did you find out anything new?"

She shook her head. "I haven't been able to talk to her alone, but I'll keep trying."

"Does she remember anything else?" Gessilyn repeated.

"I can only guess at this point. When I look into her eyes, I swear I see her wheels turning, but she won't open up to me. I think we need to look into the jaguars some more."

Everyone nodded.

"What do you know?" Gessilyn asked.

"Aside from them being super rich?" Soleil asked.

"I've heard some things," Brick said.

We all turned to him.

"What?" I asked.

"Rumor has it they practically rule certain parts of the world—well, the supernatural creatures, though their influence does seem to creep into human territory, too."

"Where?" Gessilyn asked.

"Mostly Mexico and Central America, but as we've seen, they're moving north."

"But what do they have to do with Victoria?" I exclaimed. "Are they behind her memory loss?"

"That's what it seems," Gessilyn said. "Before you found her, all my locator spells came up with jaguars, remember? They seemed to be protecting her."

I frowned. "From me?"

"Who knows?" Soleil asked. "It could be anything."

"Between us, we should be able to figure out something." I

stared at Gessilyn. "You're learning new spells every day, right?"

"It's more complicated than that, but basically, yes."

I turned to Soleil. "And you can learn people's secrets by drinking their essence."

"But I can't get to what she doesn't know."

"Can't you find a way to get some jaguar essence? Like that one she was dancing with?" My stomach tightened at the memory.

"They're hard to get that close to. I can't get it from across the room, and like I said, I can't get into their club."

I turned to Gessilyn.

"I'm not a jaguar."

"But you're a witch. Can't you concoct something?"

"I can look into it. The problem is that I know so little about them. This is the first I'm aware of them being so far north. They're probably going to hate how cold our winters are."

I sat back, feeling full of resolve. "Then I'm going there."

Brick's eyes widened. "What are you going to do, sir?"

"See what I can do. I won't know until I try."

"I'm going with you."

"I think I should go alone. Otherwise, they may feel threatened."

His face tensed. "Then I'm going to follow you, and watch from a distance. No way I'm letting you walk into that alone."

"I've already been there once."

"When?"

"As a wolf."

"So, that's where you went."

"And I'm going back, and I'm not leaving until I have some answers."

"Wait," Gessilyn said. "Give me a chance to work on a spell for you. Do you want me to cloak you with invisibility? I'd offer to disguise you as one of them, but I'd need some jaguar blood."

My teeth gritted. "I'd gladly supply you with some."

CHAPTER 18

Toby

I CROUCHED LOW AT THE edge of the woods. The building looked the same as I remembered it, though now I could read the sign. The Jag—how clever. At least I knew I had the right place.

The parking lot was pretty empty. Just a few expensive cars sprinkled throughout.

Jet sniffed the air. "Those jaguars have a strong odor."

Brick turned to me. "Sir, if we can smell them, they'll be able to smell you. We'd better have Gessilyn whip up something to disguise your scent."

I shook my head. "There's no time." I sniffed the air. It didn't appear Victoria was anywhere in the area, though I caught a faint trace, indicating that she'd been there recently—probably within the last day. "I need to go now."

Someone drove up and parked near the front. He got out and went to a door I hadn't noticed. A bouncer let him in, disappearing inside, also.

It was now or never. I rose and dusted some dirt off my pants. Then I headed for the building like I owned the place. I had more than enough money to start something like it if I wanted to, but I didn't. I was happiest teaching and taking care of my pack. No, that wasn't true. I was content. I wouldn't be happy until Victoria was back at my side.

As I walked across the parking lot, I could feel Brick's and Jet's gazes on my back. The others weren't far behind. If I ran into trouble, at least I wasn't alone.

My skin prickled with excitement. I was on the hunt and in my element. My ears were hyper-aware of every sound. All the smells intensified. My muscles prepared themselves for action, whether it be running or fighting.

I approached the door, and it opened before I reached it.

A tall, dark, muscular man stepped outside. He frowned and crossed his arms and turned his nose down. "We don't allow your kind here."

"I need to speak with someone."

"Then call and make an appointment."

I stopped about a foot from him and shook my head. "No, I need to talk now."

He glowered at me. "To whom, exactly?"

"Whoever's in charge." I narrowed my eyes.

"Not if you don't give me a name."

We stared each other down. I tried glancing inside, behind him.

He closed the door behind his back, leaving it open only a crack. "No name, no entrance."

"Can I leave a message for the person in charge?"

"Sure, tell me who and I'll gladly pass it along."

"It's regarding Victoria."

His eyes widened, but then he quickly recovered, returning to his stoic expression. "So, you want to leave a message for

Victoria? She's hardly in charge."

"No, I can speak to her myself. I'm sure you'll tell your boss about this conversation whether or not I tell you his name. You can tell him that I'm not going to back down until her memories are restored. She deserves to know her past."

He seemed to be fighting to keep his expression resolute. "You need to leave."

"Assure me you'll pass it along."

"I promise you nothing." His brows came together. "Leave before we have to escort you and your wolves off our property."

I didn't flinch at the mention of my pack in the woods. "This isn't the last your boss will hear from me. Pass *that* along." I spun around and marched into the woods until I was out of sight from the club.

Brick, Sal, and Jet hurried over to me.

"What's going on?" Sal asked. "Do you need me to tear them apart?"

I shook my head. "I'm going to sneak in."

"Sir?" Brick exclaimed. "Is that such a good idea?"

Jet and Sal looked at me like I was crazy.

When I was a wolf, I saw what I'm pretty sure is a staff entrance.

Sal growled. "I don't like it."

"Me, neither," Brick said. "You've already spoken with that bouncer. He's sure to pass along the message. I doubt he's going to let it sit that a wolf tried to come in."

"As do I," I agreed. "But I can't just walk away. I need to get inside and find out what's going on."

"You don't think they'll smell you a mile away?" Sal asked.

"They probably know we're all out here."

"What am I supposed to do, then?"

"Wait and see what they do," Sal said. "Give them a chance to come to you."

"No. I've waited long enough for Victoria. Those jaguars have some kind of hold on her, and I need to find out what."

"Then I'm going in with you," Sal said. "I can't let you do this alone."

"Don't encourage him," Jet said. He turned to me. "You have the pack to think about, too. Not just Victoria."

I glared at him.

"She's fine, right?" Jet asked. "They're not hurting her."

"No, they've just stolen all her memories," I snapped.

"I mean she's safe. In no imminent danger."

"That we know of. I'm going in."

Jet's nostrils flared. "This is a bad idea. I feel it in my bones. You said Gessilyn's working on something, right? Have some patience. That's what you always tell us."

I stared at him, hating that he was using my own advice against me.

"Look, I don't want to see you get hurt. Especially before you have a chance to get back together with Victoria."

A low growl escaped my throat. My wolf urged me to get in there and fight for our wolfess. We were only half an alpha without her on our side. If it were possible to shift right then, I would have. Instead, I burst into a run, heading for the backside of the building where I recalled seeing someone take the trash out.

Footsteps sounded behind me. I didn't want to bring anyone else in with me. Not only would I be putting them in danger, but it would make our wolf scent twice as strong.

I stopped and spun around. Jet nearly ran into me. He skidded to a stop only inches from me. "You go, I go."

"I order you to stay back. This is my fight."

"We're a pack. That's stronger than family. You're stuck with me."

"No. Go back and check on the others at home. Ziamara needs you."

"You need me more right now."

Sometimes wolf loyalty had serious drawbacks. "I'm going. You're not. End of discussion." I narrowed my eyes and stared him down until he looked to the ground in submission.

"Okay, but know I don't like it."

"Noted."

He glanced up at me. "And I'm going to keep watch from the woods."

"Great."

"If I even sense trouble, I'm going in."

I wanted to argue, but I couldn't turn down backup. "Not if you sense it. You have to be sure of it." I glowered at him until his nose faced the ground again.

"Fine."

"I'm serious."

"Yes, I understand."

Brick and Sal caught up.

"What's going on?" asked Sal.

"Make sure he stays down unless I'm in trouble."

They both stared at me.

"I mean it."

"Yes, sir."

I spun around and ran toward the dumpster before anyone could try to talk me out of it. Once there, I hid behind it and glanced at the building. The dance hall was empty and dimmed. I scanned the building, nearly missing the entrance. It was tucked behind some delivery trucks and on each side sat stacks of lumber.

Glancing back, I could see my three pack mates at the edge of the woods. I took another look all around. There were no jaguars in sight.

This was my chance. I crept out of my hiding spot and ran over to the door. I pulled on the handle, but it didn't budge. Biting back a curse, I tried again.

Nothing.

I'd come too far to give up now.

The others watched from a distance. They'd moved closer to the edge. Jet waved me back.

"Over my dead body," I muttered. Gessilyn and Soleil could continue trying to find answers, but I was done waiting for them.

I knocked on the door and then scurried behind some lumber.

A minute later, the door opened. A guy with a chef's hat opened the door and looked around. He closed it before I had a chance to decide what I was going to do.

I went over and knocked again. This time, I hid where the door would open and hide me.

The door opened, nearly ramming into me.

"Who's there?" the chef demanded. "Smells like roadkill out here."

I shoved the door, slamming it into him. He stumbled and I jumped in front of him.

"What the—?"

"Sweet dreams." I grabbed at his hat and shoved his head against the wall.

His eyes closed and he crumpled to the ground.

I couldn't have done that to the front guard, so luckily the cook was easy to take care of. I had no idea what to expect with whoever I ran into inside.

Stepping over him, I went inside and closed the door, making sure it locked behind me. I was in a hallway littered with brooms, mops, buckets, and other cleaning supplies. It smelled like dirty laundry and wet towels. I stepped in puddles of what I hoped to be water as I made my way down the hall.

The smell of jaguar—musky and catlike—grew stronger as I came to a wider area. Food aromas came from the left, making my mouth water. To the right, cigar smoke tickled my nose and masculine laughter sounded.

I followed the sounds until the white tile turned into a dark carpeting and bright lights gave way to smaller, dimmed ones. I came to a doorway, where laughter and conversation bellowed.

The door was cracked, so I peeked in, careful not to be seen. I couldn't see much, but I did see part of an intricately decorated chandelier and the corner of a table which appeared to be etched with gold decorations.

Footsteps sounded from inside and I jumped back, ducking down an adjoining darkened hallway. A couple waiters walked past silently, carrying platters of empty plates. I followed them a little ways, but stopped.

She was nearby.

I sniffed the air. It was definitely her. I'd know that sweet aroma anywhere. I crept down a dimmed hallway until I came to an empty restaurant. Judging by the air, she was close and she wasn't alone.

Following the scent led me to a booth in a back corner.

Victoria sat with the same well-built guy—a jaguar. He was holding her hand and gazing into her eyes.

Inside me, my wolf howled. I struggled to keep myself from growling. I moved a little closer, careful not to be seen.

Her face and arms were scratched and bruised.

What had he done to her?

My wolf clawed to get out—not that he could no matter how much either of us wanted to shift. I restrained myself from attacking the kid.

Maybe whatever had happened to her hadn't been at his hands. Victoria didn't seem uncomfortable around him. In fact, she seemed entirely too comfortable.

I studied her cuts and bruises. They didn't appear too bad, as if she'd been through something life-threatening. Maybe a tumble.

Oh, how I wanted to ask her what had happened but that would have to wait until tomorrow if she would even be willing to tell me. The way she'd run off earlier made me nervous about her opening up to me again.

Footsteps sounded, heading toward their table from another direction. I headed back the way I came from without any fewer questions that when I'd started. Having seen her, I had even more.

"There he is!"

I spun around. The chef I'd knocked out pointed to me.

Two men twice his size ran at me.

I had nowhere to go.

CHAPTER 19

Victoria

"Are you sure you're okay?" Carter asked.

I glanced up from my laptop and nodded. "Really, it's just a few scratches. I'm fine."

"Promise me you won't go jogging in the woods." His eyes filled with concern. "You could've really gotten hurt."

"I promise I won't go running in the woods *barefoot* again."

His mouth crooked. "How about you won't go in alone?"

"I like running in nature."

"What are you going to do when it starts to rain for days on end?" He reached across the table and took my hand, rubbing his thumb across my knuckles.

My heart fluttered. "I'll get a poncho. Maybe some boots."

"We have a state of the art gym here, you know."

Why didn't that surprise me? "I like the outdoors."

"What if I go jogging with you?" He flipped my hand over and traced my palm, tickling it. "I can double as a protector and a workout buddy."

"Maybe, but sometimes my runs are spontaneous like today. I promise to wear shoes, okay?" My feet still throbbed, reminding me what a dumb idea going barefoot had been.

"I can be flexible. Call me next time." He stared into my eyes.

A familiar scent drifted my way. Something woodsy and rugged—entirely out of place for the Jag. Something inside me pushed me to find out what it was.

I ignored my loud inner voice and squeezed Carter's hand. "I'll try."

He tilted his head. "Try?"

"Maybe I'll buy mace or something."

"You'd be better off with bear spray around here."

A server came to the table and topped our glasses. "Would you like more appetizers? An early dinner, perhaps?"

Carter ran his finger across my hand. "What do you think?"

"An early dinner sounds great."

We ordered, but I couldn't get my mind off the rugged aroma. My inner voice was practically screaming at me to investigate. It was probably the same one that had told me to go for a run without any shoes. I ignored it.

"There he is!" someone cried from the other end of the restaurant.

I let go of Carter's hand and peeked around the corner. I couldn't see anything, but it sounded like people were fighting.

"What's going on?" I turned back to Carter.

He shrugged. "Someone probably broke one of the rules."

"What do you mean? What's going to happen?"

"He'll probably get kicked out. Or worse." He shuddered.

"Worse? Like lose his membership?"

A strange somber expression crossed Carter's face. "Something like that."

It sounded like someone was being dragged away. I tried to look around the other booths and tables, but couldn't see anything. "Does that happen often?"

He shook his head. "Most people don't want to do any-thing to risk their membership."

"How much does it cost?" I asked.

"What? Oh, I wouldn't know. Family discount, remember? How's your psych paper coming along?"

"Better than the last. And Massaro replied to my email saying he got the first one."

"Oh, good." He took my hand again. "Hey, I have an idea. Do you want to take the dinner back to my place? I need a break from all this studying."

"Your place?" My inner voice again fought me. It clearly thought that was a bad idea.

"Yeah, you've never been there. I'd love to show you around."

My heart thundered in my chest. Was he planning to take things to the next level? And more importantly, was I ready for that? Especially with everything going on? My inner voice answered each question with a loud, resounding no.

He traced my palm again. Chills ran down my back.

"Do I make you nervous?" he asked.

I shook my head and pushed my conscience down. It needed to chill. Carter was a good guy and I was an adult, capable of making my own decisions.

"Then let's go. I'll tell Yurika to give you the night off. You deserve it after what you've been through today."

"Thanks."

Carter squeezed my hand. "You like nature, right? You'll love my garden. I based it off the famous ancient hanging gardens."

I stared at him. "Really?"

"Yeah. It's hard to say how close it came, but I like to think it's accurate." He winked.

"Now you've got me curious."

"I'll tell Renaldo to box up our meal and then I'll pop in and talk with Yurika. Just keep working on your paper and don't worry about anything." He kissed my hand and walked away.

I tried to focus on my paper, but couldn't. Luckily, this one wasn't due the next day.

My mind wandered to Carter's place. Did he have his own house? How else would he have his own replica of Babylon's hanging garden?

I glanced around the restaurant. If his family owned the Jag, then it wasn't surprising. They probably lived in a mansion with plenty of servants.

Would Carter take me into the garden and run his finger along my palm again? Maybe gaze into my eyes and kiss me under a flowering tree?

My inner voice screamed at me to go back home to study.

"Shut up," I muttered. Now I was talking to myself. Great.

It continued pushing me to stay away from Carter's place.

Had I been a nun in my forgotten life? Why else would my mind be so much against a relationship with Carter? He was caring, gorgeous, and incredibly fun. Not to mention the fact that he liked me and made me feel sane. I'd be crazy not to be thrilled.

I turned back to my paper and focused on that. At least the voice in my head had quieted itself. I needed to find a way to make it go away. All it seemed to want was my misery.

It wanted me to feel crazy. I wanted to be sane. I would win the war it was waging because I was in control of myself.

I managed to get a few more paragraphs written before Carter returned with takeout boxes. He smiled. "We're all set."

We packed up our laptops and textbooks and headed outside to his car.

"Where do you live?" I asked once he pulled out of the lot.

"Not too far. Dad wants me close, so I am." He turned onto the main road and punched the gas.

"He drives you nuts, doesn't he?"

Carter groaned. "You have no idea. In fact, he's the reason I wanted to get out of there so bad tonight. He was eying me and I could tell he wanted to pull me into the meeting he has planned. Thank God for homework, right?"

"I guess."

He slowed and turned right onto a gravel drive. We went up a hill and around through the woods before finally stopping in front of a mansion bigger than the one I shared with fifty other students.

"I hope my maid cleaned up. If not, I apologize for the mess. Tidying isn't my strong suit."

"It's no big deal." I wouldn't bother if I had someone to pick up after me, either.

Carter got out and opened my door. He led me to the front door, where I half-expected a butler to let us in. He put his palm up to a black box next to the door. Something clicked and the door opened automatically.

"Welcome to my humble abode." He gave a slight bow and ushered me inside.

Everything sparkled, reminding me of the Jag. The entryway had a high, open ceiling and showed off an enormous living room to the left and a beautiful spiral staircase to the right.

I gasped. "This is gorgeous."

He kissed my cheek. "I'm glad you like it. Would you like to eat outside or in the dining room?"

"Uh..." I glanced around, imagining the dining room to be just as elegant as everything else.

"How about the garden?" he asked. "I could use some air. Then I can give you the grand tour."

"Sure."

He looped his arm through mine and led me through the living room. I stared in wonder. Everything was so fancy, it seemed to belong in a museum. Actually, the house *felt* like one. It was hard to believe Carter lived there.

We went out through a sliding glass door. I gasped at the sight. His garden was bigger and more gorgeous than I had ever imagined the ancient one being. Beautiful and unusual plants hung down as far as I could see.

"This way." He laced his fingers between mine and we followed what felt like a maze until we reached a picnic bench. It had a lovely lace covering, plates set out, and two tall lit candles on either side of a bottle of champagne.

Carter gestured for me to sit and then he scooted next to me.

A man in a black suit came over and emptied the food from the boxes onto our plates. Then he popped open the champagne and poured it into glasses.

"Do you need anything else, Master Jag?"

"No, we're fine."

"Very well." He bowed and walked away.

I turned to Carter, my eyes wide. "Why do you spend so much time at the club when you could be here?"

"Usually, it's lonely here. Not today, though." He tipped my chin and pressed his soft, warm lips on mine. "Now it's the perfect getaway. Let's eat before the food gets cold."

My pulse raced. This was all too much. But I wasn't about to complain.

As we ate, I took in the scenery. Flowers and buds of every shape and color surrounded us. It felt like a magical kingdom rather than a garden just outside town.

I'd been hungrier than I thought and emptied my plate when Carter was only about halfway through. I sipped my champagne and enjoyed the sweet aromas surrounding us. The bubbly drink helped me to relax further and seemed to repress that annoying inner voice, and that was probably the best part.

Carter set his fork down. "How do you like my garden?"

"I could live here." I laughed awkwardly. "Okay, that was weird. Sorry."

He grinned and ran the back of his fingers along my jawline. "Not at all. I love how you adore nature—even if it does get dangerous."

"It doesn't. I just like adventure." I grabbed his hand and kissed his fingertips.

Carter held my gaze and leaned closer, leaving barely an inch between us.

My breath hitched.

"As do I." He pressed his palms against my face and moved them back, combing his fingers through my hair.

My skin felt on fire. I longed to feel his mouth on mine again.

The inner voice urged me to pull away.

Shut up, nun.

I reached for his arms and ran my hands up them, enjoying every ripple of his muscles. He flexed and I leaned closer, able to smell his cologne and hair gel. I could see a few faint freckles sprinkled across his nose.

His fingers cupped the nape of my neck and he leaned closer, brushing kisses in front of my ear and trailing down to my neck. I gasped and instinctively raised my chin, giving him easier access. His lips tickled my skin, sending a fire through me.

I moved my hands up to his face and guided his mouth to mine. He wrapped his arms around my back and pulled me closer, kissing me with an intensity that made me shudder.

He purred.

Wait. He *purred*?

I pulled back and stared at him. "What was that?"

My inner voice urged me to run. I didn't budge.

Carter made the purring sound again. "You light me on fire, Victoria."

The way he said my name sent a warm shiver down my spine. I leaned in and pressed my mouth on his. He forced my mouth open and pulled me even closer, so that I could feel every curve of his muscular frame.

The annoying voice screamed at me to leave. It only made

LOST WOLF

me want this all the more. After all I'd been through, I deserved some fun and relaxation.

Carter pulled back and trailed kisses to my ear. "Do you want to take this inside?"

Toby's face appeared in my mind's eye.

I leaned back, surprised.

"We can stay out here," Carter whispered. "It's perfectly fine with me." He nibbled on my earlobe.

A gasp escaped my mouth.

"You like that?" He ran his fingers down my bare arms, giving me the chills.

I ran my fingers through his hair. It was so soft. I pulled on it.

He purred again and ran his fingers up my arms and to my back. He tugged on the zipper, pulling it down.

My inner voice screamed and yelled. Images of Toby from my dream ran through my mind—of him gazing into my eyes with nothing other than undying love.

I pulled back, gasping for air.

Carter let go of my zipper and stared at me, his eyes wide. "Is this too fast for you? I'm sorry. We can slow down. I'd never pressure you to do anything you don't want."

I struggled to breathe normally. Though I was looking at Carter, all I could see was Toby. I shook. The harder I tried to stop, the worse it became.

Carter pulled me close and held me in an embrace. "I'm so sorry. What did I do wrong?"

"I… I don't know what's the matter with me. I'm sorry."

He kissed my forehead. "Don't be. I know you can't remember anything—I should have gone slower." He drew in a

173

deep breath. "It's just that after one kiss, I couldn't control myself. You're intoxicating."

Toby's image flashed in my mind again.

"It's not you."

CHAPTER 20

Victoria

THE COLD PLASTIC BENT IN my grasp as I clung to my iced black coffee. I'd gotten next to no sleep again. Carter had been so upset by my stupid freak-out that he'd insisted we relax by watching a movie in his personal theater. He kept his arm around me the entire time and hadn't placed his sweet lips on me even once.

Then when I was back at the Waldensian, Landon and Sasha bombarded me with questions about Carter and the Jag. When I finally climbed into bed, my dreams terrorized me with images of deadly wolves and hatchets aimed at my head.

I sipped my drink and took a seat next to Grace.

She arched a brow. "What happened to you?"

Absentmindedly, I rubbed a scratch. "Just clumsy, I guess."

Her eyes widened. "You must be a level ten on the clumsy scale."

"It would appear so." I pulled out my laptop and textbook.

"So, what happened?"

"I tripped in the woods."

"Ouch." She cringed and then went on to tell me a story about crashing her bike while camping.

I kept watch for Toby from the corner of my eye. It was nearly time for class to start, and he usually arrived early. A prick of worry tugged at me. Hopefully nothing bad had happened to him.

Of course it hadn't. I wasn't going to turn into a worry wart—or was I already one? I sighed, wishing I knew something about myself.

By the time Grace's story was over, it was a full five minutes past the start of class.

"Where's Professor Foley?" she asked, glancing at her fitness watch.

Others were whispering about him, too. At least I wasn't the only one worried.

Five minutes turned into ten, and then fifteen.

One guy put his stuff away and stood up. "I'm leaving."

Several others followed.

My twinge of concern was growing by the minute.

"Someone should check his office," a guy said.

A group of girls agreed and left the room.

I took a deep breath. Something seemed wrong. Even though I didn't know him very long, showing up late was out of character.

"What do you think?" Grace asked.

"Maybe he's sick or something."

"But wouldn't he tell someone?" she asked.

My stomach twisted in knots. I remembered running off the day before after lunch. Had I upset him when I'd done that? He wouldn't skip class to avoid me, would he?

The more I thought about it, the worse I felt. He'd gone out of his way to be nice to me—more so than anyone else other than Carter or Sasha. He had paid for my meal and then offered to help me over lunch. My stomach churned acid.

What if his absence had something to do with me?

Or more than likely, I was being paranoid and full of myself. Why would the professor not showing up have anything to do with me?

Everyone whispered theories, and to my relief, some of them were far wilder than the ones running through my head. I was pretty certain he hadn't been abducted by aliens or eaten alive by any wild animals.

The girls who had gone to check his office finally returned.

"He never showed up this morning," said a blonde. "Another instructor told us to do whatever he has in the syllabus for today. Basically, we're free to go."

Cheers erupted around the room, and the majority of people hurried out. A few remained, reading from the textbook.

"What are you going to do?" Grace asked.

I shrugged. My pulse was elevated, and I felt sick to my stomach. Something was wrong.

The card. He'd given me his number.

"You okay?" she asked.

"Yeah. I need to make some calls. Mind if I meet you later to drive across campus?"

She glanced at the time. "I have time to walk. I'm just going to do that."

"Are you sure?"

"Yeah. See you tomorrow." She packed up her things and left.

I glanced at the doorway, hoping he'd walk through. Maybe he'd even give extra credit to those of us who had stayed.

But I knew that wasn't happening.

I put my stuff back into my backpack and headed outside. The warm sun felt good, but did nothing to help me feel better. I dug into the pocket with Toby's card, entered the number into my contacts, and called him.

Straight to voicemail. I ended the call.

Maybe I should leave him a message. What if something really was wrong?

I went over to a secluded area and called again.

"Hi, you've reached Toby. I'm not available right now, but if you leave a message, I'll get back to you as soon as possible. Thanks."

My hand shook as I waited for the beep. "Hi Professor Foley, this is Victoria. You didn't show up for class this morning and I just wanted to make sure everything's okay. Hope you're having a nice day."

I ended the call and shook my head, embarrassed. *Hope you're having a nice day?* He was probably violently ill stuck in a hospital bed somewhere. It wouldn't be long before he thought I was a total idiot, and I already had one teacher who thought that.

Sighing, I leaned against the closest tree. What could I do? Running off, excited about getting to miss class wasn't something I could do. Not when I was so sure something had to be wrong.

Maybe I could go to his office. I didn't know what I could find that the other girls hadn't, but at least it was something. It was better than doing nothing.

I pulled out his card again. His office was across campus. Maybe a brisk walk would help to clear my head. I secured my bag over my shoulders and headed for the building.

When I got to his floor, some professors were gathered together, talking about Toby.

My stomach twisted into tighter knots. Something was definitely wrong. I continued heading toward his office, anyway.

A tall blonde sat in the chair behind the desk.

"Is this Professor Foley's office?" I asked.

Her eyes widened when we made eye contact.

"Soleil?" I asked, remembering the girl who had spoken with me at the Jag. "What are you doing here?"

"I'm friends with Toby." Her expression was somber.

"What's wrong?" I exclaimed. "Where is he?"

She gestured for me to come inside. "Close the door."

I did and then sat across from her. "Is he okay?"

"We don't think so."

I felt like throwing up. "What happened?"

She took a deep breath. "It's rather complicated, and you don't remember anything."

"Huh?"

Soleil bit her lip. "I'm not sure how much he would want me telling you."

I stared at her. "You do realize I'm just his student?" Though I was sure I was about to find out more about not only him, but my memory issues as well.

She held my gaze. "You and I both know that's not true, honey."

My shoulders dropped and a lump formed in my throat. "I don't know *anything*."

"You know more than you're letting yourself admit to."

"Stop talking in riddles!"

"This would go a lot faster if I could drink from your essence again."

I stared at her. "What are you talking about?"

"This." She got up, walked around the desk, and stopped inches from me. She closed her eyes and opened her mouth. Mine opened on its own. The same silky feeling from our last interaction pulled up from deep within me and out through my throat.

My eyes fought to shut, but I forced them open as a warm tingle ran through my body, massaging every inch of me. A sparkling purple mist swirled in between our mouths, appearing to travel from mine to hers. If that wasn't weird enough, wings appeared behind her, taking up the entire office. A slight breeze brushed over me with each movement.

The pulling sensation continued and the tingle grew warmer as the mist grew darker in color. Finally, my body went limp. I couldn't remember what I'd been so upset about just moments earlier.

Soleil closed her mouth and everything stopped. I jerked backward. She opened her eyes—and they were an unnatural shade of green. She blinked and they returned to normal. Her wings disappeared.

I stared at her, breathless.

"Okay, now that I'm up to speed—"

"What was that?" I demanded. "You did that to me at the Jag, too."

"For Toby."

My mouth gaped. "What?"

She returned to the seat. "Your dreams—those are actual

memories."

"I-I… How do you know about my dreams?"

"When I drank your essence, I gained access to everything."

I scowled. "Everything? My memories, you mean?"

"Only what you allowed, and—"

"I didn't allow anything! You didn't even tell me what you
were doing." Anger tore through me. "How dare you?"

"Look, Toby needs our help. Are you willing or not?"

"Where *is* he?"

"Being held against his will."

The room seemed to spin around me. "What?"

"Look, I don't want to overwhelm you. There's a lot you
don't know, but I know you remember Toby—even though
you doubt."

I felt completely naked. Her essence drinking, whatever
that was, had given her access to all my thoughts. "Well,
whatever you just did to me, you should know what I'm
willing to do," I snapped. "And how do you know he's being
held against his will? Did you steal his essence, too?"

She muttered under her breath. "He was trying to protect
you."

Everything disappeared around me as I stared at her. I
couldn't find any words.

Soleil reached around me and helped me to stand. "Here,
come sit in the comfortable chair." She helped me around the
desk and sat me in the soft seat.

"We need to get him out, but you're the only one with a
way in."

"You've got to be kidding me." I leaned my elbows against

the desk and accidentally knocked over a stack of papers—I really was a klutz.

"Nope. None of us can get near him."

"Why me?" I picked up the fallen papers and put them on the desk. A framed picture sat on the desk, face down. I pulled it upright and gasped.

It was a photo of me.

Or someone who looked just like me. I held it, trying to make sense of everything. The girl looked just like me, down to a barely-noticeable scar in front of my right ear. Only she was wearing an outfit I'd never seen and was sitting in front of a pond I'd never been to—at least that I was aware. I hated my memory.

"Wh-what's this?" I shoved the frame at Soleil.

"His favorite picture."

I pushed the chair back, shaking my head. "This is all a joke. A really cruel prank." I glanced around for hidden cameras.

She shook her head. "It's not, and he needs *you*."

The room seemed to close in around me. My stomach lurched. "I'm going to be sick."

"The toilet's down the hall and to the right."

I ran past her and found the bathroom just in time. As soon as I rinsed my mouth, I hurried out of the building as fast as I could.

Why did he have my picture? What did it all mean? Whatever the answers were, I couldn't face them.

CHAPTER 21

Toby

MY HEAD SNAPPED BACK, WAKING me. I blinked my eyes, trying to get rid of the bleariness. My arms ached from being tied over my head for so long. I pulled on them, but the metal only dug into my skin again.

I steadied my legs underneath me, using them rather than the chains, to keep me standing upright. If only I had something to lean against. Or to drink. I was parched.

How long had I been in the dark dungeon?

Over to the side of the room lay a human skeleton, still in chains.

That didn't offer me much hope. The only thing I had going for me was that Brick, Sal, and Jet knew I'd gone into the club. But was I even still there? Surely this room wasn't advertised in their brochures.

My right eye throbbed, reminding me of the beating I'd received after being chained. The owner had sucker punched me a few times before unleashing a couple of his men on me.

I coughed, which only made sharp pains shoot out from my ribs. At least all the pain distracted me from the hunger and thirst.

The doorknob jiggled.

My head shot to attention. Was I in for another beating, or would they give me something to drink finally?

The door opened, and in walked the owner. He looked at me and laughed. "How's it going?"

I clenched my teeth, refusing to give him the pleasure of an answer.

"The strong, silent type, are you? We'll see how far that gets you. If you want any water, you better answer my questions."

I groaned involuntarily.

He laughed again. "That's what I thought. What were you doing inside my building?"

"Looking for answers."

"More specific." He punched me across the face.

Blood gushed from my nose. It dripped down my face and onto my bare chest. Instinctively, I tried wiping it, but the chains stopped me. Sharp pains shot through my shoulder.

"Why were you here?"

"Victoria."

"Ah, now we're getting somewhere." A slow, sly smile spread across his face. "My son had a nice make out session with her last night."

I lunged at him, not that it did any good.

"I've got the video to prove it." He pulled out a phone and slid his finger around the screen. "One of these days, Carter will find out about the cameras I have everywhere and be pissed." He chuckled. "But what can he do?"

I turned away from him, ignoring the shooting pains in my neck.

"Here we go. Look at this."

"No," I grunted.

The jerk grabbed my face and forced me to look at the screen. It showed Victoria with the guy she'd been eating with the night before. They sat at a candle-lit table surrounded by plants, just talking.

"Wait for it."

Carter turned to my Victoria and ran his hand along her face. She then kissed his fingertips.

I closed my eyes, refusing to watch anymore.

My captor made a noise in his throat and then something wet hit my eye. "I said to watch," he growled. "Should I turn the volume on?"

I opened my eyes and glared at him through the spit hanging on my eyelashes.

He squeezed my chin and shoved the screen closer to my face.

Carter ran his hands through Victoria's hair. She had her hand on his arms as he flexed. From the expression on her face, she was enjoying herself.

My stomach twisted in knots. The wolf inside me raged, eager to escape. I averted my eyes, unable to watch.

The fingers around my face tightened. I brought my gaze back to the screen.

Now Carter kissed her face. Her neck. The look of enjoyment on her face made me sick.

"What have you done to her?" I demanded.

He laughed. "I didn't plan on this—but it worked out nicely. Carter was just supposed to keep an eye on her. I didn't expect a jaguar to fall for a lowly wolf, but I'll take it for now."

I lunged at him, not caring about the metal digging into my flesh.

"Watch the show." His fist hit my temple with a sickening crack.

On the screen, my captor's son passionately kissed my love. His hand went for the zipper on the back of her shirt and he started unzipping.

The screen turned black.

"You've seen enough. I suppose you've earned a sip of water. I'll let someone know. Have fun imagining what's on the rest of the video." He smirked and left the room, slamming the door behind himself.

Bile rose from my stomach as I tried not to think about the rest of the video. Had that sleazy jaguar…? I couldn't even finish the thought. Victoria and I had decided to save ourselves for marriage—back in those days, there was honor in such a decision.

Images from the video replayed over and over in my mind. The harder I tried not to think of them, the more vivid they grew. I thought of Victoria's sweet scent, her soft hair, those supple lips…

And now that jerk knew them as intimately as I did. Maybe even more.

Vomit rose into my mouth and I threw it up onto the floor until my stomach could only dry heave. Once I escaped, I would tear that conniving, greedy bastard to pieces—in front of his father. They would both pay. Heavily.

I fought against the chains as my flesh ripped all the more. Fresh droplets of blood dripped down my arm. I shouted, allowing my wolf to release all his anger along with me.

Once my throat was raw, I stopped. I'd exhausted myself.

A few minutes later, the door opened again. A different jaguar came in carrying a glass of water. "Finally quieted down, I see." His face turned green. "It reeks in here. What did you do?"

I stared at the drink, longing for even just a sip.

"What did you do?" he shouted.

"Only what's natural, given my circumstances."

He gagged. "I'm glad I'm not on janitorial duty tonight." He plugged his nose and walked around my vomit. "Disgusting."

"Maybe you shouldn't lock people in here."

"Like I have any say." He shoved the glass to my mouth. "Hurry up before I puke all over you from the stench."

I drank as quickly as I could. The water had a funny taste, but I didn't care. I just wanted to quench my thirst and get the horrible sourness leftover from vomiting out of my mouth.

He yanked the glass from my mouth before I'd finished it. "I can't do this." He ran out of the room, gagging.

The inside of my mouth felt better, but I was growing dizzy. Everything spun around me. Maybe that was a good thing. At least it kept me from thinking about Victoria and that jaguar making jaguar-wolf hybrid babies.

Everything turned black.

CHAPTER 22

Victoria

I CLIMBED INTO MY CAR, sure Yurika would fire me. It had been the worst day ever. I couldn't concentrate, worried about Toby and agitated by my run-in with Soleil. I kept trying to convince myself I'd imagined everything from her drinking my essence to her bright green eyes and wings. But I could still feel the strange purple mist leaving my body.

My only saving grace was that Carter probably wouldn't allow Yurika to let me go, despite my having spilled crimson nail polish on a lady's silk dress, making it look like she'd had a monthly mishap. If that wasn't bad enough, I'd also put the wrong lotion on another lady's hands, leaving her skin red and irritated.

After that, Yurika had given me papers to file and she'd worked double-duty with the clients.

Sighing, I started the car.

My phone buzzed, indicating I had a text.

Carter: *Sry. Stuck in mtg still*

Victoria: *Can I cu l8r?*

Carter: *Hope so*

Victoria: *Having the worst day*

Carter: *:(Ill try 2 get out asap*

Victoria: *Thx*

Carter: *<3 Sry*

Victoria: *Me 2*

I hadn't seen him all day because I'd skipped my next two classes, hyperventilating in the woods. Alex, the friendly wolf who always seemed to find me, had found me yet again and helped me to calm down. But by then, I was due at the spa.

My body ached, and I didn't want to see anyone other than Carter. Well, and Toby. But if there was any truth to what Soleil had told me, no one would see him anytime soon.

Guilt shot through me.

What if they really did need me to help find him? No, that was ridiculous. What could I do? It wasn't like I had any superpowers. No hero was half as clumsy as me. Either she was crazy or I was. Whichever it was, I couldn't help Toby no matter how much I wanted to.

I pulled out of the parking spot and onto the road, heading for the Waldensian. I'd just claim to have a headache—it wasn't far from the truth—and then I'd climb into bed, sticking my earbuds in. Hopefully that would make the rest of the world disappear for a while. At least until Carter was able to get out of his dad's meeting.

When I got to the campus, groups of people were posting fliers on utility poles. I slowed to look at one. It had the word *Missing* in large letters and a picture of Toby with information about him.

Someone turned to me. "Have you seen him?"

Tears stung my eyes. I shook my head and pulled back onto the road. My vision blurred, but I blinked the tears away.

Once I got home, a couple dozen people were crowded into the living room, watching the news. Toby's face flashed on the screen. It was the same picture as was on the flier.

Sasha ran over to me. "Can you believe it? That professor seems to have disappeared into thin air."

"I know." I cleared my throat. "It's crazy."

She leaned closer. "I heard he was involved in a cult."

I gave her a double-take. "Huh?"

"It makes sense if you think about it. He lives in a huge house in the middle of the woods."

"And that makes him a cult member?"

"Leader." Sasha nodded her head knowingly. "Their whole compound is blocked off with an electric fence. My friend heard they shoot visitors on sight."

"That doesn't sound like him."

"How would you know?"

My face warmed. "I'm in one of his classes."

Sasha pulled me into the next room. "Why are you blushing? Do you know something?"

"I'm not blushing." My face heated all the more.

"Liar. Tell me everything."

"Nothing to tell. He's my professor and a nice guy, that's all."

"So, cult leaders can't be nice?" She arched a brow. "How do you think they lure everyone into—oh my gosh!"

"What?" I asked.

She stared at me.

"What?" I demanded.

"He's luring you in!"

People in the living room turned and stared.

I grabbed her arms and dragged her into the kitchen. "No, he's not. Stop talking crazy. He's just a professor."

"A really hot one. He doesn't even look old enough to be a teacher."

"Obviously, he is."

"He really has you under his spell."

"No, he doesn't!" I spun around and marched up the stairs.

"Hey," Sasha called. She caught up to me. "I didn't mean to upset you."

"Then stop making wild accusations against someone who's missing. What if he's in danger? Maybe he's dead!" Hot, angry tears blurred my vision. I blinked and they fell to my face. "Just think before you gossip about nice people."

I ran past her, went through our room into the bathroom and slammed the door, locking it. I dropped my backpack on the floor.

She knocked. "Hey, I wasn't trying to upset you."

"Too late." I leaned against the wall and stared at my reflection. My eyes were red and puffy, my hair was coming loose from the ponytail, and my scratches were hideous. I slid to sitting.

"I'm sure none of it's true," Sasha said. "People say stupid things for attention all the time around here. Have you noticed that?"

"Yep." Including my roommate.

"Look, I'm sorry. I should've stopped once you said he was your teacher. I'd probably be upset if one of mine disappeared. Come out, please?"

"I have a headache."

"We'll talk about something else. Are you going back to Carter's place tonight?"

"Do I *look* like it?"

"He doesn't care about that. Have you seen the way he looks at you?"

"Go away."

"If you won't come out, will you at least let me in? I hate talking through this door."

"I just need to be alone. Nothing personal, but I don't want to be around anyone right now."

"You need a friend. I'll just sit with you. I promise to shut it."

I shook my head, too exhausted to argue.

"Is that a yes?"

"Fine." I reached up and unlocked the door.

She came in and sat next to me. "I'm sorry. I didn't realize you were so… attached to your professor."

I sighed. "It's not that, okay?"

"Not that I would judge."

"Great." I put my forehead on my knees.

We sat in silence for a few moments.

"So, how long are we going to sit here?" she asked.

"No one's making you stay."

"I know. How are things going with Carter? That's not why you're upset, is it? You guys didn't have a fight, did you?"

I shook my head. We might have, if he'd have been upset about me wanting to slow things down. "He's practically perfect."

"Good! See, you don't need to worry about the professor."

"What does that have to do with anything?" I turned and looked at her like she was crazy. "He's a nice guy, and nobody knows where he is."

"If there's any truth to—"

"There's not."

"How would you know?" she asked.

"I thought you came in here to be supportive."

"Sorry. Tell me about last night again. Carter's home sounds as impressive as the Jag—which I still haven't seen any pictures of, by the way."

I counted silently to ten. "Can you go downstairs and see if there's anything new about T… Professor Foley on the news?"

"You think there might be?"

"Never know." I shrugged.

"Sure. You okay?"

"Yeah, I think I'm going to jump in the shower."

Sasha gave me a hug. "I'm sure he'll be just fine. Maybe he'll show up in class tomorrow, ready to hand out gobs of homework."

My inner annoyance perked up. I tried to ignore it. "That would be one time tons of homework would make me happy."

"I'll let you know if they've found him." She got up.

"Thanks. Speaking of assignments, I'd better get started on tonight's work. My psych professor is probably already mad at me for skipping today."

"Massaro?" she asked. "I heard he's the devil."

"Pretty much." I closed the door and climbed in the shower, letting the water get as hot as I could stand it. I just stood there, letting it run over me for at least five minutes before reaching for the shampoo.

Not that I had anything to compare it to, but it wouldn't have surprised me if this had been the craziest week of my life.

When I got out of the shower, I had a new text from Carter.

Carter: *Sry. Stuck here l8.*
Victoria: *Its OK. Tons of HW*
Carter: *Ill make it up 2morrow*
Victoria: *No worries*
Carter: *I promise <3*
Victoria: *Thx <3*
Carter: *Sweet dreams*
Victoria: *u2*

I got comfortable on my bed and spread out all my stuff, starting with psychology. According to the syllabus, we were just supposed to read. I could handle that.

By the time I finished all my studying, Sasha still hadn't returned. I took that to mean Toby was still missing. My heart sank a little as I pulled my covers up.

I closed my eyes, and my interaction with Soleil replayed in my mind. Something was seriously wrong with me since I was more freaked out by finding that picture of me than I was by the whole essence-sucking thing. Her temporary electric-green eyes and wings should have shot fear through me, instead the relaxed feeling returned as if she were pulling the purple mist from me again.

It helped me to drift to sleep…

Toby and I sat on a blanket next to a pond. A wicker picnic basket sat between us. He gazed into my eyes, holding me happily captive. He reached over the basket and took my hand. "I can't believe we finally got away together."

I squeezed his hand and smiled. "I think we're alone now."

The only sounds around us were of birds singing in the distance and some frogs in the pond.

He pushed the basket away, scooted closer, and pulled me onto his lap. I squealed with delight.

Toby put his mouth next to my ear and brushed some hair out of the way. "What would our parents say if they could see us?"

His breath tickled my skin. I shivered. "My father would kill you."

"Mine would join him." He kissed my ear and laced his fingers through mine.

"Aren't you afraid?" I turned and brushed my lips across his. He smelled so good—so masculine and woodsy.

"No. Being with you is worth any risk." Toby deepened the kiss. He tasted even better than he smelled.

He pulled back, and I had to catch my breath. "Are we going to spend our lives sneaking away to see each other?"

"We might have to start our own pack." He pressed his lips on mine again, pulling me closer.

"Mmm… but how?" I ran my hands across his rock-solid chest. "We're both the eldest children of alphas." Rival alphas. My father had sworn to take out all of Toby's pack if it were the last thing he did. I shuddered.

"We'll run away together. Just you and me."

I leaned my head against his. "Nothing sounds better."

Footsteps sounded.

"There they are!"

Sasha's alarm woke me up. I bolted up. I'd forgotten to set mine. It took me a minute to realize I was no longer in the woods with Toby.

"What time is it?" I demanded.

She mumbled something incoherent. I flew out of bed, threw on the first clothes I grabbed, ran a brush through my hair, and pulled it into a ponytail. No time for makeup. I grabbed my backpack and headed for my car, with my heart racing.

I slid into my seat next to Grace. "Please tell me it's Friday."

"It's Friday."

"Is it really?" I exclaimed.

She nodded. "I can't wait to sleep in."

"Sleep in?" I asked. "I want to sleep through both days."

"Not me. I have a soccer match tomorrow evening." She glanced toward the door. "Do you think they're going to have a sub? Or even a new professor?"

My heart sunk. I only wanted to see Toby's gorgeous face walking in through the door. I sighed, fighting a lump in my throat.

"Only like half the kids are here," Grace said. "Did you notice?"

A handsome thirty-something wearing a tie and trendy glasses came into the classroom and set a bag on Toby's table. He unbuttoned his cuffs and rolled up his sleeves, exposing well-defined arms. "I'm Roger Fredrickson, and I'm going to be your professor temporarily."

Grace leaned over and whispered, "This place has the best math department ever."

"He's got to be twice your age."

"I don't care." She sighed dramatically without taking her gaze from the new guy.

The professor held up a paper. "It looks like Professor Foley has you working on unit three. Let's open up to page—"

"Can't we post fliers?" asked a girl on the other side of the room.

"Yeah," said another. "We can catch up on math later."

Fredrickson took a deep breath. "Yeah, I'd rather do something to help find him, too. Okay, here's the deal. You guys need to stay on track with the syllabus, but if you need help, I'll set up a study group over the weekend. Sound good?"

"I'm there," Grace said. Others agreed.

"Okay. I'll reserve one of the library's study rooms for Sunday at two. Now if you want to hand out fliers, there are stacks of them in the Student Union Building and also where our offices are. Let's get to work."

Everyone packed their things away and filed out of the classroom. Grace and I headed for the student building—I didn't want to go near the offices in case Soleil was there waiting for me.

Grace and I spent the next half hour posting papers on every blank pole we could find. I found it hard not to stare at them. In the picture, it felt like he was looking right at me. Like he was trying to tell me something.

Someone tapped my shoulder. I turned around to see a lady in a nice dress, holding a microphone. A cameraman was only a few feet away.

"Did you know Tobias Foley?" She shoved the mic in my face.

"He's my stats professor."

"All these students handing out and posting fliers, are they in his classes, too?"

"Most of them. Our stats class decided to do this instead of studying."

"What do you think happened to him?" The lady pushed her mic closer, practically into my mouth.

I backed up. "Excuse me, I'm going to hand the rest of these out."

Another girl from our class hurried over and spoke with the reporter.

Grace gave me a knowing look. "Pushy, much?"

"I thought she was trying to feed that to me for breakfast."

She rolled her eyes. "I see some empty poles over there."

"Let's go."

CHAPTER 23

Victoria

DAYS TURNED INTO WEEKS WITHOUT any news on Toby's disappearance. The warm sunny days were giving way to chilly, rainy ones and most of the fliers were now tattered and falling off the poles.

Each weekend, I joined a group of students and professors who handed out fliers around town, but the size of that group hand dwindled down. It was like almost nobody expected him to return anymore.

Professor Fredrickson had taken over the stats class and a couple others had taken Toby's other courses.

Carter and I continued our daily study and dinner sessions, but now they were mostly at his house. He didn't want to be anywhere near his dad, who he said had been in a bad mood for nearly a month.

I'd settled into a routine at the spa and was confident I could give a mani-pedi in my sleep. I hadn't had any more embarrassing mishaps since the day Toby disappeared.

Thunder rumbled in the distance.

Carter glanced at me from the other side of the picnic table in his garden. "We'd better take this inside."

The sounds of large raindrops hitting his plants surrounded us. Little wet splashes landed on my face.

In haste, we gathered our laptops, papers, and textbooks. We ran inside just as a flash of lightning lit up the garden like a bright summer day.

He slammed the sliding glass door. Thunder boomed, shaking the glass.

I ran to the middle of the room, not wanting to be anywhere near the storm. The outside lit up again, followed immediately by more rumbling.

Carter came over and dumped his stuff on the couch and wrapped an arm around me. "You'll be safe, I promise."

I nodded, breathless.

"Want me to have someone make some hot chocolate?" He gazed into my eyes and ran his fingers through my hair.

"Or we could make it ourselves."

He arched a brow. "For real?"

"Of course."

"Do you know how to make it? I sure don't."

"I think so. Do you have dried cocoa powder?"

Carter shrugged. "Let's go see."

We went into his kitchen and started going through the cabinets until he pulled some out. "Is this it?"

"Yeah. Now we just need milk, sugar, salt, and… something else?"

"Is it important?" He pulled a jug of milk from the fridge.

"Let me think." I found the salt and sugar, then scanned the spice cabinet. "Oh! Vanilla. That's right." I grabbed the little bottle. "Can you start boiling a third of a cup of water?"

His brows came together and he tilted his head. I'd never

seen anyone so confused about boiling water—of that, I was sure, despite my lack of memories.

I shoved him playfully. "I didn't ask you to translate *War and Peace* into Swahili. Can you at least find the measuring cups?"

"Uh… sure?"

"Oh my gosh, you're such a princess," I teased.

He burst out laughing. "I know I should be offended, but you're too cute."

I shook my head. "I'll find the measuring cups, but you're going to help me pour and stir."

"Whatever you say, boss."

Before long, we had our mugs of steaming cocoa. I found a box of candy canes and crushed one. Then I sprinkled the crumbs in the two drinks.

Carter held his up to his face and took a deep breath. "This smells fantastic."

"Wait until you taste it."

A crack of thunder sounded. Everything went black.

"Great," he muttered. "And we never replaced the generator. So much for a romantic evening."

"Do you have candles?" I asked.

"Of course."

"Then it'll be even more romantic."

"I like the way you think. Should we take it up to my room?"

My internal nun yelled at me louder than usual. I'd been putting Carter off for weeks.

"Not yet?" he asked. "Okay, no biggie. The living room, it is. But I'm turning on the fireplace."

We managed to make our way to the couch without spilling the drinks. With the flip of a switch, we had a gas fire.

"Still want candles?" Carter asked.

"No, this is nice." We made ourselves comfortable and watched the fire, sipping our hot chocolates.

After we set the empty cups on the coffee table, Carter grabbed a quilt and covered us. My heart thundered against my ribcage. I was nervous he'd try something, but he kept his hands above the blanket, sliding my hands into his.

Watching the fire lulled me to sleep. Just before dozing, my head leaned against his. He kissed my forehead.

Once again, I found myself in the woods with Toby. These dreams had become a common occurrence.

This time, we were next to a bubbling stream. The sky was colored with bright hues behind the trees and the moon was full.

Toby brushed his lips across mine. "Are you ready?"

"As always." A sharp pain shot through my spine.

"Are you sure you want to do this together? You know, with the clothes situation…" He cleared his throat nervously. "I mean, I'm used to undressing in front of others—don't get me wrong. It's just that with you, I want it to be special. Not just for a shift."

Pains prickled through my shoulders. I held back a groan. "Me, too. We can undress behind bushes. I really want to run together as wolves."

"Okay. We'll…"

His voice faded away as fire spread through my legs and down into my toes.

Something shook me.

"Victoria, are you okay?" That was Carter's voice.

My eyes flew open. I was back in his living room.

"I think you were having a nightmare."

All my aches and pains were real. I grasped my legs, unable to speak through the agony.

"What's the matter?" he exclaimed. Terror covered his face.

I cried out, unable to control myself any longer.

This was just like what I had gone through after moving in. I'd eaten enough for ten people at lunchtime, having suffered the same ravenous appetite. The manager at the cafeteria had even asked me to leave.

"What can I do?"

I tried to remember what had happened the last time I'd been ravaged with the pain. "Medicine."

"What?" he exclaimed.

"Painkillers." I doubled over, nearly falling off the couch.

He caught me. "You're going to be safer on a bed."

I moaned, unable to argue. With my body hurting this badly, I was likely to pass out. I couldn't remember if I had even managed to stay conscious the last time.

Carter wrapped his arms under me and pulled me up to his chest. "I'll put you in a guest room."

Every step he took added to my suffering.

Why did this keep happening?

Finally, Carter laid me in a bed and covered me with blankets. "Do you want regular painkillers or something really strong? I've got some prescription stuff from when I broke my leg."

"Strong," I mumbled.

"It'll knock you out for a while."

I rolled over and screamed into the pillow. When I was done, I had the room to myself.

A few minutes later, Carter returned with an orange pill bottle and a glass of water. "Can you swallow one, or do you want me to mash it up?"

My bones felt like they would melt and explode at the same time. I cried out, my back arched high into the air.

Once the torment eased, Carter handed me the glass. "I mashed up the pill and put it in there. Just drink. Hurry." His eyes were wide with worry.

He helped me sit up and I drank the bitter, clumpy water.

Once it was gone, he laid me against the pillow. "Stay there. I'll be right back."

"Where would I go?" I mumbled.

Carter tucked the blankets around me and left the room. He returned with a damp washcloth and put it on my forehead, cooling me. He held my hand. "I'm right here, and I'm not going anywhere."

Grogginess overtook me. I drifted into a deep, dreamless sleep.

CHAPTER 24

Toby

A NEW GUARD CAME INTO my cell. He set my daily tray of food on the dirty floor and strutted over to me, keeping his gaze averted. He unlocked my shackles and shoved me against the stone wall. I braced myself and managed to not have the wind knocked out of me that time.

He spun around and marched out, slamming the door behind him. It clicked as he turned the lock.

I scrambled over to the tray. It was my usual, leftovers from the restaurant thrown into a single bowl. It wasn't much, but I'd adjusted—and lost weight. But I'd kept my muscle tone, exercising with the meager free time I was given after my meals.

My bones were starting to ache, indicating that it was probably almost the full moon. I wasn't sure how close, since I'd been locked in the dark room for so long.

Not that I cared when my food waited for me. I picked up the bowl and dug in, eating as though I were in my wolf form. Aside from using my dirt-crusted hands, I had no other option. If the jaguars had cameras on me, they were sure to enjoy reducing me to acting like my inner animal.

Let them gloat. I was determined to have the last laugh one way or another. I'd survived Victoria's death so many years earlier. Now that she was alive again, I would find a way out of this and get her back.

I finished the scraps and dropped the bowl onto the tray. It was only a matter of time before someone returned to lock me up again, so I didn't waste time allowing my food to digest. I simply stretched and ran around the room a dozen times. Then I dropped to the floor and did as many push-ups as I could. I ran again to give my arms rest before doing chin ups on the pipe that stuck out of the ceiling, which was also the hated carrier of the chains that I hung from most of the day.

Since I had some extra time, I rested and then did sit-ups until the doorknob jiggled. I jumped back and leaned against the wall, pretending to be bored.

The club owner came in, holding his dart gun—my constant reminder of what would happen if I tried to take him down again.

He stared at my tattered, dirty pants. "You really should do something about those." He laughed. "Ready to be chained back up?"

My bones were growing sorer, preparing for the impending shift. "I'm going to shift soon."

"Oh, right. I nearly forgot about the full moon. I've been so distracted watching all the videos of Carter and Victoria."

I jumped up and lunged for him.

He held out the dart gun. I skidded to a stop, only inches from him.

"They've got extra tranquilizers today. I wasn't sure if you'd already be in your wolf form."

"If your son is already in love with Victoria, why don't you let me go? What use am I to you?"

"You think that's why you're here?" He shook his head.

"Why then?" I shouted.

"She was here as bait for *you*."

"What?"

"That's right. I've got you exactly where I want you, Foley."

I stared at him, confused. "What do you want with me?"

"First, we're going to continue torturing you."

"And then?" I clenched my fists.

He shrugged. "Then we kill you. But don't worry, we have plenty of time before that, wolf. Let's get you locked up."

"You can't seriously—not now."

"Why not?"

"You'd have me shift while tied to the ceiling?" I cringed, imagining my wolf form hanging from the shackles.

"Like I said, we're going to torture you, even in your wolf body."

I backed away, my pulse drumming in my ears. There was a lot I could power through, but not that. "Can't we work something out?"

A sly smile spread across his face. "I like to see you squirm. This is kind of fun."

"What about some other chains?" I gestured toward the ones still attached to the skeleton in the corner. "I'd still be in chains, but I won't be hanging in the air."

He appeared to think about it. Then he turned to me. "No. I like the other one better. That's why you've been there this whole time."

"I'll go without my meal tomorrow."

"Stop begging. It's pathetic."

"I'm negotiating."

"No you're not. You have nothing to offer. Now move, before I shoot you."

I stared at the darts. Being tranquilized would be my best option if I had to hang in shackles in my wolf form. I jumped at my captor, knocking him onto the ground. Apparently, he hadn't seen that coming.

The dart gun flew from his hand and spun across the room. Our gazes met for a moment before we both scrambled to our feet and jumped after it.

He reached it first, turned to me and aimed for my chest. I didn't bother trying to move out of the way. It stung as it broke through my skin. A moment later, the hard ground flew toward my face.

When I came to, I was still in my human form and chained to the ceiling. This time, my ankles were cuffed, also. My bones ached with a greater intensity, indicating the shift wasn't far off.

This was likely going to be one of the worst shifts of my life.

A sharp pain ran from the base of my neck down to my toes. It was probably what had woken me from the tranquilizer.

My right cheek felt tender. He had probably taken advantage of me being passed out to hit me a few times.

Acute pain squeezed my shoulders and moved around through my body. My arms and legs fought fruitlessly to free themselves from the restraints.

The door opened, though I hardly noticed because of my

torment.

"Still haven't changed?" came my captor's voice. "Because you're not out under the moon?"

My body convulsed, so close to the shift and fighting the upright position.

"I have a surprise for you."

"You're going to release me?" I struggled to focus on him.

"I'm going to shift, too. It's been a while, so I figure why not?" He turned his back to me and stripped off his clothes, throwing them into the corner. He flexed one butt cheek and then the other. "Like the show?"

I rolled my eyes and let my chin fall to my chest. My stomach and chest were already sprouting fur. I braced myself.

My wolf let out a howl. He was taking over. This time, we would shift as one. We needed to if we were going to fight a jaguar—while chained to the ceiling.

A roar echoed around us. Our captor had shifted, and his glowing yellow eyes stared right at us.

The door opened and two men in suits appeared. They threw off their clothes and shifted before my eyes.

Blinding pain overtook me. My wolf yelped. We fell to the ground, landing on our tail. My pants—what was left of them—lay next to us shredded into rags.

Our paws had been too small to keep us restrained in the shackles.

Three spotted jaguars crept toward us, growling and baring their teeth.

We scrambled to our feet. I felt myself melting into him. As one, we stood a chance. Fighting each other, we didn't.

One of the jaguars lunged at us. We ran in the other direction, needing time to think. The other two ran over and blocked us, growling.

What did they expect? That I would fight both of them? If it were true that they wanted to keep me alive for a while, they wouldn't kill me. But he seemed so giddy at the thought of making me suffer.

Play dead, my wolf whispered.

What?

Get bitten, and then we'll fall to the ground, tongue hanging out.

Maybe.

If they hold the door open for any amount of time, we can make a run for it.

It sounded better than anything I could think of. *Okay.*

He took over and ran to a corner. One of the jaguars cornered us. He jumped, roaring.

I tried to run out of instinct, but my wolf held us still.

Bitter pain surged through our shoulder as the beast's teeth sank into our flesh. Blood pooled into our fur.

Though it wasn't enough to take us down, my wolf threw us down. He forced our eyelids shut and our tongue hung out, resting against the nasty floor. It tasted of dried blood, vomit, and feces.

The jaguars bumped and nudged us. My wolf did a great job of keeping us still. Our captors would likely think they'd killed us.

One let out a howl. Another growled. One jumped on the other, and the two of them rolled around, hissing at each other. The third continued pushing us around.

Finally all the commotion stopped. Bones crunched, and I assumed they had shifted back.

"I can't believe you killed him," the owner exclaimed.

Something hit a wall.

"Hey, I didn't bite him that hard."

"Oh, right." Sarcasm dripped from our captor's voice. "Our end of the deal is to hand the wolf over *alive*. It's pretty hard to do that if he's dead."

Sounds of pulling on clothes echoed around us.

"Check for breathing."

"I don't have time for this. You better hope he's still alive."

"He *is*."

"Like I said, you better hope so. I have to focus on the wedding."

My ears perked. Surely, he couldn't mean Victoria and his son. He just couldn't.

Disappointment, fear, and anger ran through me. I couldn't tell which belonged to me and which belonged to my wolf.

The three humans left the room. My wolf and I were too shocked by the mention of the wedding to even consider attempting to escape.

The door slammed shut. After a few minutes, I got up and paced, limping on our bad leg. It felt like the jaguar had torn the muscle. Luckily, we healed pretty quickly in this form. The ache eased with each step.

It couldn't be Victoria's wedding. She'd just met the jaguar at the beginning of the school year. That had been—what? A month? The last full moon had occurred right before school started.

My chest constricted. Guilt tore through me. This was my

payback for having had a relationship some years earlier. That's what this was. Even though Victoria had long been deceased, I should have never allowed myself to fall for another.

Wolves mated for life.

Technically, we never mated with Victoria, my wolf told me.

I growled and snapped. *I'd given my heart to her.*

You also spent almost all of your years since her death alone.

But I gave myself to another for a time. I wanted to go back in time and knock some sense into my younger, dumber self.

And you also knew the girl's heart belonged to another. We all knew it wouldn't last. Let it go.

I shook our head and picked up our pace. Even though Victoria had been dead at the time, I'd betrayed her. If I did manage to win her back, I'd have to tell her about my indiscretion.

Then you'll be even, my wolf said. *She's seeing that jaguar kid now.*

But she doesn't remember being with me! I remembered her when I dated Alexis.

You couldn't have known Victoria would return. Also, it's not like you set out to date her. You were just trying to pull the girl out of a depression, right? Then one thing led to another...

Guilt continued stinging. *But still. My heart belonged to Victoria.*

Hey, I told you dating a vampire was a bad idea.

I hung our head in shame. *I should have listened.*

What if I'd lost Victoria forever?

CHAPTER 25

Victoria

WHEN I WOKE, THE SUN shone brightly through the blinds. Carter slept next to me, on top of the covers, with one arm resting over me, holding the now-dry washcloth on my forehead.

My body no longer hurt.

Could my dreams of Toby be real? If they were, that meant I was a werewolf.

That was totally crazy.

But then again, so was having my essence sucked out by a... a... whatever Soleil was. I'd been avoiding her like the plague, so I'd had no chance to find out what exactly she was.

Carter's arm twitched and he rolled onto his back, letting out a little snore. He shivered.

I pulled the comforter up from me, covered him, and crept out of bed without disturbing him. I tiptoed over to the window and lifted a blind. Water dripped from everything, the only remnant of the previous night's storm. Otherwise, it looked like a sunny autumn day with so many trees showing off their beautiful array of colors.

Carter whispered something. I went over to him. He

mumbled something about cats.

I grinned. He was a cute sleep-talker.

He'd probably stayed awake a long time keeping an eye on me, so I decided to let him sleep. I went into the hall, found a bathroom, and took a shower. Normally, I wouldn't have been too excited about wearing the same clothes, but I didn't mind. I'd survived that horrible pain and other than that, had had a wonderful date with Carter—and he'd been the perfect gentleman, not trying anything.

My heart warmed, thinking about him. He was such a great guy. I'd really lucked out meeting him.

I went back to the bedroom and dug some makeup out of my backpack—Carter must have brought it upstairs. He was seriously the most perfect guy ever.

Once I was happy with the way I looked, I pulled out my laptop and worked on my midterm psychology paper. I had five thousand of ten thousand words.

After a while, Carter rolled over and rubbed his eyes. "How are you feeling?" he asked, his voice raspy from sleep.

"Like new. Thanks so much for everything." I set my computer aside and pressed my lips on his.

He backed up, covering his mouth. "I probably have morning breath."

"Me, too. I have no toothbrush here." I kissed him again.

Carter grabbed me and pulled down next to him. "We'll have to fix that, won't we?"

I giggled. "Maybe."

"How about we start with me giving you the day off?" His voice was husky and gave me the chills.

"Oh, that sounds heavenly."

He smiled and ran his knuckles along my jawline.

I took his hand and kissed a fingertip. "Oh, wait. I can't do that to Yurika."

Carter frowned. "Why not? I'll send one of the bouncers in to replace you if I have to."

"As much as I'd like to see that, I can't do that to her. There's a big wedding party, and we have to get them all ready."

He smacked his forehead. "My cousin's wedding! I'm supposed to usher. Crap, I totally forgot about that."

I checked the time. "We'd both better get going, in that case. I don't have much time—I told Yurika I'd be there a little early."

Carter scrambled out of the bed. "Let me just take a quick shower. Five minutes, I swear."

"Okay."

"Wanna join me?" He gave me pouty eyes.

"Sorry. I guess I'm just not that kind of girl."

He leaned over and planted a kiss on my lips. "And that's part of what I love about you. You're old-fashioned, and you won't bend on your standards."

My eyes widened. Love?

"I'll get you there on time, I swear. Five minutes."

I nodded, unable to speak.

Carter ran out of the room and soon I heard a shower running. I packed up my bag and mentally prepared myself for a busy day. So far, the spa had never had too many clients at a time, but Yurika had warned me today would be crazy—and that it was extra important that we do everything perfectly.

I'd been doing well, getting better every day. I could do

this. In fact, I would impress Yurika.

He ran into the room, his hair slicked back and water dripping down his face. "Like I said, under five minutes. Let's go."

I wiped some drops from under his eye and brushed my lips across his. "You're simply amazing."

Carter closed his eyes. "You're going to have to stop, or neither of us will leave here."

"Right." I stepped back and grabbed my backpack.

"Let's go. Do you want me to drop you off at the Jag or take you to your car?"

"I'd better take my car to work. You're probably going to be busy with the wedding."

"You could always join me." He frowned and ran a finger across my mouth. "I'd love to show you off." He cringed. "That sounded bad. I mean to introduce you to everyone."

First love, and now he wanted me to meet his entire extended family? I adored him, but I wasn't ready for all of that. "You're the sweetest, but I have to work on Massaro's paper tonight."

Carter scowled. "That slave driver. Yeah, I should be working on that, too. Looks like another all-nighter for me."

We grumbled about our professor until we reached his car.

"Your car's at home, right?" he asked.

"Yeah. Sorry, I hope it's not too far out of the way."

"Nah. And if I show up late, Dad has it coming after the jerk he's been lately." His phone rang. "Speak of the devil."

"When do I get to meet him?"

Carter flinched. "You want to meet the scum bag?"

"Um, not so much when you put it that way."

"Trust me. I'm protecting you. Besides, he's really busy and thinks he's too important to meet my friends."

"Oh, okay." It seemed strange, but I pushed aside those feelings.

When we reached the Waldensian, he got out and held my door open for me. He stared into my eyes. "I'm going to miss you tonight." He pulled me close and gave me a long, sweet kiss before climbing into his car and speeding away.

I went inside, my heart fluttering. People said hi as I passed, but I barely noticed. Now I understood what it meant to have my breath taken away.

In my room, I tossed my backpack onto my bed before digging through my closet for some fresh clothes.

Sasha came out of the bathroom and gasped and squealed. "Were you…?"

"What?" I pulled out some dressy slacks and a lavender silk top—my wardrobe had improved dramatically since working at the Jag.

She gave me a once-over. "Same clothes as yesterday. Gone all night. Your handsome prince?"

"Wait, it's not what you're thinking."

"Girl, we have to talk!"

"Seriously, I got sick after the power outage and—"

"What power outage?"

"His place lost power during the storm."

"You *were* at his place." Her eyes widened.

"I. Got. Sick." I took a deep breath. "Look, *nothing* happened."

"Where'd you sleep?"

"In a guest room."

Her expression drooped. "Oh. Hey, where'd he sleep?"

"He was busy taking care of me. I have to get to work. Seriously." I took off my clothes for the second time that morning.

"Where'd he sleep?"

"Nothing. Happened." I put on my new clothes and went into the bathroom to style my hair.

Sasha followed me in. "Well at least you've forgotten about the professor."

I froze, holding the hot flat iron on my hair.

"You're going to burn your hair!"

I put the iron down. "What do you mean?"

"You've been so mopey since your math instructor vanished. I can't even think of his name."

"It's plastered all over town."

"I know, but I haven't paid attention in a while."

Sighing, I picked up the flat iron and continued straightening my hair. "His name is Professor Foley, and I wasn't moping over him."

She gave me a knowing look. "Anyway, I'm more interested to hear about your night at Carter's. Did you remember to get any pictures yet?"

"Just some selfies of the two of us."

"Before you got sick, right?" She arched a brow.

"Precisely." I put the iron down, fluffed out my hair, and fixed my mascara.

"Your lipstick is smudged." Sasha threw me a playful smirk.

I fixed it. "He did kiss me," I admitted. "But that was it."

She sighed dramatically. "You're either the most boring

person alive or the most exciting, and totally holding out on me."

I sprayed some perfume and spun around. "I gotta get to work."

"Details. Later."

"Okay. I'll tell you all about us doing homework and making hot chocolate."

"Boring. Well, if you want your secrets, I can't blame you. But I'm going to use my wild, vivid imagination. Your choice."

"Texting my boss now."

Victoria: *On my way. Hope I'm not late.*

She was so formal with everything, I even had to properly spell out my texts.

Yurika: *The wedding party is having lunch. You have an hour.*
Victoria: *Thanks!*
Yurika: *Carter said something came up, but please be on time.*
Victoria: *I will. I promise.*

Sasha pouted. "Are you sure you don't have time to spill just one juicy detail?"

"Sorry. I gotta go." I grabbed my purse, hurried to my car, and then parked on the side of the road near campus. My mind was racing, and my conversation with Sasha hadn't helped.

One of Toby's missing fliers hung loosely on a pole. I climbed out and stared at the faded picture.

Someone bumped into me. "Sorry. You know what I heard?" He glanced toward the flier.

"What?"

"That his cult chopped him up and put the pieces into stew."

"You're disgusting."

He shrugged and kept walking.

I clung to the paper and got back into my car. It wasn't until I tried starting it that I realized I was shaking. I took a few deep breaths and finally drove to the Jag. I put on soft instrumental music. There was no way I could afford a repeat of the day I'd spilled nail polish on that lady's dress.

By the time I pulled into the Jag's lot, my mind had calmed down. I waved to the doorman as I entered ahead of the line.

Yurika shot me a grateful expression when I arrived. "A couple of the girls are already here. I'm going to start them with pedis. When the next ones get here, start them with facials."

"Do we have any help?"

She nodded. "Lucy and Julia will be here after their break."

"Oh, good."

"Tell me about it. We're going to need all the help we can get today."

And I was going to need all the focus I could manage. My mind kept wandering to both Carter and Toby, and when I was at the spa, I always found myself hoping Carter would pop in and surprise me. He rarely did, though, because his father kept him busy when he wasn't studying.

But it didn't keep me from wishing.

CHAPTER 26

Victoria

I RUBBED THE LAST BIT of cream on the bridesmaid's face. "Just lay there and relax for a few minutes."

"This feels so nice."

"Good. Is the music okay?"

"Perfect."

Yurika ran in, her eyes frantic. "We're running out of nail polish remover. I thought we were fully stocked."

"Do you want me to get some more?"

"Yes," she snapped.

"Where is it?"

"Ugh. You really don't know?"

I shook my head. "It's always been in the cabinet."

She threw her hands in the air. "If I had time, I'd get it. It's in the big utility closet in between the kitchen and Master Jag's office suite. You know the one?"

"I think so."

Her eyes narrowed.

"Yes, I'll find it."

Yurika ran out of the room.

I turned to the bridesmaid. "I'll be back in a few minutes.

The cream will be fine—it's working to both cleanse and moisturize your skin. If you need anything, just ring this bell here." I took her hand and guided her to the tray with the bell. "Julia's in the next room. She'll hurry over."

"I'm too relaxed to move."

"Sounds like it's working." I adjusted the warm blankets around her body and hurried out of the spa.

A line of people carrying what looked like a truckload of flowers walked by. There was no way I was going to get around them, and when Yurika was rushed, so was I.

I darted down a different hallway, hoping I was headed for the kitchen.

By the time I'd gone down a few turns, I realized I was lost. It was just a maze of dimmed halls, and I wasn't sure which one had brought me where I was.

Conversation sounded down from my left. I thought I heard the word wolf. Something inside me perked up. I pressed myself against the wall and listened.

"…supposed to find out if he's dead."

I gasped. Someone was dead in the Jag?

"Did you hear that?"

I covered my mouth.

"No. Did you check him?"

"I haven't."

"Stupid. When the boss says jump, you do it."

"I've never seen a dead body."

"So? Check the dungeon."

"Won't you do it for me? I'll owe you all my vacation days or something."

Somebody sighed. "What's his name?"

"Foley."

"You mean that guy who's plastered all over town?"

"Right. He's down there."

A cry escaped my mouth.

Footsteps sounded.

I glanced around. There was a door a few feet away. I had no other choice, so I ran inside and closed the door fast and as quietly as I could. Clothes hung all around. I darted behind some and pressed myself into a corner.

The door opened, lighting up the closet full of suits just like the waiters wore in the restaurant.

I held my breath.

"No one. Are you sure we heard something?"

The door closed.

I breathed again and slunk down to the ground, my heart pounding so loudly I was sure they could hear it out in the hall. I gasped for air and tried to listen for the men outside the closet once I calmed down. I waited a full five minutes, counting out the seconds, before I dared to open the door.

The hallway was empty.

I smoothed down my hair and went down the way the two men had been talking about Toby. There were a few doors, and I checked all of them. Most were utility closets, but the one at the very end opened to a dark staircase.

If there was a chance Toby was down there—locked in a dungeon—I had to see. Especially if they thought he might be dead. Tears stung my eyes. My insides felt like they were jumping around.

I clung to the rusty railing as I descended down the staircase. It was steep and narrow. Water dripped somewhere.

When I got to the end, I came to another door.

Barely breathing, I opened it. I came to a hallway, and it was better lit. There were a few doors off to my left. I pressed my ear against the first one, but didn't hear anything. I opened it anyway.

It appeared to be some kind of cellar. Old, dusty canned food sat on shelves. Underneath them were brown bottles. Some were labeled moonshine.

This place was as old as Prohibition?

I opened the next door and found another closet full of old food and drinks. When I got to the next door, I fully expected to find more of the same.

Instead, it was a mostly empty room with chains hanging from the ceiling and the walls. It smelled of bile and urine.

Someone jumped out from behind the door, positioned to attack.

I screamed, my voice echoing around both the cell and the hallway.

"Victoria?"

I stared at the man. It took me a moment to realize it was Toby. And he was naked.

My eyes shut and I turned my head. "Toby! What are you doing here?"

"They're trying to kill me."

"We've got to get you out of here, but first I need to get you some clothes."

"There isn't time."

"You want to run through the Jag like that?" I exclaimed. "I know where some clothes are. Stay here."

With my eyes still closed, I spun around and ran up the

stairs. He called after me, but I ignored him. I made sure no one was in sight, ran to the closet, and grabbed a suit.

When I got back down to the dungeon, Toby was standing outside his cell. I looked down at the ground and handed him the clothes.

"Thank you."

I turned around and tried to pretend he wasn't naked. "So, do you need anything?"

The sounds of him putting the clothes on echoed all around us. "To get as far away from this place as possible."

"Have you been here all this time?"

"Right in that room."

"What happened?"

"I'll explain later. Someone could come down any minute." He walked over to me.

I covered my eyes.

"I'm dressed now."

"Come on. We'll get out of here." I opened one eye, and sure enough, he looked like a server. Only the clothes barely hung on and his face was bloody and bruised.

"What did they do to you?" Instinctively, I reached for his face. "You poor thing."

"Let's go. The way I came in is pretty secluded."

"Because that worked out so well for you?"

"That wasn't where I was caught."

"Where—?"

"Come on." He grabbed my arm and led me up the stairs. I followed him down the maze of halls until we neared the kitchen. He took me down another turn. We passed a line of mops and then he opened a door, which opened to the outside.

Toby glanced around and then ran for the woods.

"We can take my car."

"Which is probably parked in the main lot, right?"

"Okay, never mind."

"I know the way to my home. Are you up for a run?"

"To your house?" All the rumors of cult members chopping people up ran through my mind.

His expression softened. "What's the matter?"

I shook my head. "Nothing. Let's just get out of here."

"How did you find me?" He took my hand and ran.

"I had some help. Are you going to be okay running barefoot?"

He glanced at me. "We used to do this all the time."

My mouth gaped. Had my dreams actually been real?

"Let's go. We'll answer each other's questions at home."

We darted through trees and bushes, jumping over exposed roots and ducking under branches. Unlike with my solo runs, I didn't fall once. I felt completely in my element, like all the pieces of a puzzle had finally come together.

Finally, we came to a large gate. He punched in a code and it opened. We ran inside and the gate closed behind us. A gorgeous blue home with plenty of decks and pointed peaks loomed in front of us.

"This is where you live?" It was even more impressive than Carter's place.

"Yeah, it reminds me of the one you always had your eye on." He squeezed my hand and led us up the stairs to the front door.

Before we reached it, the door opened, and a group of people piled out, cheering and talking over each other. I let go of his hand and watched as everyone hugged him and expressed their gratitude of seeing him alive.

I followed everyone inside. Toby put his arm around me, and it felt like the most natural thing in the world. "I have someone I want you all to meet."

Eyes widened around the room. They apparently knew who I was without Toby needing to say a word.

He squeezed my shoulders and kissed the top of my head. "This is Victoria—she's the one who rescued me."

All the attention turned to me, and the group of strangers practically piled on top of me, embracing and thanking me. Several people mentioned a pack.

"Give her some space, guys," Toby said.

"And get this man some food," I added. "They've been starving him."

We all went through a living room and then came to an enormous kitchen with a table big enough to seat an army. Toby introduced me to everyone, but the only names I could keep straight were the odd ones—Jet and Brick.

Everybody talked over each other. Toby leaned back in the chair, grinning wide. Even with the bruises and cuts covering his face, he was exquisite. I couldn't take my eyes off him.

He kept glancing over at me, seeming to enjoy my sight as much as I was his. Brick and another guy brought over plates and platters of steaming food, setting them all in front of Toby.

Toby waved his arms to the others. "Eat up, you guys." He turned to me, holding my gaze. "You, too."

"I couldn't. You need the food more than any of us."

"Yeah," said Jet.

"Eat," urged Brick.

"We don't need it," said another.

He laughed. "Okay, then. I can't tell you how nice it is to have actual fresh food."

Jet's brows came together. "Didn't you eat?"

"Scraps from a restaurant." He dug into some roast beef.

"Gross," someone said.

My stomach dropped. All the times I'd stuffed myself at the Jag with Carter, Toby had been in the cell forced to eat everyone's leftovers?

"In your human form?" someone exclaimed.

My head snapped up.

"Dillon," Jet exclaimed. He nodded toward me, still looking at his friend. "Remember? Memory issues." Jet looked at me. "Don't mind him. He's an idiot. Always has been, always will be."

"Hey!"

"Guys," Toby said. "Remember what we talked about before I was taken hostage?"

Both Jet and Dillon's heads fell.

"Sorry, sir," they said in unison.

I stared at them. As odd as their behavior was, it was also strangely familiar.

Toby pushed a platter of grilled salmon covered in a yellow sauce and spices in front of me. "Eat up. You need fuel after that run."

The smell of the meal not only made my mouth water, but conjured warm feelings.

He tilted his head. "We ate that together on several picnics."

My cheeks warmed and I glanced away. "Thanks."

Toby piled some fish on my plate. "Come on, people. I don't want to be the only one eating."

"You don't have to tell me twice." Brick grabbed a plate and piled on food.

I couldn't help smiling.

The front door slammed. "I heard Toby's back," came a familiar feminine voice. Soleil entered the room and her face lit up. "You are!" She ran over and hugged him, nearly knocking him out of the chair. "So good to see you!"

He chuckled. "Who told?"

"I'll never tell." Soleil winked. "But I was at the Faeble and I might have mentioned it to Tap. Loud enough for everyone there to hear."

Toby shook his head. "Did everyone know about my imprisonment?"

"Just about." She sat on the other side of me and dished up some lamb and vegetables. "Once you've had a chance to rest, you'd better head over to the bar and say hi to everyone. Tap was worried sick—as was your pack. Gessilyn's been working nonstop on locator spells, but coming up with nothing." She turned to me. "How was it you found him?"

"How'd you know—?"

"Valkyries know just about everything."

My mouth dropped. Valkyrie?

She winked. "It's because we're so nosy. And we can drink people's essence. But you know all about that." She went on to talk about the fliers all over town and gossip from Toby's colleagues.

While she rattled on, I tried to make sense of everything. It hit me like a ton of bricks that I was at Toby's home. Everything had happened so fast—me finding him and then us fleeing the Jag to this mansion.

Was I really surrounded by paranormal creatures?

Could I be one myself?

CHAPTER 27

Victoria

TOBY AND I SAT ON the porch swing. He put his arm around me and smelled of a different soap than I seemed to remember. "I hope this is okay."

I nodded. Sitting there with him, it didn't feel like the majority of my life had been taken from me.

"Sorry about my... family. They can be a little overwhelming at times. Even for me."

"You mean your pack?" I glanced up at him.

"Yes. How much do you remember? Anything?"

I swallowed and held his gaze. My lips longed for his. But I couldn't bring myself to budge. Not when I'd been kissing Carter earlier that same day. Not when the man with his arms around me was my professor.

"What do you remember?" he asked.

Instinctively, I reached for his hand.

He laced his fingers through mine and leaned his head against mine.

"I have no idea. I've had some dreams, but who's to say if they're real or not?"

"Perhaps I can help."

My body shook.

He tightened his hold around me. "Or we can just sit here."

I took a deep breath. "I really want to remember everything. It sucks so bad to only be able to remember the last month of my life."

"Don't I know it." He kissed the top of my head again. "I really hope this doesn't make you uncomfortable. I get that I'm just your professor, but you don't know how much restraint it's taking me to hold back."

I turned and studied him. "Why don't you give in?"

Toby closed his eyes. "It certainly wouldn't be appropriate for a student-teacher relationship."

"We both know this goes way beyond that." I reached for his beard and ran my palm over it. "Have I ever seen it this long?"

"No, I like to keep it short."

"It's kind of sexy."

His face broke into a wide smile. "You say you want me to let go of all restraint?"

I bit my lower lip. "Maybe it'll help restore my memories."

Toby swallowed, making his Adam's apple bob up and down. "You don't know what you're asking."

I leaned closer to his face. "But I want to find out."

"Are you sure?"

"Wholly."

Toby reached under my arms and stood, lifting me into the air. He spun me in circles and then pulled me down against him. "I can't tell you how long I've waited to do this." He pressed his lips on mine and spun around again, stopping in front of a wall. Desire burned in his eyes and he pinned me against the house, kissing me again, but taking it deeper this time. His arms wrapped tightly around me and one leg curled around me.

My heart raced and I kissed him back greedily. It was like a well-choreographed dance that had been practiced for hours on end. I explored his mouth—the tastes so familiar, his aroma like a trip back in time. My hands went to the back of his neck and my fingers ran themselves through his soft hair.

This was what I was meant for—*he* was what was missing from my life. Even if no other memory ever surfaced again, I had all I ever needed.

His hands moved to my hair, pulling it back. "Is this okay?" he whispered.

I grabbed his face and pulled him into another exploratory kiss. His hands moved down to my waist and rested there.

A moment later, he pulled back and gasped for air. "That was just like old times."

"Let's bring the past to life." I kissed his ear. "Help me restore my memories."

"We should slow down."

"Now?" I exclaimed.

He nodded toward the window. "We have an audience."

Five faces were pressed against the window.

I turned back to him. "I don't care."

Toby took a deep breath. "I need a moment." He took my hand and led me back to the bench.

Groans sounded from inside.

Toby rested his hand on my leg, just above the knee. "That was... It was like... like no time had passed."

"How much time *has* passed?"

He squeezed my leg and gazed into my eyes. "Years."

I paused, doing the math. "That doesn't add up, especially given the age difference."

Toby's smile faded. "There is no age gap."

"Wait, what?"

"It's complicated. I don't know where to begin."

"How about with how a college professor has no age difference from someone who just graduated high school?"

He kissed the top of my head. "You didn't just graduate, sweetness."

"When did I?"

"Like I said, years ago."

I tilted my head. "I don't understand."

Tears shone in his eyes.

"What's wrong?"

"Promise to keep an open mind?" His voice wavered.

My heart shattered, seeing him in pain. "After everything I've been through, that shouldn't be hard."

Toby cleared his throat. "You died some decades ago."

"Died?"

"In my arms. I never thought I would get to see you again."

I stared at him, trying to make sense of it. "How is that possible?"

"The easy answer is that you were brought back to life."

"Is that why I can't remember anything?"

He shook his head.

"How do you know?" Everything seemed to spin around us. I clung to him.

Toby held me tighter. "Because others came back to life

around the same time as you, and they all remember every-thing."

My mouth dropped.

"Like I said, everything is really complicated. I don't want to drop it all on you right now. Hopefully it'll all come together when your memories return."

White dots danced around in the air. My eyes fluttered and I fell toward Toby's chest just as everything turned black.

I woke up in an unfamiliar bed and sat bolt upright, gasp-ing for air. The room was pretty, decorated in lavender and silver hues with the sun shining in brightly.

It took me a minute to remember everything that had happened before I blacked out. Everything came flooding back—well, not everything, everything. My life before college was still a mystery, but I recalled finding Toby and coming back to his home. That had to be where I was. Maybe a guest room or something. Such a feminine room wasn't his.

A girl with rainbow hair came in and smiled. "You're awake. Hi, I'm Ziamara."

I stared at her. A strange odor lingered in the air. I couldn't place it. "Are you... part of the pack?"

She sat at the edge of the bed. "Kind of an honorary mem-ber. I'm married to Jet."

"Oh."

"I'm a vampire."

My eyes widened. "I see."

Ziamara winked. "I won't bite, I promise. Want me to tell Toby you're up?"

"Sure, if he's not busy."

"He is, but he's been waiting for you to wake."

"You'd think he would be the one sleeping after all he's been through."

"That dude is as tough as nails." She walked to the door then turned around. "Oh, do you need anything?"

Just my memories. I shook my head and leaned back against the pillows.

She left the room and I thought back to my conversation with Toby after dinner. That kiss... It was unbelievable. I sighed, wishing I could remember our life together before—especially since that had reminded him of kisses from then.

"Knock, knock," came Toby's voice.

"Come in." I sat back up.

He smiled widely and stepped inside and paused after a couple feet. "It's so strange being in a bedroom with you."

"Is it?"

"We've never been alone in a house before. Because our parents hated each other, we could only sneak away in the woods."

"I wish I could remember. Maybe you can help me." I climbed out of the bed and pursed my lips.

He arched a brow, the corners of his mouth curving upward. "What are you thinking?"

I moved toward him slowly. "A replay of earlier. Isn't it a kiss that wakes the sleeping princess?"

Toby ran at me, scooped me up, and fell onto the bed. "If that's what you want, I have no other choice except to oblige."

"You talk too much." I pressed my mouth on his, taking in a whole new array of scents and tastes. He smelled of cologne and tasted like maple syrup.

"Anything yet?" he asked.

"Nothing."

He planted kisses all over my face. "Now?"

I giggled. "No."

"I'll have to keep trying." He trailed his lips along my jaw and down my neck. "How's that?"

"Nice, but it's not jogging any memories."

Toby trailed over to my mouth, gave me a kiss so passionate that it made my toes curl, and then he sat up. "We're either going to have to slow it down or get married real quick. Wow."

I didn't even flinch at the mention of marriage. "Were we engaged?"

He took my hand and kissed my palm. "Not formally. We were planning on running away together and starting our own pack. You wanted to have lots of pups."

"I can see why." I ran the back of my fingers along his newly shortened beard.

Toby gazed into my eyes.

We sat quietly for a minute. "So, what did you do all those years while I was gone? Did you marry anyone else? You said we were together decades ago."

He cupped my face and brushed his lips across mine. "I never married."

"Did you see anyone else?"

"Is this a conversation you really want to have?" He traced my lips with his fingertip. "Can't we just enjoy being together?"

"Well, I can't remember anything from *my* life."

Toby frowned. "I can't pretend to know how frustrating that must be. Let me contact a witch I know. She helped me figure out that you were in this area."

"Wait. When did she do that? Before you ran into me?"

"Yeah. She discovered you were with the jaguars."

Blood drained from my face. "Jaguars?"

"Shifters."

"You mean like were-jaguars?"

"Exactly. They own that club you work at. Your boyfriend, he's one."

"Carter?" I asked. "He's not my boyfriend."

"Don't feel bad about it, sweetness. You had no way of knowing about us."

I scooted away. "He's not my boyfriend—we've never agreed to go exclusive."

"His dad showed me the video. I'm not upset. Don't worry."

"Video? What are you talking about?" My voice was growing higher pitched by the moment.

Toby took a deep breath. "Of you two... at his place. Close."

My mouth dropped. "When? How? I-I... This can't be happening."

"Whatever you two did, it's not my business. I didn't want to watch." He closed his eyes. "I'm sorry. I shouldn't have said anything. I don't know what I was thinking."

"What did you see?" I demanded.

He frowned. "You two kissing and then him unzipping your shirt. His dad turned off the video and essentially said—"

"Did he show you the part where I told Carter to stop?"

Relief flooded Toby's face. "You did? He led me to believe—"

Anger burned within me. "Was I with them before school

started? Do you know?"

"Gessilyn saw you early in the summer, if I remember correctly."

"Why? What did they want with me?"

"According to Carter's dad, you were bait."

I stared at him.

"They wanted me."

"But… they… you mean they used me to get to you? For what?"

"He wanted to torture and then kill me."

Terror ran through me. "Kill you? Why?"

"Your guess is as good as mine."

"They used me so they could try to murder you?"

"That's the way it looks."

"I think I'm going to be sick."

CHAPTER 28

Victoria

I STEPPED OUT OF TOBY'S Hummer across from my home and held his gaze for a moment. My mind was still spinning out of control—there was entirely too much to process. Carter and his dad using me. The fact that Carter had anything to do with it infuriated me. But looking into Toby's eyes helped calm me, momentarily at least.

"Are you sure you don't want me to go with you?" I asked. He was going to tell the news media he was back after dropping me off.

"I'd like nothing more, but it's best to keep you out of it."

"Because I'm your student."

He nodded. "We have to pretend that nothing has changed—at least until you have a new professor. But also, I don't want the jaguars catching wind of this. It's going to be bad enough that I'm going public with my return."

I bit my lip. "Okay. Well, I need some time to sort my thoughts anyway. When can I see you again?"

Toby stared at me, mirroring the same mixture of longing and needing time alone as I felt. "I'm leaving it up to you. Call me when you're ready. Day or night."

Realization hit me. "I don't have my phone. It's in my purse, which I left at the Jag. I'm not going back for it—or my car. All of that has been paid for by them. And it was them! *They* cut off my credit cards."

Toby's face shadowed. "You're better off cutting out anything that has to do with them. The car, the phone, everything."

My mouth dropped. He was right. "But they're even paying for my room and board." I started shaking.

He waved me back in the truck and wrapped his arms around me. "Everything will be okay, I promise."

"H-how? I'm about to be homeless. I have nothing."

Toby kissed the top of my head. "You won't get kicked out of school or your housing. Those are usually prepaid. Just act like everything is normal. I'll get you set up with a car and phone. I have to get another phone myself. Do you need anything else?"

"I don't know. Do you think they're monitoring my laptop?"

"More than likely. I'll add that to my list."

"Are you sure? I don't want—"

"There's nothing I wouldn't do for you, sweetness. Nothing at all."

Tears pooled in my eyes. I blinked and they fell, landing on Toby's hand.

He cupped my chin and guided me to look at him. "I promise it'll all work out, and I'll take care of everything. I don't want you worrying about finances or anything else. And I'll contact Gessilyn about finding a memory spell for you."

"Thank you, Toby." My lips quivered.

Toby glanced behind me. "Some people are coming our way. You'd better go. Let me give you Jet's number in case you need to get hold of me before class tomorrow."

He pulled out a pen, scribbled down a number, and squeezed my hand.

I hurried out of the Hummer and into the mansion. Sasha looked up from her bed, where she was on her laptop. "Did you spend another night in Carter's guest—what's the matter?"

"You wouldn't believe me if I told you." I dug into my backpack and pulled out my computer. I put everything I needed onto a cloud server—which Carter probably had full access to. He probably also knew all my passwords.

I'd never felt more violated. Well, in recent memory. Once I was sure all my schoolwork was safe, I threw the laptop on my bed.

"Victoria?"

"I'm fine."

"Obviously."

The screensaver on my laptop turned on. A picture of a jaguar lounging in a tree.

Fury tore through me. I grabbed the computer and threw it across the room and hit the wall. Pieces flew off and the screen cracked.

"Do you want to talk?" Sasha slid off her bed and crept toward me.

I picked up what was left of the laptop and threw it on the floor.

"Or maybe you'd prefer to destroy a thousand-dollar computer."

Ignoring her, I jumped up and down on the biggest piece. I pictured Carter's traitorous face with each crushing blow.

Someone pounded on our door. "What's going on in there?"

"Nothing!" I ran over to my nightstand and picked up a framed photo of a picture Carter had taken of us. I threw it across the room, shattering it much more nicely than the computer.

"Oh…" Sasha nodded. "Trouble in paradise. Gotcha."

"You have no idea." I leaped over the laptop remains and pulled the photo from what was left of the frame. Then I tore it into as many pieces as my fingers could manage.

"Again, I ask, do you want to talk?"

"Not unless you can breathe fire on his fat, ugly face."

She snickered and then covered her mouth. "Sorry."

"Wait!" I could probably have Soleil suck out his essence. Maybe she could take all of it.

Pounding sounded on our door again.

"Go away!" I shouted.

The door flung open. Landon came in. "Turn on the news! They just found that professor."

"Alive?" Sasha asked.

"Yeah, they're interviewing him now."

Sasha glanced at me. "That's good news. You were worried about him. And this'll get your mind off what's-his-butt."

Landon's mouth dropped. "You and Jag broke up?"

"Ugh!" I grabbed Sasha's arm and dragged her past Landon. "Let's go downstairs and see for ourselves."

"Wait," Landon called. "Details. I need some."

I ignored him and ran into the crowded living room. Everyone was talking about Toby, so I couldn't hear the interview. Not that I needed to—I was the only one who knew what had really happened.

On the screen, Toby appeared to be in front of the building where his office was. His hair was jumping around in the wind and he had close to a dozen microphones shoved at his face.

Sasha turned to me. "He looks like he's been through hell."

"Yeah, I know." What would she have thought if she'd seen him before he showered off all the dirt and gunk? He looked leaps and bounds better than when I'd found him. Now it was just bruises, cuts, and swelling. He was lucky nothing had gotten infected.

Watching him on the screen made me want to run out from the Waldensian and down to campus to throw myself in his arms. I didn't want to deal with school or anything. Not homework, midterm papers, or reading. None of it.

I turned to Sasha. "I'm going to clean up our room and then go to bed."

"This early? You haven't even had dinner, have you?"

"I don't care. And if Carter tries to find me, can you tell him I've moved?"

"Um, okay?"

"Thanks." I pushed my way through the sea of people up to our room.

Little pieces of the laptop and picture frame were all over the carpeting. I cursed Carter the entire time I cleaned. If they'd had me—against my will?—before I could remember, he had probably brainwashed me to fall for him in the first place. All the jaguar stuff seemed to make that clear.

I wanted to break more stuff, but the thought of cleaning it was enough to stop me. My stomach rumbled, but I ignored it. I just wanted to go to sleep and forget about everything for a little while.

At least Toby was going to help me break the Jag family's hold on me. I climbed into bed and tossed and turned for a while, my mind racing. Everything with Carter had been a lie. He'd used me. Pretended to know nothing about why I couldn't remember anything. Acting like I was just some random girl that he met at the barbecue.

The worst part was that I should have seen through it all. Hadn't someone told me that he never talked to most girls? Yet I'd eaten it up when he showered me with attention.

Stupid.

If I was dumb enough to fall for that, could I be equally idiotic for believing Toby? Did he have anything to gain by a relationship with me? As crazy as it was, I believed every bit of his story of our decades-old love for one another. That I'd died in his arms.

I sighed and pulled my pillow over my face. If only I had somewhere to call home, I'd run there to the safety and security of my family. Except that Toby was as close to that as I had.

When Sasha came back to our room, I was still awake, but I pretended to sleep.

I must have fallen asleep because my alarm woke me from a sound sleep. Eyes closed, I found the snooze button and sat up. I felt like I'd been hit by a truck.

Everything from the previous weekend hit me like a ton of bricks. Anger pulsated through me at the thought of Carter. But then I relaxed, knowing I might see Toby in my first class of the day. I wouldn't be able to wrap my arms around him—or could I? The day he returned from being missing, no one would question a student giving him a hug, right?

I turned off my alarm and bounced out of bed. Humming, I got ready and spent extra time on my hair and makeup.

"You seem happier," Sasha said. "Feel better than last night?"

"Sure do." I smiled at her. "I'm not going to let a stupid guy get the best of me."

"Good for you. Oh, he did stop by last night. Said he and his cousin were dropping off your car. That your purse was in the trunk. Said the keys are behind the front driver tire or something."

"Jerk," I muttered. All the better to keep me under his thumb.

She lifted a brow.

"Did you tell him I moved?"

"Yeah, but he didn't believe me."

I frowned. Did the jackass have some other way to follow my every move? Had I led him to Toby's house accidentally?

"Are you okay?" Sasha asked. "You look like you've seen a ghost."

"I just want him out of my life."

"Remember, you're not going to let a stupid man get to you."

"You're right." I plastered on a fake smile. "Have a good day. I sure plan to."

By the time I got to class, I was late because I refused to take the car. Not that it mattered, Professor Fredrickson was there. He gave me an annoyed glance and continued talking math. I took my regular seat.

"Did you hear they found Foley?" Grace whispered.

I nodded.

"The school's making him take a week off to recover, then he'll be back here."

The rest of the morning flew by in a blur. I ate lunch by myself, scarfing down two plates of food since I hadn't eaten since lunch the day before.

My stuffed stomach twisted in knots as I walked toward Massaro's class. If I could've skipped class, I would have, but I was already on his list. One wrong move, and he'd likely fail me. Then I'd be stuck with him another quarter—assuming someone would pay for me to continue schooling.

I held my head high, walked in the classroom like I owned the place, and acted like I didn't see Carter. Out of the corner of my eye, I could see him, though. He sat up taller when I entered, and I could even see his face light up. I went to the other end of the room and sat in an empty seat.

Carter came over to me. "Hey, didn't you see me sitting over there?"

I opened my backpack and pulled out the pad of paper and pen I'd been using all day.

"What's going on?"

I wrote the date on it and the name of the class.

"Victoria?"

Massaro came in and set up his things.

"I've been calling you," Carter said. "Didn't Sasha tell you your stuff was in the car?"

I kept my gaze on the professor. He started speaking about the papers we were working on. Or in my case, supposed to be working on.

"What's the matter?" Carter whispered.

Massaro glared at him. "Mr. Jag, when I am talking, you are not."

Carter spent the entire class whispering to me when Massaro's back was turned. I spent the entire time ignoring his lying words.

When the hour was finally over, I stuffed my notebook and pen into my bag, trying to ignore Carter. As he spoke, I started to think of some of the good times we'd had. It almost made me want to hear him out. He'd been so good to me the entire time we'd been together.

Lies. All of it. That's what I had to keep in mind. He'd stolen my memories and lied about it.

I fled the classroom, eager to get away from him. He followed, keeping up all too easily.

"Why are you ignoring me? Talk to me, Victoria. I have no idea what's going on." And on and on he went. People stared, but he didn't seem to notice. He must have really missed having so much control over me.

I headed for the library, which I knew was in the opposite direction of his next class.

He grabbed my arm. "I'm not going to leave you alone until you tell me what's going on."

Finally, I turned and looked at him. Seeing him made a lump form in my throat, but there was no way I would let him know he could upset me like that. I narrowed my eyes. "I'm going to need you to apologize to Yurika for me. I have to quit."

"She already figured that out when you left her high and

dry the other day and didn't show up the next day. What's going on? This isn't like you."

I pulled my arm from his grasp. "You should be able to put the pieces together. Leave me alone."

Hurt and shock covered his face. "What did I do?"

"Just leave me alone." I spun around, unable to look at him any longer.

"Victoria," he pleaded. "Please. I have no idea what I did. Everything was going great, and now you seem to hate me."

"Then you'll have to think out of the box, won't you?"

He stepped in front of me and grabbed me again. "Just tell me. This is eating me up."

"Good!"

Carter flinched.

I clenched my teeth. "You really want the truth?"

"It would be nice." He shot me an exasperated look.

"First, begging doesn't suit you. Second, Carter, I know *everything*."

His brows came together, probably in mock confusion. "About what?"

"Are you so dense?" I exploded.

He frowned. "Apparently."

"About me."

His head tilted. "Can you explain what that means?"

I sighed, beyond annoyed. "My memories. *You* stole them, so thanks for that. But I don't need you to save me. I've made other friends, so I don't need any more of your lies."

Carter's mouth dropped. "I don't know what you're talking about."

"Seriously?"

"Yes!"

"Stop with the lies. I can't take it anymore. It's bad enough that you're behind all of this, but at least man up and take responsibility for what you've done."

He let go of my arm. "I really don't understand."

"Just leave me alone, and please take the car back. I won't use it."

Carter held my gaze, appearing deep in thought. "I don't know what's going on, but I have a feeling my father is behind this. I'm going to get to the bottom of whatever's going on."

"Great. Have fun." I spun around and stormed away.

"I'll make it right," he called. "I promise."

CHAPTER 29

Toby

"YOU SURE SHE'S COMING?" TAP asked, sliding me another drink.

I caught it and took a swig. "I'm sure Gessilyn was just held up."

Tap leaned closer. "I've learned it can be tricky trusting her kind."

"She's not just any witch, she's the high witch."

"Even more worrisome."

I finished the drink and set the empty glass down. "Trust me. We go way back—long before she had any clue of how powerful she really is."

He shrugged. "It's your funeral."

"Thanks. I'll take my chances."

"Another drink?"

I shook my head. "I need to be able to think clearly."

"Wise man."

Gessilyn came around the corner, wearing purple yoga pants and a black tank with her hair pulled back.

Tap glanced at me and arched a brow. "She's your witch?"

"Yeah."

"Huh."

She came over and wrapped her arms around me. "Hey, Toby. It's so good to see you again. You had us all worried."

I returned the embrace. "You know me. Nothing's going to keep me down."

"Still, we were worried. Where did you find this bar? I almost didn't find it."

"That's how I like it," Tap said. "It's open to all supernaturals, but I don't want just anyone stumbling upon it."

Gessilyn glanced around. "I can see why. Nice place."

A look of pride crossed Tap's face. He held out his hand. "I'm Tap."

She shook his hand. "Gessilyn."

"Pleasure. Do you want something to drink? First drink's on the house."

I arched a brow. "You never told me that."

"Sorry, you aren't that pretty."

Gessilyn laughed and ordered something I'd never heard of before. The she turned to me. "Mind if we sit somewhere quieter?"

I turned to Tap.

"Take one of the private rooms. I'll have Quinn bring your drink."

"Thanks." She smiled at him.

I got off my barstool. "The rooms are this way." We chose the one farthest down the hall. It was a small room with some cozy recliners. We both sat in one and I filled her in on what had happened with Victoria. "Do you know of any spells to restore her memories?"

"It's going to be tricky without knowing exactly what removed them in the first place."

I groaned.

"I said tricky, not impossible."

The door opened, and a teenage siren came in and handed Gessilyn a magenta drink and left.

"Do you have anything in mind?" I asked.

She sipped her drink, looking deep in thought. "There is one that might work in this case."

"What is it?" I leaned forward, eager to hear about it.

"True love's kiss."

"Come again?"

"It's similar to the ones you hear about in the faerie tales, but this one isn't a myth. Truth is, it's potent. Most don't end up liking what they find. In fact, many regret ever using the spell in the first place."

"We need her memories restored."

"But she remembers you, does she not?" Gessilyn arched a brow, continuing to sip her drink.

"It's not that simple. She remembers *me*, but not our time together." I closed my eyes, remembering the way she'd kissed me. Victoria definitely remembered us—she still had the very same passion she'd always had.

"That'll help," Gessilyn said, bringing me back to the present.

I opened my eyes. "I sense a but."

"On the plus side, it should be easier to access her memories, but that also includes the ones she doesn't want."

"Except that it's not like she blocked out the memories herself. This was done to her—against her will. She wouldn't have agreed to forget me."

Gessilyn put her hand on top of mine. "Is it possible she agreed in order to forget something more painful?"

Irritation rose in me. "No, actually it's not. My Victoria never would agree to forgetting us."

"Okay. I'm just asking. It's going to take me a few days to gather the ingredients and get everything ready."

My heart sank. "Even with rune travel?"

"Yes."

"Okay. Thanks, Gessilyn. Is there anything I can help with?"

She shook her head. "Just make sure she knows the risks."

"What do you mean?" I asked.

"That she probably won't like everything that comes back to her."

"I'm pretty sure she'd rather just have her memories back, but I'll mention it to her."

She rose. "I'd better get started."

"Wait."

She glanced at me. "There's more?"

"Do you know anything about why she wouldn't be able to turn at the full moon?"

"No, but maybe that'll be something this spell will reveal. If I can help, I will."

"Is there any way around the curse of the moon for the rest of us? The jaguars aren't held to it. They shift at will."

Gessilyn frowned. "I can look into it, but I really need to focus on one spell at a time."

"I understand, but there has to be a way. You're able to help vampires go into the sun, so surely you can help werewolves shift when we feel like it."

She rubbed her temples.

"I'm sorry, Gess. Don't worry about it. I'm getting ahead of myself."

"I understand. I wouldn't like being under the moon's curse. What if I ask my parents? They've been around practically since time began. One of them might know something."

My face lit up and I gave her a hug. "Thank you. I owe you."

"You sure do." Her tone held a hint of teasing. "But seeing you get back together with Victoria is all the payment I need."

"Thanks, Gess. Speaking of true love, how's Killian?"

She beamed. "Great. We'll have to set up a double date when everything settles down."

I gave a slight nod, and then she left. I sat back in the recliner and took a deep breath. After everything I'd been through, I couldn't wait for life to return to normal. I'd been through so much since the days Victoria and I had planned on running away to start our own pack. Now I was well-versed in running packs.

My phone buzzed. It had been going off nonstop since my TV appearance. I checked my texts. Fifty-six new ones, but not one from Victoria. I replied a quick thanks to all the ones expressing appreciation for my safe return.

I checked the time. Her last class was long over. She'd emailed me from the library earlier saying she'd stay there and wait for me.

Hopefully she'd had enough time to study, because I couldn't stay away any longer. I had her new phone and car, and couldn't wait to give them to her.

I hurried from the Faeble, waving a quick goodbye to Tap and some others I knew before making my way through the woods to my place. I got in my Hummer and headed for campus. It shouldn't have surprised me, but people kept stopping me on my way to the library. I tried to be appreciative but quick.

When I finally made it to the library, more people surrounded me, expressing their gratitude for my safety. I felt bad for being annoyed.

At long last, I made it to the study rooms, where everyone was too busy to notice me. I found the room she was in and went inside.

Her face lit up when she saw me. I made sure no one was looking in the room and then I wrapped my arms around her. She squeezed back tightly. "How are you?"

"I've had the worst day."

"I'm sorry." I sat in the chair next to her and took her hand. "I have some good news."

"You're here. That's all I need."

"How about a phone?" I pulled out her new phone. "It's all set up and ready to go. I preloaded it with my number in the contacts." I couldn't help smiling.

"You've just made my day." She threw herself into my arms.

"That's not all," I assured her. "Your new laptop is in my car and we still need to pick up your car."

Victoria squeezed me tighter. "I can't thank you enough. Fleeing from the Jags isn't something I could've done on my own. I have a little in saving from working at the club, but that wouldn't last me long." Her voice cracked.

"Shh." I rubbed her back. "It's going to be okay now, and I have more good news."

She looked at me, wide-eyed. "You do?"

I nodded. "Gessilyn's working on a spell to restore your memories. She sounds pretty confident about it. We just have to give her some time to prepare it."

Victoria threw herself against me again.

I kissed the top of her head. "Everything is going to work out. Are you ready? I paid for your car to be dropped off at my house so I could check it out first."

She took a deep breath and sat back, her eyes shining with tears.

"Victoria…"

"These are happy tears. After everything I've been through, I just can't believe—" She shook her head. "Listen to me. You've been through so much more, and yet you've done all this for me."

"I'd do anything for you."

Her lips shook. "I don't deserve that."

I pressed my fingertip against her mouth, wanting to kiss those soft, sweet lips. "Stop. You deserve everything I have and more. Let's get going, but we're going to have to take a back way. You'd think I was a celebrity the way everyone's acting."

"You kind of are. Everyone spent so much time handing out fliers and trying to find you."

"I saw some of those. It's kind of weird seeing my face on them."

"Everybody was disappointed you weren't in class today."

"The college won't let me come back this week. Come on." I helped her pack her things and led her a back way to my

Hummer. A few people stopped me, but it wasn't the constant barrage I'd received on the way in.

We finally made it, and on the drive to my place she asked, "What kind of car is it?"

"Definitely not a Jaguar."

"I appreciate that." She laughed. "What is it?"

"Guess."

"Really?"

"Yeah, I want to see if you get it."

"Okay. Beamer?"

"Try again."

"Audi?"

"Nope."

"You've gotta give me a clue."

"Where's the fun in that?" I struggled to keep my expression straight. It was so nice to be teasing her again.

"Will you at least tell me if I'm guessing in the right ballpark?"

"Maybe."

"Ugh." She blew on her hair, just like she always had when she was playfully irritated.

"A Fiesta?"

I laughed. "Now you're in the wrong ballpark for sure."

She sighed. "I really don't know that much about cars."

"We're almost there now." I pulled onto the dirt drive.

"You'll tell me?" she asked.

"If you guess it."

"Have you always been this annoying?"

"Me? Annoying?" I asked in mock offense.

"I'll take that as yes. And I'll just wait to see it."

I snickered. "One thing I will tell you, you've always been fun to tease."

"Wonderful."

We went the rest of the short drive in silence. When we got to the gate, I unlocked it with a remote and waited for it to open.

"Do I get one of those?" she asked.

"A gate?"

"No." She shoved me. "A remote."

Excitement ran through me. "If you want one."

She squeezed my hand. "I do."

I pulled through the gate, remote locked it, and then pulled up next to the Bentley.

Victoria glanced at the white car and over at me. "Whose is that?"

I raised my brows.

Her mouth gaped. "I... You got me... Really?"

"You think I could let those jaguars outdo me?"

"But a Bentley?"

"You'd prefer something more expensive?" I teased, trying to keep my voice steady.

She put her hands up. "No. Not at all."

"Let's check it out. I just want to look under the hood real quick and you can take me for a spin."

"This is unreal."

"No, having you back from the dead, that's unreal." I leaned over and finally pressed my mouth onto hers again.

CHAPTER 30

Victoria

THE COLD WIND FLUNG MY hair into my face. I pulled it away and stepped into a deep puddle, covering my new pump. I took a deep breath, tightened my coat around me, and shook my foot off.

I glanced up at the darkening sky. The full moon was already coming into view in the horizon. There wasn't much time. Gessilyn had finally found the last rare ingredient for my true love's kiss spell and it would expire in less than twenty-four hours from the time she mixed it. But Toby was due to turn into a werewolf soon, and as much as I adored him, I couldn't imagine puckering up to a wolf.

Another breeze picked up, this time sending soggy leaves against me. I hurried toward the Waldensian to drop off my backpack and change my clothes.

A bear and a lion jumped in front of me from behind an SUV, roaring and screaming.

I jumped back, heart pounding.

They held out bags. "Trick or treat!"

"Go away, Landon." I rolled my eyes.

"You're no fun. Oh, look. Here come the Ferdinand twins.

Let's scare them." He and his friend ran off.

I shook my head. Halloween, a full moon, and a spell to bring back my memories. What could possibly go wrong?

Despite having just eaten at the all-you-can eat place, my stomach growled. At least my bones weren't aching as bad as they had during the last two full moons.

My phone vibrated.

Toby: *U no how 2 get 2 the Faeble right?*
Victoria: *Yeah. B there soon.*
Toby: *Hurry.*
Victoria: *I am.*

My heart raced. I'd had to stay later than expected in the library because I'd run into Massaro, who thought that was the perfect time to lecture me about how important the next day's quiz was. If I hadn't already thought him cruel, having such an important quiz the day after Halloween would've proven it.

I ran inside and was attacked with silly string from both sides. The two guys aiming at me burst into a fit of laughter.

"Thanks." I pulled it off and threw it on one of them before heading upstairs.

Sasha stood at our vanity wearing a tight black body suit with a tail. She was painting something on her face. "You going to the party at the Beta Kappa Pi frat house?"

"No, I have other plans."

She turned to me and frowned. "You never do anything fun."

"Sure I do."

"Fine, I'm sure your mystery guy is great, but I never see

you anymore."

"We'll go somewhere fun soon. I promise."

Sasha turned back to her makeup and gave herself whiskers. She put on a headband with black pointed ears. "It's obvious I'm a cat, right?"

"Best one I've seen yet."

She beamed. "What are you going as?"

I doubted anyone was dressing up at a bar for paranormal creatures. "Nothing."

"On Halloween?" She shook her head. "I think I need to drag you to the frat party. I heard they have bobbing for apples in a tub of vodka."

"Maybe I'll stop by later. I'm going to a bar."

Her eyes widened. "I didn't know you had a fake ID."

"I have connections." I stuffed my backpack in my closet under some clothes. Toby had bought me the most expensive laptop available, so I never left it where it would be easily found.

"Nice. Well, you *have* to dress up for Halloween. Come over here."

I shook my head and backed away from her. "Really, I just need to change my clothes." I kicked off my shoes, setting the soaked one next to the heater. Then I turned to my closet, trying to figure out what exactly one wore to a spell that would restore her memories. I settled on skinny jeans and a scoop neck shirt—all black for the holiday.

Once I was dressed, I turned around to ask Sasha something, but she lunged for me, painting something on my face.

She smiled. "Perfect."

I groaned. "Thanks."

Then she put some necklaces with bats and pumpkins on me. "Now you at least look like you tried."

My phone buzzed.

Toby: *U almost here?*
Victoria: *Yes.*

"Thanks, Sasha. I have to go."

"Have fun. Stop by the party if you get a chance."

"Sure." I found my midnight blue running shoes and put them on. With the Faeble being in the middle of the forest, I would need them. I grabbed a coat and hurried down the stairs, managing to avoid another silly string attack.

Outside, I double-checked that my car was locked up tight and then headed for the woods, pulling my hood up over my head. The wind had picked up and blew raindrops against me.

Once in the cover of the forest, I found it easier to run. The trees kept the ground from getting too wet. Before I made it too far, a gray and black wolf ran over to me, keeping up with me.

"You again?" I asked. "I hope you're in the mood for a run, Alex. I can't stop today."

He howled.

I felt a little better having him there. Somehow, he always managed to find me out in the woods when I needed a friend. "I'm headed to the Faeble. Hopefully that isn't too far from where you're willing to run." I should have felt dumb talking to him like he could understand, but he'd sat through my ramblings enough times, he actually felt like a friend.

Alex howled again.

"I'll take that as a yes."

He let out another sound and turned to the left.

"I'm going this way, buddy."

Alex turned over to me and took the cuff of my coat in his mouth. He gave a muffled bark.

"You want me to go this way? I'm in a hurry."

He pulled on my coat.

"Okay, as long as we don't get too far off the path to the Faeble."

Alex let go and ran off. I followed, since he wasn't too far off the path. Part of me wondered if I was crazy for following the wolf when I needed to get to Toby before the full moon reached its point in the sky.

I was about to turn and go a different way when the Faeble came into sight. My mouth dropped. "How did you—?"

The wolf turned to me and stared. I got the feeling he was proud of himself.

"I don't know how you did that, but thank you." I rubbed his head and then ran inside. The place was filled with Halloween decorations, costumes, and festive music.

Tap came over to me and arched a brow. "I didn't realize you came ready to party."

I'd forgotten about whatever makeup Sasha had put on me. "I'm not. It's a long story."

"They're all waiting for you downstairs. I have a private room where you won't be disturbed."

"Stop!" came an all-too-familiar voice from behind.

I spun around. Carter.

"What are you doing here?" I demanded.

Tap's face scrunched. "What is a jaguar doing here? I thought you were all too good for us—that's why you built the

Jag."

Carter kept his attention on me. "You have to hear me out, Victoria."

I shot him a glare, wishing looks could kill.

He grabbed my arm.

Tap jumped between us, baring the sharpest teeth I'd ever seen.

Carter let go of me and backed up. "This is important."

"This more so." I turned to Tap. "Take me to Toby."

"Who's Toby? You don't mean—?"

I glanced out a window. The moon was moving higher in the sky. "Come on, Tap."

Carter grabbed my arm again. I yanked it out of his grasp. Tap bared his teeth again.

"Want me to tear him to pieces?" Tap asked.

"I don't care what he does, just take me to Toby."

Tap glowered at Carter and then dragged me down a hall-way I'd never seen.

"I'm coming with," Carter called.

I groaned.

Tap turned to me. "Seriously, I'll send him home in pieces. Just say the word."

I had no doubt he meant it literally. "No, he needs to see this." I turned and glared at Carter. "Maybe you'll finally understand that we're through."

We entered a dark area, reminding me of the basement Toby had been kept in. Tap flicked on a light, showing instead a beautifully decorated room with items that looked like they belonged in a castle. "This way."

I followed him farther down the hall. He opened a door

into a candle lit room. Gessilyn stood at a table, mixing something in a black pot. Toby, Soleil, and several wolves circled around her.

Upon seeing me, Toby broke free of the circle and pulled me close. "Why's he here?"

I stepped back and glared at Carter. "I think he followed me."

He stared at everything, horror covering his face. "What's going on here?"

"We're going to fix my memory. You'd better not try to interfere." Oh, how I wanted to slap him. "You know, since you did this to me."

Carter shook his head. "I swear I didn't. I came to tell you I finally figured out what my dad did—you were right. He was behind everything, including your memories."

I narrowed my eyes.

"But I didn't know about any of it. You have to believe me."

A pop sounded.

Gessilyn stopped stirring. "It's ready."

Toby let out a cry and stepped back. "We need to hurry." He rubbed the back of his neck. "I can try to hold this off, but it won't last long, and I'll need to save my energy."

My heart thundered in my chest. Was I really about to remember everything?

"How does this spell work?" Carter demanded.

"Who is this guy?" Gessilyn asked, sounding irritated.

"Nobody," I said.

Hurt crossed Carter's face.

Gessilyn waved me over and poured some black liquid

from the pot into a small glass cup.

Soleil strutted over to Carter. "It's true love's kiss."

"What?" Carter asked.

She turned to me. "Want me to find out if he's telling the truth?"

"Maybe later."

Gessilyn handed me the drink. The thick goo bubbled and the glass was cold to the touch.

Toby cried out in pain again.

"Drink it," she urged.

"What's going on?" Carter demanded.

I brought the glass to my face. It smelled like tar and gasoline. I closed my eyes, plugged my nose, and swallowed. It was freezing and sticky.

The other werewolves ran from the room, fur growing all over their bodies.

Soleil explained the spell to Carter, and I tried to focus on her voice rather than the gross drink.

"Done."

Gessilyn took the glass from me. "Let's hope this is enough. I made double what the spell called for just in case."

"Thanks. What do we do now?"

"Your true love kisses you and everything floods back. Although, it might not be that simple. You might have a rough night ahead of you, given all the years of memories stolen from you."

I turned to Toby. His face was contorted. I hoped he could make it.

He turned to me and took a deep breath. "I don't know how much longer I can hold off."

"Wait," Carter said.

Toby glared at him. "Who invited you?"

"I want her to kiss me first."

"What?" Toby exclaimed.

"Are you kidding?" Gessilyn asked.

"Get outta here." Soleil lunged for him.

Carter narrowed his eyes. "Victoria *does* love me. And besides, my family did this to her. It only makes sense that my kiss would fix this." He turned to Toby. "Unless you're too chicken to let her try."

Toby's nostrils flared. "I'm not afraid of you."

Carter turned to me.

I shook. "I've never hated anyone more than I hate you right now."

"How would you know?"

I lunged for him, fists flailing.

Soleil blocked me. She turned to Gessilyn. "How much time do we have left?"

"Not a lot."

Toby stood taller and glared at Carter. "Go ahead and let her try. It won't do any good."

I swallowed. "Toby—"

"No, I'm serious."

Carter stepped forward. "Are you afraid it might be true?"

"Never! I'd be glad to prove you wrong." I turned to Gessilyn. "What happens if I kiss more than one person?"

"Nothing, as long as you kiss your true love. You could kiss everyone in this bar before kissing Toby—"

"You mean her true love," Carter said.

Gessilyn glared at him and turned back to me. "But just so long as you kiss your true love before the time runs out, and it's ticking."

I turned to Toby.

He held out his arm toward Carter.

I glared at Carter. "This is just so you can't ever say you're my love." I went over to him and put my lips on his. My body relaxed as memories of good times with him flooded my mind.

Fear tore through me. He wasn't actually my true love was he? It couldn't be. He was a cruel traitor. A liar.

He pulled me close and deepened the kiss.

I had to fight my weakening body to pull away.

"Do you remember anything?" he asked.

"No." Not that I would have admitted if it had. I turned to Toby.

His arms were wrapped around his middle and his face was contorted in pain. Cracking noises sounded and then fur sprouted on his arms.

I threw myself into his arms and pressed my lips on his. He wrapped his arms around me and deepened the kiss. I melted into him and knew he was the one.

He pulled away. "I'm sorry, I can't keep the change away any longer." He brushed his lips across mine and ran from the room.

I stared at the empty doorway, breathless.

"Do you remember anything?" Carter asked.

I closed my eyes. The only thing in my mind was Toby's mouth on mine.

"Do you feel any different?" Soleil asked.

Nothing had changed from before I drank the potion. I opened my eyes and glared at Carter. "Did you do something to break the spell?"

CHAPTER 31

Victoria

I ESCAPED FROM THE BAR, tears spilling onto my cheeks. Why had I agreed to kiss Carter? The only thing I would have needed to prove my love of Toby would have been to kiss him.

Gessilyn and the others called after me, but I needed to be alone. I ran until my legs grew tired and my lungs burned. My bones ached, reminding me that they longed to shift.

I leaned against a tree and gasped for air. Not a single memory had formed. I turned around and punched the tree, digging the bark into my flesh.

At least the pain was something to distract me from the stupid mistake I'd made. I never should have trusted Carter. How could I have been so foolish?

Footsteps sounded.

I jumped up, ready to beat the crap out of my former jaguar friend.

Instead, a guy about my age with light brown hair and bright gray eyes walked over. He was handsome and seemed familiar, though I was sure I'd never seen him before. He wore a dark blue polo shirt that I thought I'd seen on Toby once.

Clearly, my mind was playing tricks on me.

"Are you okay?" he asked.

"I'd rather be left alone, if you don't mind."

He frowned. "I understand, but if you'd like to talk, I'd be more than happy."

I gave him a double take. "I don't even know you."

"Actually, you do. You've shared all kinds of secrets with me."

My heart practically leaped into my throat. More memories I would probably never recover. "What do you mean?"

He stepped closer, extending his hand. "I'm Alex."

"Alex?" I studied him. "I don't know an Alex."

"Did you get to the Faeble in time?"

I gave him a double-take. "The wolf?" My face heated. How was that possible? "I d-don't understand."

"Have a seat." He sat at the base of the trunk. "I'll understand if you don't want to rub my ears this time."

My face and neck grew inflamed with heat. I slid down to sitting.

"I'm a werewolf, too," he said. "Only I live as a wolf and only turn human on the full moon."

"What?"

"We're called wolfborns. Instead of being born human, we come out as wolves. Many consider us a bad omen. Most are drowned at birth."

I gasped.

"But those of us who were spared have formed our own pack."

"I'm so sorry."

He shrugged. "I don't know any different."

"But wouldn't you rather be human most of the time?"

"It's actually pretty peaceful living the way we do."

I tried to wrap my mind around it.

"You want to talk about what's bothering you?" he asked.

"Are you sure that's how you want to spend your one night as a human?"

He laughed. "It beats spending another evening in the Faeble. Not that it's a bad place, but it's nice to have someone else to talk with—especially someone who trusted me in my wolf form."

"Wait. Where's the rest of your pack? I've never seen you with any others."

Alex frowned. "Some hunters came through recently. They took most of us out. The rest of us were separated. I think they left the area, not that I can blame them."

"Why did you stay?"

He shrugged. "It's my home."

"But aren't you lonely?"

"Of course. But someone needs to stick around to take care of the new wolfborns. We find several a year. They'll never survive on their own—unless born to another wolfborn."

"Why don't you stay with Toby's pack?"

Alex shook his head. "Like I said, others view us as an abomination."

"Not these guys. They have a vampire living with them. Surely, you can't be worse than that."

He gave me a double-take. "They've got a vampire? Like, as a pet?"

I smiled. "No, she's married to one of them."

"No way."

"I'm serious."

"Well, maybe they *would* accept me."

I patted his shoulder. "I'm sure they will. Plus you could keep an eye on the property, as a wolf when they're humans and as a human when they're wolves."

He seemed to be considering it.

"Let's go. I'll introduce you to Ziamara."

"Maybe you should talk to the other wolves first."

"I'm sure they'll be happy to have you on board. They pride themselves in being a pack that accepts everyone. You'll add to the diversity."

"But what about when I find a newly abandoned wolf-born?"

"I'm sure they'll let you raise him there. I—" Everything spun around me.

Alex grabbed my shoulders. "Are you okay?"

White dots formed all around. "I…"

"Talk to me!" He shook me.

My eyelids closed and I couldn't fight them…

When I opened them, I was in a strange house. I shot up in bed. No, this wasn't a new place. It was my childhood home.

I sniffed, smelling eggs, bacon, and coffee. Noise sounded outside the room. It sounded like my family was already up, getting ready for the day. I got up and rummaged through my dresser, finding an outfit that had once been my favorite.

After I had brushed my hair, I went into the bright, cheery kitchen. My father sat at the table, reading a newspaper. My mother was flipping bacon. Two of my three brothers were wrestling in the corner near the door.

"Take it outside," my father barked, not looking up from the paper.

"They're just being pups," my mother said. She turned to me and smiled. "Go wake your sister, would you? I don't need you kids late for school again."

I returned the smile and turned around. My sister bounded down the hall. "I'm already up."

"Good," said Mother. "Everyone sit for breakfast. It's getting close to the full moon, we need to eat up."

I took my normal seat.

"Boys!" Father snapped.

My brothers stopped wrestling and came over to the table, still eying each other.

"Can we please go to the school dance?" asked my sister.

Father folded over the top of the paper and glared at her. "No."

"But, Father."

"I said no. There will be no more discussion."

"But we don't have to go with regular boys. We can—"

"No," roared my father. He slammed the paper down. "Are you all trying to test my position as alpha? If you don't respect me, how do you expect the rest of the pack to? There will be no dances." He paused to make contact with all of us kids, his dark brown eyes narrowed. "You each have your own mates picked for you. We're not following the world's ridiculous dating trend. Bring it up again, and there will be blood."

"Let's eat," Mother said, her voice chipper. "We don't want to be ravenous the day of. Build up our strength now."

Father pulled the paper back in front of his face. "She said to eat."

We all grabbed our forks and dug in.

"There's plenty. Have thirds, kids."

The room was nearly silent as we filled up. I already noticed a greater than usual hunger.

My sister poured some juice. "I heard an unmarried girl from our pack is seeing someone from our rival pack."

Father slammed down his newspaper again and glared at her. "Elsie, you need to stop. If something that ludicrous was going on under my nose, I'd know about it—and deal with it severely. Death would not come swift enough for that girl. Stop trying to go to the school dance."

I held my expression steady, but my insides shook. How had anyone found out about Toby and me? We'd been extremely careful. Or was she referring to another couple? Maybe she was making it up, having no idea how true it really was.

Elsie scowled. "You might want to consider getting with the times, that's all I'm saying."

"Are you trying to bring down my wrath on you, child?"

She took a bite of eggs and shook her head. "Just saying that times are changing. Maybe we should try to—"

"To your room! Now. Before you say something that brings your death."

My mother's mouth dropped and she begged Elsie with her eyes.

"Death would be better than living here," Elsie muttered and rose from her chair.

"What did you say?" demanded Father.

"I said, yes sir." She pushed in her chair and stormed into the hall. Her bedroom door slammed shut.

"You people had better talk some sense into that girl," Father said. "She's close to finding herself as an example for the entire pack. I will not allow the world's ways to pollute the pack. Do you understand?"

"Yes," we all muttered and went back to eating.

My heart thundered, not only for how close Elsie was walking the line but also for myself. Toby and I had fallen in love, hard. He was all I could think about, and we wanted to get married, even if it meant running away to do it. I would so much rather live as his wife than under my father's thumb for the rest of my life.

Not only was he always a tyrant, but the jerk he'd picked for me to marry was no better. I shuddered just thinking about Franklin. Though not even engaged, he acted like I was his property.

I avoided him like the plague, using studies as my excuse. But soon, I would graduate and the engagement would begin. There was no getting around it. The alpha picked marriage partners for everyone at birth, and no one dared dispute Father's decision.

I was determined to be far, far away from the pack before Franklin had an opportunity to propose. As it was, every time he saw me, he spoke of nothing other than the large home we would own and how well I would keep it, all while giving him a new pup each year for the duration of my fertile years.

He made me sick. Toby was his polar opposite, kind to a fault and never using his strength to intimidate anyone.

We needed to make our move soon, which meant I would have to talk with Toby. School was easier, but still tricky.

The day went by in a blur, and I wasn't able to get any-where near him because he was always with someone from his pack or someone from my pack was near me.

That night, I was woken to a loud clatter, followed by shouting. My father was yelling—that was no surprise—but I couldn't tell who the other person was. It sounded like either my mother or sister. Worried that he might hit one of them, I climbed out of bed and crept out to the living room.

A glass vase lay shattered on the floor between my father and Elsie. He was in his pajamas, but she wore her nicest dress and hair ribbon. Maybe even a little of Mother's makeup that we weren't allowed to wear. Father said not until our wedding day.

"Back to bed," Father commanded, not even turning to me.

"What happened?"

"You needn't worry yourself over it. Back to bed!"

"C-can I help?" I asked and gave Elsie a look to let her know I wouldn't leave her alone.

"Did you not hear me?" he bellowed, finally glancing my way.

"I—"

"Fine. Your sister snuck out to the dance. You stay here and watch. It'll teach you both a lesson."

My stomach twisted so tight I was sure I'd throw up.

Elsie shot me a pleading expression.

I swallowed. "Maybe we can talk about this in the morning after everyone has had a chance to calm down."

"Calm down? I need to take care of this while my anger is still fresh. Why do you think an alpha is given so much power and fury?"

"To fight off enemies."

Father snorted. "It's sure a good thing women aren't alphas. Nature got that right." He turned back to Elsie. "You are going to regret disobeying my orders. Everyone else will learn never to cross me."

She turned to me, tears in her eyes.

He grabbed her chin and forced her to look at him. "You have humiliated me on top of insubordination. What do you think will happen now? The pack will think I'm weak. That I can be walked over and ignored. And why? All because my daughter showed everyone it's all right."

"Father, I'm sorry."

He sneered at her. "I'm sure you are, but sorry doesn't change anything."

"I'll do anything."

Father pulled out a long, thick knife from his pocket and aimed it at Elsie.

"No!" I ran to him and pulled on his arm, keeping the blade from touching her.

She ran for the door.

He shook me off and bound toward her. He slid the knife right into her abdomen. The blade stuck out through her back. He pulled it back and replaced it in his pocket.

Elsie's eyes widened and her hands reached for the wound. Red oozed over her hands.

I cried out and lunged for her.

Father blocked me and held me back, digging his fingers into my arms.

"Elsie!"

She opened her mouth, but no words came.

I turned to Father. "How could you?"

"Let it be known that this is the fate of anyone who dares

to defy me."

My sister crumpled to the ground.

I turned and struggled to free myself from Father's grasp. He only clung to me tighter.

"Elsie," I cried.

Her face had paled and she stared at me with eyes nearly vacant. The pool of red around her grew bigger.

Then her eyes shut.

I screamed.

CHAPTER 32

Victoria

MY FATHER STARED AT ME, his eyes wild and crazy. "Go to your room and pack your things. Tomorrow morning, you're marrying Franklin. No more school—it clearly corrupts young minds. I won't have that for my pack any longer. We're forming our own school."

"Father…"

He let go of my arm and shoved me toward Elsie. "I won't make another mistake again. I've given you children too much freedom, and that is over. Right now. Prepare for your wedding."

I flinched, ran to my room, and got dressed. I packed quicker than I'd have thought possible, but it wasn't to be with Franklin. No, I was nothing more than a means to an end to him. A maid and pup-producing factory.

Toby cared about me. He wanted what was best for me, even though it meant he would lose his position as future alpha of his pack.

I packed one bag and sneaked out my window. In the background, Father screamed at my brothers about the upcoming changes. No more wrestling and acting like brats.

As quietly as I could, I slid out of the window and landed on the ground. I closed the window and crept toward the woods. If anyone saw me sneaking away, they would report it to Father right away. I took the longest way possible to Toby's village, again being as careful as possible not to be seen. Everyone knew I was the rival pack's highest daughter.

One wrong move and... I winced just thinking about the decapitation.

I found the alpha house and crept around trees and bushes until I got to Toby's window. I threw a pine cone against the window, hoping he was in his room, and alone.

His curtain moved. An eye peeked out from a small opening.

I waved. He held up one finger and then the curtains closed.

My pulse was on fire. So many things could go wrong, yet I was left with no other options. Not when I would be forced to marry Franklin in a matter of hours.

Toby came around the house. "What's going on?" he whispered. "Not that I don't want to see you, but my father's preparing—"

"We have to go now." I couldn't bring myself to think about Elsie, much less talk about what had happened. Not even with Toby—not then.

"Right now? We were going to plan—"

"I'm sorry, but I don't have time to explain anything. It's now or never." I glanced around to make sure no one was watching us.

Toby took a deep breath. "Are you in danger?"

I nodded. "I have to leave with or without you. I'd prefer

with you."

"You think I'd let you go alone?" He shook his head. "Let me grab some things."

"Okay." I leaned against a tree while he ran back inside. It took him a while to come back out. I started to fear something was wrong, but finally, he ran out with a pack slung over his shoulder.

"Sorry about that. My father started questioning me, but I convinced him I just needed to get outside on my own." He took my hand in his and we ran deeper into the woods.

"Where are we going to go?" I asked.

"There's an abandoned home a few towns over. I thought we'd start out there. I'd hoped to set it up first, but I'm sure we can make do."

"As long as we're together, I don't care if we live in a swamp."

He squeezed my hand. "Don't worry. I wouldn't do that to you."

We ran through the woods for several miles before I heard something. It sounded like half a dozen sets of feet running in our direction. "What was that?"

"Hopefully just some wild animals."

"You don't think one of our families are after us?"

"I wouldn't say it's impossible, but can you go faster?"

My father's angry face popped into mind. "Yes."

We picked up our speed, but the running only grew closer. Horse hooves.

I turned to Toby, panic-stricken.

"Could be wild horses." He sounded less sure than I felt.

The clomping footsteps grew closer, closing in. Then the

horses and their riders surrounded us.

I clung to Toby. His father and several key leaders glared down, aiming rifles at us.

"You, son, have made a grave mistake."

"No," I pleaded. "It was me."

He bared his teeth. "Clearly. Shall I behead you rather than him?"

A cry escaped my mouth.

Toby scooped me up and ran, darting between two of the horses.

"Put me down," I insisted. "I'll only slow you down."

"I'm not letting them kill you."

"And I don't want you to die, either. Let me run."

He refused, and continued running.

"Toby."

"Let me do this."

"I'm only slowing you down." I glanced behind to see the horses chasing us.

Toby darted between trees and around other plant life.

"Please," I begged.

"I know a shortcut up ahead. They'll never see it coming, and we'll—"

A shot rang through the air.

"Let me go." I squirmed, but he held tighter. "I don't want to get us killed."

"You won't."

Another shot. The bullet flew right past us, only inches from Toby's head.

"Come on," I pleaded.

"Okay." He slowed and let go.

I jumped down and ran. We went much faster without him carrying my weight.

Bang! Bang! Bang!

Toby grabbed my arm and pulled me into a thick bush. Thorns scratched me as we fell into the shrubbery. My arm hit a thick branch, bruising it.

I gasped for air. "What now? They're going to find us easily enough."

He put a finger to his mouth and then pointed toward the other end of the bush. We crawled through, with thorns scratching my arms the entire way. My bag also kept getting caught on the branches. I was determined to keep up with Toby, though.

More shots rang through the air. They sounded close.

I shuddered.

Toby led me through a maze of bushes until we came to an empty den, barely large enough for the two of us. He pulled me inside and wrapped his arms around me.

"What lives here?" I sniffed, smelling a mixture of smaller animals.

"Nothing. Sometimes in my wolf form, I sneak away here to get away from my father."

I leaned my head against him. "How long before they give up, do you think?"

He groaned. "I'd give it a while. He's stubborn as a mule."

At least we were snuggled together and had a chance to rest. I couldn't have asked for anything more—aside from his pack not chasing us with rifles.

We sat quietly for what felt like hours. It was hard to tell for sure, though. We laced our fingers through each other's and gazed into each other's eyes a lot, neither daring to speak. Not with the excellent hearing wolves had.

I had so many questions about our future, it was torture to keep them inside.

Everything grew silent in the woods.

Unnaturally so.

Toby's back straightened. My ears perked up.

Something was wrong, but it was impossible to tell what, exactly.

An explosion sounded to our right. A branch flew off the bush in front of us.

Bang! Bang!

My heart sank. They'd found us.

Toby jumped in front of me to protect me from the shots. "If I'm injured, run!"

"No. I won't leave you." Tears stung my eyes at the thought of leaving without him. I'd already lost my sister. I couldn't lose him, too. I just couldn't.

He turned to me. "I want you safe. Promise me."

The bushes moved in front of us, and Toby's father appeared. "You think I didn't know about your little hiding spot, son?"

"Let us go."

He sneered. "Never. An act such as this requires death."

I shook, unable to handle any more dying.

"Father, it doesn't have to."

"You know the laws of our pack."

His father and a couple other men grabbed Toby's arms and pulled him away from me.

"Run!"

I froze. I couldn't leave him. If he was going to die, so was I. There was nothing left for me to live for without him, anyway. I crawled out from the den, watching from the bushes.

Toby knelt, execution style on the dirt with his hands on his head.

Terror shot through me. I couldn't let this happen.

His father aimed a rifle at Toby's heart.

I ran out from my hiding place and jumped in front of Toby, knocking him back.

A shot rang through the air.

Pain exploded in my chest. I hit the ground with a sickening thud.

Arms wrapped around me. Toby pulled me into his lap. "How could you?" Tears dropped onto my face.

I glanced up at his father. "Don't… hurt… him."

"I won't need to. Your death will destroy him." He laughed and motioned for his pack mates to follow him toward the horses.

Toby turned me so I was looking at him. His eyes were red and his face tear-stained. "Why did you jump in front of me?"

"You… can't… die."

"But now you're going to." Tears spilled onto his cheeks. He ran his hands along my face.

I took a deep breath, struggling to speak. "But my last moments are with you." Not my father and not Franklin. I reached up and ran my hands along his scruff. "I love you."

"Don't…"

White crept into the outer edges of my vision. "Live your life well."

"Without you?" His voice cracked.

He leaned down and pressed his lips on mine. "I swear I'll make my father pay."

The white took most of my vision. I could only see him— barely. My arms went limp and my eyelids started to close.

"Victoria!"

My eyes closed all the way.

"I love you, too. I'll never stop."

CHAPTER 33

Toby

I SAT AT THE EDGE of the bed. Though sleeping, Victoria clung to my hand, and I dabbed her forehead with a damp cloth. She continued flailing around, muttering.

"Is this supposed to happen?"

Gessilyn frowned. "Everyone reacts differently. Her memories are flooding back through dreams."

"How much longer is she going to have to endure this?" I dabbed her forehead some more.

"As long as it takes."

Killian, Gessilyn's husband, came in with a tray of food in each hand. He handed one to her and one to me. "Eat up."

"Thanks, but I have no appetite."

"All the more reason to eat." He sat next to Gessilyn and pulled some of his dark hair behind his ears.

I glanced back over at Victoria. It seemed cruel to eat while she was obviously suffering in her sleep. I took a bite, anyway. Killian was right. I needed my strength in case—no, when—Victoria woke. Who knew what the flood of memories would do to her?

She would remember dying in my arms at the hand of my

father. Then she would remember returning to life, and whatever had happened in death and also her time with the jaguars before starting school.

"Did anyone ever figure out what's going on with the wolf outside?" Killian asked.

"Poor thing probably needs a pack," Gessilyn said.

I swallowed a bite of chicken. "He probably sensed us while we were in our wolf form. I'm not worried about him."

Victoria sat up, eyes wide, gasping for air.

I nearly dropped my tray of food, but managed to set it on the end of the bed. Gessilyn moved it to the table near her.

"Victoria," I whispered, taking her hand.

She turned to me, her face pale. The way she stared at me, it was like she didn't recognize me.

"It's me. Toby." I squeezed her hand gently.

Victoria continued studying me.

"You're safe, sweetness. We're here in my home and I'm going to take care of you."

She looked around the room, her eyes darting about erratically.

"Did you remember the past?" I pulled some hair from her eyes.

"Her memories might not have caught up with the present," Gessilyn said.

I kissed Victoria's palm. "Do you need anything? We've got some food."

She turned back to me. "Your father…"

My stomach sank. I knew where this was going. "Yes?"

"He, he killed me." She threw herself into my arms, burying her face into my chest.

I rubbed her back, a lump growing in my throat. "I know. I alone buried you."

She sobbed, soaking my shirt with her sweet tears.

"I wish I could take it all back."

Victoria shook her head. "Don't wish it away."

"What do you mean?"

"I had no other choice but to run from my father. He flew off the handle, insisting I marry Franklin early. It was either stay and endure them my entire life or risk leaving to spend my life with you. The short time we had was worth it."

"You never told me about that."

She clung to me. "I never had time because I needed to get away."

I took a deep breath, trying to make sense of it all. "He wanted you to marry Franklin right away?"

Victoria sat back and nodded, holding my gaze. "Elsie went to a school dance with a boy from her class. Father found out, and he killed her in front of me." Her eyes filled with tears and they poured down her face. Her lips trembled and she shook.

It broke my heart to see her in such pain. I held her close and rubbed her back. "I'm so sorry, sweetness. I never knew."

She sobbed, and finally sat up and took a deep breath. "Th-then he said he would put a stop to the family's rebellion, starting by forcing me to quit school and marry Franklin. That's when I fled to you."

"It all makes sense now."

Her eyes shone with tears again. "I know. It was all my fault."

I shook my head. "No, it was your father's. And my father's. All we wanted was to be together, but their stubbornness and old ways prevented that."

Gessilyn came over and sat on the other side of Victoria. "I know you've just been through so much, but do you remember everything?"

"I know Toby tried to save me. He did everything he could."

Gessilyn put her hand on Victoria's. "I don't doubt that. What I mean is, do you remember anything after that?"

Victoria glanced up, looking deep in thought. "No, I don't think so. Why?"

"The spell is going to keep working until you recall everything, and I want to stay here until it completes its course."

"Okay." Victoria leaned against me, shaking.

I wrapped my arms around her. "I'm really sorry you have to deal with all this."

"Do you remember anything about why your memories were wiped?" Gessilyn asked.

Victoria shook her head.

"It's coming. You should eat." She reached for the tray I'd eaten from and handed it to Victoria. "You'll need the nourishment."

"She's right," I urged. The next round of memories might even be worse—it was too hard to say. There was no telling what had happened to make her forget everything. Had it been a spell? Or had she experienced something so traumatic, her mind could do nothing else except block it all out?

Either way, we were sure to find out soon.

Victoria nodded and picked up the fork.

I couldn't help fearing what might be found. She'd kissed

both me and that vile jaguar after drinking the tonic. A part of me kept asking the question I didn't want to think about—what if something had changed, and he was her one true love now?

A lump formed in my throat. I wasn't sure that was something I could deal with. I'd lived without her all these years, and now that I had her back, could I let go? I might not have a choice.

She handed the empty tray back to Gessilyn. "Thanks. I'm feeling sleepy now."

My pulse drummed in my ears.

Gessilyn spoke to Victoria, but I couldn't hear a word. All I could think about was whether or not Victoria would still love me when she woke up.

She lay down and pulled the covers up, her eyelids starting to close.

I leaned over and brushed my lips across hers. "I'm not leaving your side. When you wake up, I promise to be here."

Her eyes closed. "I love you, Toby."

"And I love you, forever and for always."

Please remember that.

CHAPTER 34

Toby

"GET SOMETHING TO EAT," GESSILYN urged. "I won't take my eyes off her. I promise."

I glanced down at Victoria. She seemed to be sleeping peacefully, and had been for a while. "Do you think she's remembering anything else?"

Gessilyn put a hand on my shoulder. "It's possible. She could also just be recovering from such an emotional trauma."

"Trauma? That seems like a strong word, don't you think?"

"She just recalled her death, and not just that, but her sister's, too."

I frowned. "True. I can't imagine what it's like to go from remembering almost nothing to having all that flood back."

Gessilyn squeezed my shoulder. "But now you two can move forward together. I know how long you've wanted this."

"And how badly." I leaned over and brushed my lips across Victoria's. Then I turned to Gessilyn. "The moment she wakes, let me know."

"You have my word."

Relief swept through me, and I realized how hungry I was. "Do you want anything?"

She shook her head. "I ate not long ago. You can send Killian up, though."

"Sure thing." I rose from the chair. "Thanks again for everything, Gessilyn."

"Don't thank me yet."

I arched a brow.

"Not until I've figured out how to break the curse of the moon."

My heart nearly broke in two.

"What's going to happen to her if she doesn't shift?" Gessilyn sat in the chair.

I shook my head, not wanting to talk about it.

"I need to know what I'm dealing with."

"The truth is, I can only speculate. Maybe she'll lose the ability to shift, or maybe she'll finally shift into the wolf and never return to this state."

She gave me a sympathetic glance. "I sense another *or* coming."

I frowned and then whispered, "She could die again—worst case scenario."

Gessilyn jumped up from the chair. "We're not going to let that happen. Do you hear me?"

I nodded, not trusting my voice.

"Toby, I'm serious. I won't let that happen. I'll move in here and work day and night if I have to. The jaguars have found a way around the curse. So can I, and I will."

"Thanks, Gessilyn." My voice cracked. "If anyone can, it's you."

"Darn straight. In fact, while you're eating, I'm going to call my parents. They've been around longer than me. Surely, one of them can think of something I've never heard of."

"I can't tell you how much I appreciate it." I glanced at Victoria. "I'd do anything for her."

"That's why I'm going to put in everything I've got into this."

"And if you ever need anything from me…"

She pulled out her phone and waved me away. "Just get something to eat. Or just talk with your guys. You need a break."

It was hard to pull myself away from Victoria, but Gessilyn was right. I needed to think.

I went downstairs. Everyone was gathered in the kitchen.

"How's it going, sir?" Brick asked, standing from his seat.

"She's still sleeping, and she doesn't seem to be having any bad dreams."

Relief swept over his face. "I'm so glad to hear it."

Soleil jumped up from her spot next to him. "Me, too. Is there anything we can do?"

"I just need to clear my head."

"There's nothing like a good meal to help with that." Brick spread his arm toward the table, which held enough to feed our pack right before shifting. "I can also put some roast beef in the oven."

"This is fine." I took my usual seat and filled the plate.

"How's Gessilyn?" Killian asked.

"She wants you to go upstairs and sit with her."

He finished up his drink and turned to me. "I'm really glad Victoria remembers you."

"Me, too." I dug into my food. My emotions were too raw, and I didn't want anyone to see them.

Everyone spoke around me. I was grateful for the distraction as I listened to them discussing possible cures for the curse of the moon.

Once I'd finally had my fill, I glanced around the table. Each member of my pack took a turn giving me a reassuring expression.

Strength filled me, replacing my aching emotions. My family had my back and the high witch was deeply invested in fully restoring Victoria to her natural state. And the best news of all was that Victoria remembered me and our time together before her death.

We had each other, and that was something I'd desired for so long. Too long.

The love of my life was now back with all of her memories. We were together once again—really together. And with Gessilyn working on curing the moon's curse, that left me with only the worry of when and how to give her to the proper proposal. Now we had nothing standing in our way of getting married and running the pack together.

I glanced around the table. Everyone was joking and laughing, blissfully unconcerned with the vampire or the valkyrie sitting with us. Brick, especially, seemed pleased with Soleil's presence. He was grinning wider than I'd ever seen as she shared a story about an unfortunate encounter with a pharaoh's daughter.

Killian came over to me. "Victoria's starting to wake."

My heart leaped into my throat. I jumped from my seat and bolted up the stairs.

CHAPTER 35

Victoria

I SQUEEZED TOBY'S HAND AS Moonhaven came into sight. The sun sat behind it, creating a show of bright pinks and oranges against the darkening sky.

He turned to me and took my other hand in his, gazing into my eyes. "Have I told you how happy I am to have you back?"

"One or two *hundred* times," I teased. "But I can't hear it too much. Not after everything we've been through. I wish I could remember why I forgot everything."

Toby pulled me closer. "It doesn't matter. The only thing that does matter is that we're together now."

My heart fluttered. "I couldn't ask for anything more. Deep down, I missed you horribly. I just didn't understand it."

He stepped closer and brushed his lips across mine. "That's because our love is too powerful for a memory loss. What we have goes deeper than memories. It reaches into the depths of our emotions. It's part of who we are. You're as much a part of my soul as I am. Without you at my side, I was only half a wolf—half a man. You make me whole."

My mouth gaped and tears filled my eyes, pooling and

blurring my vision. "You... you're equally part of me. I just can't say it as eloquently now that you've melted me with your words." I blinked, causing tears to spill.

He wiped them away and held my gaze. "There's only one thing I need to be fully complete."

"What?"

Toby stepped back and knelt on the grass.

My heart rate sped up.

He reached into his pocket and pulled out a diamond ring. "I've never loved anyone more than you, Victoria. Even your death couldn't keep my feelings at bay. You're the most important person in my life, and I couldn't be happier to have you back—and remembering me, no less."

I laughed and wiped new tears from my eyes. My knees wobbled, so I lowered myself to the ground, also.

Toby took my left hand. "I want nothing more than to lead this pack with you. I love you, Victoria. Will you marry me?"

"Yes! We've waited too long for this." I laughed while more tears ran from my eyes.

Smiling, he slid the ring on my finger. It was a perfect fit.

"You've just made me the happiest man alive." He beamed.

"But you can't be any happier than I am." I wiped my tears away.

"I beg to differ." Toby pulled me onto his lap and pressed his mouth on mine. I wrapped my arms around him and kissed him greedily, excited about our future together. After all these years, we would finally get married—and this time, there was no one around to stop us.

Other Books

If you liked Lost Wolf, you'll enjoy the Transformed series where it all began…

The Transformed Main Series

The Gone Saga

The Seaside Hunters series

Visit StacyClaflin.com for details.

Sign up for new release updates and receive three free books.
stacyclaflin.com/newsletter

Want to hang out and talk about books?
Join My Book Hangout and participate in the discussions.
There are also exclusive giveaways, sneak peeks and more.
Sometimes the members offer opinions on book covers too.
You never know what you'll find.
facebook.com/groups/stacyclaflinbooks

Author's Note

Thanks so much for reading Lost Wolf. This book has been a long time in the making. Ever since Toby's role in my Transformed series lessened, I've received numerous emails asking for more of him. Unfortunately, his place in the series had mostly dwindled down as that world exploded, going in some directions I never imagined.

I've been excited to write his story. Not only is he one of my favorite characters, but I'm excited that so many of you love him, also! I really hope you enjoyed reading it as much as I've enjoyed writing it. As with the previous series, I have no exact plan as to how many books there will be (I like to see where the stories go on their own) but there will be at least four!

Feel free to let me know your thoughts. I'd love to hear from you. The easiest way to do that is to join my mailing list (link below) and reply to any of the emails.

Anyway, if you enjoyed this book, please consider leaving a review wherever you purchased it. Not only will your review help me to better understand what you like—so I can give you more of it!—but it will also help other readers find my work. Reviews can be short—just share your honest thoughts. That's it.

Want to know when I have a new release? Sign up here for new release updates. You'll also get a free book!

I've spent many hours writing, re-writing, and editing this work. I even put together a team who helped with the editing process. As it is impossible to find every single error, if you find any, please contact me through my website and let me know. Then I can fix them for future editions.

Thank you for your support! I really appreciate it—and you guys!

Made in the USA
San Bernardino, CA
08 November 2017